THE SPELLBINDING COURTSHIP

CALATINI TALES BOOK 0.5

KATHERINE DOTTERER

KatSpell Press

The Spellbinding Courtship

Cover by Danielle Fine @ By Definition

Edited by Angela James, Lauralynn Elliott

A KatSpell Press Book

- ISBN 978-1-955614-00-9 (ebook)
- ISBN 978-1-955614-01-6 (trade paperback)

❀ Created with Vellum

CONTENTS

ABOUT THE SPELLBINDING COURTSHIP

*W*elcome to Calatini, an enchanting Regency-inspired kingdom filled with faegifts, witches, and heartwarming romance.

Miss Selena Midor is lonely, close to destitute, and trapped far away from home with her cruel uncle. She's grown accustomed to outwitting him to keep herself safe, but when she overhears her uncle's evil scheme with a witch, Selena must make a choice no lady of quality should have to make. She must find a man to deflower her, and quickly.

Aragon, eldest son of the Duke of Childes, is caught in the rain without even a spelled cloak to protect him. So he stumbles into a brothel... and finds Selena. Though tempted, Aragon is too honorable to accept Selena's desperate overtures. He can't take from her what she should give to the gentleman she loves.

Selena is astonished when Aragon instead offers to bring her home for his family to present at court. She accepts his rescue but longs to be more than his charity case. Yet Aragon refuses to act on their attraction, and soon he isn't the only eligible bachelor spellbound by Selena. Should she wait for Aragon or choose another?

. . .

FANS OF JULIET MARILLIER, Naomi Novik's *Uprooted*, and Julia Quinn's Bridgerton series will be enthralled by the Calatini Tales series of Regency-inspired historical fantasy romance novels.

CHAPTER 1

*S*elena was sketching the family estate she'd never see again when furtive movement out her bedroom window caught her eye. Her pencil halting, she scrutinized the black-clad man as he skulked down the street and rapped on the door of her uncle's townhouse. Who was he? She'd never met him—not surprising since she'd not met anyone in the six months she'd lived in Ormas, yet his tenebrous air alarmed her.

The back of her neck prickled as Uncle Adan ushered his visitor inside. Why had he invited a man like *that* as their first visitor? Another one of his shady schemes? She must find out so she could outwit whatever he was plotting.

Selena grimaced as she uncurled from the window seat. Father used to scold Uncle Adan for his schemes, which had only inspired her uncle to escalate them. Like when he'd bound brownies to the kitchen after Father had said the estate couldn't afford to hire the pair her uncle had found. That attempt to best Father and impress Mother had wrecked the kitchen when the household spirits escaped her uncle's spell the following day.

But her parents could no longer curb her uncle. Last year a dying peddler had brought wraith flu along with his ribbons, and the virulent strain had felled her parents and half the village. Selena had nearly died as well, yet her uncle had only been ill a week. The day after her parents' funeral, Uncle Adan had sold the country estate that had belonged to Midors for generations to fund his move to Ormas. For some reason, he'd brought her along—perhaps to prevent gossip, but more likely because he'd hoped the lengthy journey across Calatini would kill her.

As she crept downstairs, the air was dead yet heavy with silence. Where were her uncle's few servants? Were they hiding from his suspicious visitor? She shivered as she locked the gamesroom door before removing the faded painting over the peepholes she'd drilled into Uncle Adan's study to keep abreast of his schemes.

"...so I must recoup the funds I squandered on her recovery and upkeep. By the Goddess, she eats more than all my servants combined." Seated at his desk across the study, her uncle scowled and snipped a branch on the miniature cedar tree he was sculpting.

Selena suppressed a snort. 'Twas because the miser didn't feed his servants enough to keep will-o'-the-wisps alive. And the magical ghost lights who misled night travelers had no corporeal form.

Uncle Adan's tone turned sly, "And I heard you're skilled at generating gold from the most burdensome dross, witch."

Sprawled in the chair before the desk, the lanky witch smirked. "I'm no Rhiannon descendant, but I'm clever at what I do. Be warned, my methods aren't for weaklings or those who care about that dross's fate."

Her uncle echoed the witch's smirk as he snipped another branch. "Good. She's all that remains of my brother, so the worse her fate, the better. I almost wish he were alive to see his precious daughter's destruction."

Selena's stomach tensed. Uncle Adan had always resented Father, but he'd never plotted her destruction before. Perhaps because now Mother was no longer alive to temper him. Selena swallowed to soothe her aching throat.

The witch smoothed his scraggly beard and eyed Uncle Adan. "How old is your niece?"

Her uncle grimaced as he moved the cedar tree to the corner of his desk. "Twenty-four last month."

The witch steepled his bony fingers. "Why is she still unwed?"

Uncle Adan snorted and leaned back in his seat. "Because Arias was too soft on her. The fool. If she'd been my daughter, I'd have forced her to wed before she reached her majority four years ago."

Selena clenched her hands. Father had been no *fool*—he and Mother had loved her and wanted her to find a lifelong love like they had. And they'd understood waiting to meet the perfect spouse. Father had been forty when he'd met Mother, the girl his much younger brother wanted to court. Within a fortnight of meeting, Father and Mother had eloped and married in a blood-binding, the most unbreakable ceremony possible.

The witch's hum brought her back to him and her uncle. "So she's still pure then?"

Uncle Adan sneered, his expression perverting his resemblance to her loving father. "No doubt. Just like Arias, my niece is so sanctimonious it nauseates me."

Selena stiffened and glared at her uncle. Sanctimonious? She was no such thing! Particular, perhaps...

The witch's dark eyes gleamed with depraved zeal. "A virgin of her age shall fetch a bundle in the right market. Especially if she's halfway pretty."

A chill skittering across her skin, Selena shuddered at the witch's smile. Whatever he meant by right market couldn't be pleasant.

Still sneering, her uncle shrugged. "She is. Particularly if you like wholesome."

The gleam in the witch's eyes burned brighter. "Even better."

Uncle Adan leaned forward, his sneer fading to a frown. "What did you mean by right market? Only a desperate man would wed a spinster with no dowry."

The witch chuckled. "True, but certain gentlemen would pay plenty for a pure, wholesome lady they can despoil without being forced to wed. Revenge against the ladies in their life they can't punish."

Selena's breath froze as her pulse surged. Oh, Goddess. She'd been correct. The right market wasn't pleasant at all. In fact, 'twas horrifying.

The witch rubbed his chin. "I'll send out word to interested parties, and we can set an auction for late next month. The season shall be well underway by then, so we'll have numerous bidders."

Uncle Adan arched a brow. "And your payment for arranging all this?"

The witch's responding grin glinted with malevolence. "A portion of her auction price, and the energy produced by her rape. A pure lady of your niece's age is rarer than a faebird's teeth and shall produce especially potent energy. A witch like myself must simply be nearby to gather it."

Ice clawing at her throat, Selena shuddered again. From his words, her uncle's visitor must be a black witch. Black witches were infamous for poisons, curses, and other evil spells. Forbidden by the Goddess, Rhiannon the founder of human magic, and kingdoms across Damensea, black witches lived in hiding. Yet her uncle had unearthed one.

Uncle Adan leaned back in his seat with a smirk. "If my niece shall generate such bounty, then I deserve more than mere money for her virginity. Perhaps you could use some of her potent energy to craft a spell for me to gain influence at court..."

Since her uncle's toadying was insignificant, Selena stepped back from her peepholes and rehung the painting. She unlocked the gamesroom door then scurried upstairs on silent feet. The black witch and her uncle mustn't discover her spying. Goddess knew how they'd retaliate.

She locked her bedroom's feeble door behind her. Her heart thudding in her ears, she snatched her sketch journal from the window seat then curled up on the lumpy chair beside her bed. Sketching always helped her think. And she must think hard to outwit Uncle Adan's latest scheme.

Her hand trembled as she began sketching. Goddess, how could she foil that auction? She wasn't a witch, and she'd little experience with magic. Her small village had only had two minor witches—sisters who spent most of their meager power divining for copper and purifying air inside the mine. And even if she were still home, both had been killed by the wraith flu last year.

She only knew the basics about magic any child learned. Rhiannon had wheedled the secret of magic from the Goddess over two millennia ago. And spells required payment in kind to fuel them, but that cost could be difficult to predict.

Selena grimaced. Unfortunately, she knew little else. She'd never used more than common spells, most of them purchased from the sisters. So she knew no spell to prevent the black witch from stealing the power produced by her rape.

Her pencil halted mid-sketch. But what if she disposed of her virginity without being raped? 'Twould surely lessen the power the black witch could gather, so he wouldn't bother to arrange the auction, and she'd escape being raped.

She sighed and licked her parched lips. She'd always hungered for lasting love to strike like her parents' had, and coupling should be an expression of that love. Could she truly surrender that?

After a moment, she jerked a nod. Somehow, she must. 'Twas the only way to escape her uncle's scheme. So she'd bed someone without love. But how?

Her fingers clenching her pencil, Selena began sketching again. Uncle Adan's servants would never touch her—not that she wanted their attentions. She knew no one in Ormas, and her uncle would never introduce her at court while plotting her destruction. And 'twould be perilous to approach a stranger on the street.

No, she must meet her deflowerer somewhere accustomed to handling such dealings—a brothel. Fortunately, her uncle couldn't afford a townhouse in one of the better neighborhoods near the palace, so multiple brothels should be nearby. And last week she'd overheard the cook and the footman discussing one on Mermaid Street. She'd start there.

Selena cocked her head as she finished her sketch. Once she was no longer pure, she must ensure Uncle Adan learned about her ruined state. Then he'd have nothing to sell to the black witch. Without the power and money her virginity would engender, she could leave without them pursuing her. Perhaps she could become a governess or find a school needing an art instructor. As long as her employer never learned of her visit to a brothel, either would be better than living with her uncle.

CHAPTER 2

*A*fter his first council meeting, Aragon gritted a serene
smile as the eleven other councilors strolled from the
room. The newest councilor couldn't let the others see his strain.
Councilors must always exude aplomb. They served as advisors
to the king, and in addition to representing their duchy, they
each headed a government ministry. And as the only new councilor, he'd yet to prove his worth.

Once they were alone, Aragon dropped his smile and turned
to Devon beside him. "Are council meetings always like that?"

His best friend leaned back in his seat at the head of the table.
"More or less. Overwhelmed, were you?"

"Yes..." Aragon rubbed his brow. His head ached like he'd
been thrust into a magical creature's kingdom without a guide.
Since the catastrophic Stone Wars before the founding of
Calatini, most magical creatures lived north of the Walle, so
humans only knew many by reputation. And suddenly living
among magical creatures would be nothing like simply knowing
of them. Just like serving on the council was nothing like
discussing council meetings with Father.

Aragon grimaced at Devon. "I knew nothing about half the

matters the other councilors mentioned. I reviewed Father's notes, but they weren't enough."

Devon cocked his crownless head. "I experienced that at my first council meeting too. Don't fret; you'll catch up soon."

Aragon sighed. Hopefully so. He couldn't fail at the first duty he'd assumed from Father. He'd placed his trust in Aragon when he'd retired after his last term. "I hope I can fulfill my duties as Calatini's Minister of Agriculture as well as he did."

Devon clapped Aragon's shoulder. "You shall. Allow yourself time. I felt the same when I became king two years ago. But now I'm accustomed to ruling."

Aragon suppressed a wince. He shouldn't be complaining. At least his father was alive, so he could seek advice whenever he wanted. Devon couldn't. Since King Sarastor had unexpectedly died from angina, Devon had no family except for Aragon and his family, who were mere third cousins.

He smiled and straightened in his seat. He should invite Devon to dinner. His friend hadn't joined them in months, and he might distract Mother's guests. "What are your plans for this evening?"

Devon shrugged. "Wading through the stack of reports on the Wildewall dispute I received this morning. If not dealt with soon, it could damage trade with our magical neighbors north of the Walle."

Aragon slouched, his head throbbing again. Due to their longstanding treaty with the nightmara, Calatini was one of the few human kingdoms other magical creatures traded with, so ensuring that continued took precedence over his little problem. He sighed. "You aren't free for dinner then. Pity. I'm not antici-pating facing it alone."

Devon arched his brows. "Why?"

Aragon grimaced. Because Mother had become more managing than a mama trolless during autumn. He loved her, and she always meant well, but when determined, she'd harp on something for ages. Sometimes not even Father could get her to relent. And right now, she was determined to see Aragon wed. "Mother expressly ordered me to attend dinner tonight and not be late."

Devon winced and slanted him a sympathetic glance. "Another potential bride?"

Aragon sighed and almost shuddered. "More than one, I suspect." And only interested in his title and fortune like her previous candidates. "She's become desperate in recent months. Apparently, no lady shall have me if I wait much longer."

"I doubt that." Devon shook his head. "Perhaps you should act like Hawke when your mother meddles and avoid dinner. Visit that tavern you like near the docks."

Aragon's head eased at Devon's suggestion. Perhaps he could —for one night at least. As heir, he must settle for one of Mother's candidates eventually, but he could escape tonight. "The Gold Griffin does serve a fine fish pie."

Devon chuckled and rose. "'Tis decided then. Play some cards for me. I must return to those reports."

Aragon and his cousin strode from the council room. Two royal guards joining him, Devon turned toward his study, while Aragon headed for his carriage at the stables.

Once Aragon returned to the family townhouse, he snuck around back and slipped inside. Please let Mother not spot him. She'd guilt him into remaining for dinner if she did. He dashed upstairs and changed into riding clothes then left the way he'd entered.

He relaxed when he rode from the stables without anyone stopping him. He inhaled the brisk spring air with a smile. Devon's suggestion was the perfect remedy to forget the grasping potential brides and stressful council meeting.

After riding through the crowded streets of Ormas, he left his bay mare at the stables at the end of Mermaid Street and strode to The Gold Griffin, grinning at the peeling sign swinging above the door. He loved the rowdy tavern and had since he first stumbled across it four years ago.

He'd been riding home from the nearby orphanage his youngest brother Hawke supported. The gold griffin sign had caught his eye because griffins were land creatures renowned for inspiring truth and taking lifelong mates—an unusual choice for a tavern near the docks. So he'd gone inside, and from the first, everyone at the tavern treated him like an ordinary man rather than the heir to a wealthy duke and cousin to the king. Unlike everyone at court and Mother's candidates. Plus, the tavern's special gold ale glowed when telling the truth, so the card games were always honest. He visited as often as his duties allowed.

Once he entered The Gold Griffin, Aragon nodded at the porter then sat at the bar. Although not packed yet, the tavern was still busy. Sailors bawled chanteys and spilled their glowing tankards of gold ale as they swayed. On the opposite wall, several groups played cards, eyeing their glowing ale after every move. Scattered about the other tables throughout the tavern, tradesmen ate an early dinner in clusters of one or two.

The huge tavern keeper wiped his hands on his tattered apron and barreled over with a broad grin. "Afternoon, Lord Treyvan. What'll you have today?"

Warmed by Micah's hearty welcome, Aragon grinned in return. "Afternoon, Micah. A fish pie and a tankard."

Micah nodded. "Right away."

When the tavern keeper returned with his steaming fish pie and glowing tankard, Aragon's mouth watered. Definitely much better than suffering through dinner with Mother's candidates. "Looks delicious, as always."

Aragon and Micah discussed the tavern while Aragon devoured his meal. Once he finished, he ordered another tankard then joined a group playing cards. Like his companions, he eyed everyone's tankards to discern deceitful plays. While he played cards over the next few hours, more patrons arrived until the tavern was raucous and oven-like.

'Twas well past dinner when Aragon tossed down his final hand and allowed the blacksmith who'd been watching for the past hour take his seat. Mother's candidates surely must have departed, although Mother would scold him for missing dinner when she saw him. Yet a relaxing evening had been worth it.

He shoved through the packed tavern but halted before the door. Rain splattered outside, and dark puddles littered the ground. He glanced at the porter. "How long has it been raining?"

The porter shrugged. "Since shortly after you arrived. Doubt it'll stop any time soon."

Aragon grimaced and blew a sigh. "Of course not." He eyed the tavern. 'Twas much too crowded to stay. He'd brave the rain. If only he'd brought a cloak spelled for it. He stepped outside and sprinted down the street toward the stables.

Halfway there, the cold and steady rain burgeoned into a numbing deluge so heavy he could barely see. Wetter than a drowned firecat, he darted into a nearby doorway to wait for the rain to ease. He should have remained at The Gold Griffin despite the throng.

When he bumped the door behind him, it swung open, and he stumbled inside. He brushed back sodden hair from his eyes and studied his sanctuary from the deluge. Although shabby, the brown entrance hall was florid with golden sconces and dark-red carpet.

A hulking man covered with scars held open the battered door. He appeared more like a brawler than a porter as he inspected Aragon without expression.

Aragon offered a weak smile. He'd not offend such a behemoth. "Evening. Wet one tonight. Could I shelter here until the worst of the storm has passed?"

The hulking porter grunted. "Not up to me. Mistress!"

A blonde woman in a scarlet gown with a precariously low bodice sailed into the entrance hall. She eyed Aragon up and down. "And who might you be, sir?"

Aragon blinked at the woman. Considering the furnishings and her attire, this must be a brothel of some sort. He'd prefer to shelter elsewhere, but he was here. To offset his bedraggled appearance, he swept a courtly bow. "Lord Treyvan, mistress."

The woman, who must be the brothel's madam, eyed him up and down again. "The Duke of Childes's eldest son?"

Aragon jerked a nod. The gleam in her blue eyes echoed that of Mother's more grasping candidates. Wonderful.

The madam smirked. "You're perfect. That'll be twenty gold."

Perfect for what? And twenty gold was a year's wages near the docks—much too steep for shelter from the rain. Aragon glanced at the hulking porter, who chuckled and held out his hand. Aragon sighed. Despite the outrageous price, at least he could dry off. He handed money to the porter.

"Follow me." With an imperious wave, the madam led Aragon upstairs then down a long hall. Muffled moans, shouts, and thumps came from the many closed doors.

Aragon fought a blush. Although not celibate like his middle brother Mel who'd become a priest last year, he was no rakehell like Hawke, who found a new lover every few nights. Honestly, he couldn't fathom that—lovemaking should be more than mere recreation. So he'd never visited a brothel, kept a mistress, or even taken many lovers.

As they reached the final door, he cleared his throat to explain he only wanted a room. "Er..."

The madam purred a chuckle and opened the door. "Go on then, my lord. Enjoy your night." She prodded him inside and shut the door behind him.

Aragon swallowed and glanced about the tawdry room. He wasn't interested in seducing its owner and would rather enjoy his night alone. But how could he refuse without insulting the girl? Perhaps more gold would help.

But then his gaze halted on the adorable lady with sandy-brown hair and freckles hovering beside the crimson bed. From her shabby yet decorous dress, she must be poor gentry and desperate. As he met her dark-gray eyes, his breath stilled, and his heart pounded in his ears. Goddess, he'd never met anyone so spellbinding.

After a moment, the lady lifted her chin then strode over and smashed her lips against his.

CHAPTER 3

The day after the black witch's visit, Selena hid in her chambers and sketched madly until her uncle strutted out the front door an hour before dinner. Thank the Goddess he'd finally left. Her hands trembling, she dropped her sketch journal to yank on her cloak and grab her reticule. She'd only be gone the evening, so she'd bring nothing else with her.

Then she slipped out to find the brothel on Mermaid Street. The footman had mentioned 'twas two doors from The Gold Griffin and three from the stables. Clutching her cloak about her, she bent her head and strode to the brothel. Her pulse surged at the brothel's unmarked door. She gulped a breath then made herself knock.

The door creaked open to reveal a hulking man covered with scars. He eyed her but said nothing.

Selena lifted her chin, gripping her threadbare reticule. She must sound decisive or he'd never let her past. "I've business with your mistress. Direct me to her."

A bisected eyebrow quirking, the massive porter stepped back and waved for her to enter.

She glanced about the hall as she entered, her stomach quivering. Although not luxurious, the furnishings were clean and just this side of tawdry. Better than she'd expected.

The hulking porter led her down a hall with sepia wallpaper, amber sconces, and maroon carpet. He knocked then opened the carob-brown door at the end of the hall. "Lady here says she got business wi' ya, Madam Lorelei."

Selena swallowed then glided into the madam's study. A prickle skittering up her neck, she shut the door and lowered her hood. "So I do. May I sit?"

Her blonde hair arranged in frothy waves that belied the sharpness in her blue eyes, Madam Lorelei raked Selena with a long glance. "What business, pray tell?"

Selena perched in the plush chair before the desk. Before revealing her plan, she must find out if the madam was trustworthy. "I've a potential proposition for you, but I must speak with some of your girls first."

Madam Lorelei arched a brow. "I'll give you five minutes to meet them, but after that, you must pay for their time."

Selena nodded and clutched the reticule in her lap. "Five minutes shall be plenty, but I must speak with them alone."

Madam Lorelei's scarlet taffeta rustled as she rose. "Follow me." She led Selena upstairs and down a long hall.

Even though 'twas during dinner, couples were raucous behind the many closed doors they passed. A blush scorched Selena's cheeks. She'd never dreamt coupling would sound like *that.*

Madam Lorelei smirked as she opened the final door. "Is this private enough for you?"

Except for the groans coming from the next room. Selena blushed harder but nodded. Would she truly be experiencing that soon?

Madam Lorelei purred a chuckle and nudged Selena inside. "I'll send three of my available girls up. Remember, five minutes only."

Selena nodded again as the madam left. Goddess, could she

really do this? She glanced about the room as she waited. Although tidy and clean, the decor was oppressive. Everything was crimson or black. It made downstairs appear tasteful.

After a rap on the door, a willowy brunette, plush blonde, and dainty redhead entered. The willowy brunette purred, "You wanted to meet us?"

Selena swallowed, eyeing the three girls. They all appeared healthy, and none appeared scared. Hopefully, they'd speak truthfully. "How do you like working here?"

The girls glanced at one another, then the plush blonde drawled, "Well enough. Madam Lorelei treats us decent and always makes sure we're protected."

The dainty redhead sniggered. "Especially you, since you're her daughter."

The willowy brunette waved a hand. "Madam Lorelei treats us little different, and you know it."

Selena gripped her reticule. "So you'd say Madam Lorelei is honest?" When the girls nodded, her chest loosened, and she smiled at them. "Thank you for your time. You may return to your prior pursuits."

The dainty redhead scowled at her. "Don't you wanna bed one of us?"

Heat swamped Selena again. That explained the madam's earlier smirk. "No, I just wanted to speak with you."

When the redhead began to protest, the lush blonde hauled her from the room with the willowy brunette close behind.

Selena wiped damp palms on her taupe dress then strode from the room as well. She refused to hear the sounds from behind the other doors as she passed. She slipped back down to the madam's study and knocked on the door. At Madam Lorelei's reply, she entered and sat before the desk again.

Madam Lorelei arched her brows as she inspected Selena. "Done already?"

Selena inclined her head, fighting another blush. She must act composed. "Yes, your girls were most helpful. Now about my proposition..."

A wry smile curved Madam Lorelei's full lips. "I should have known your proposition would be more than a night with one of my girls."

Selena gulped a steadying breath. If only she could abandon her plan, but she must continue. "I want a night with one of your patrons instead. I must be rid of my virginity before I return home."

Madam Lorelei eyed Selena. "And what do I get out of your proposition?"

Selena lifted her chin. "You may keep whatever fee you ask of your patron. I'll leave how much you charge up to you." Hopefully, 'twould be enough to tempt the madam. She'd nothing else to offer.

Madam Lorelei's eyes gleamed. "I suppose you wish to remain hidden during your time here."

Selena shook her head despite her clenched stomach. Losing her virginity would be futile if Uncle Adan never discovered it. "Only until the deed is done. Then I want you to fetch my uncle."

Madam Lorelei snorted. "I'm not inviting a furious uncle to my brothel."

Selena sighed. The madam's refusal was understandable, but without seeing Selena at the brothel, Uncle Adan would doubt her missing virginity. Perhaps she could request a healer to prove it instead. She sighed again. "Very well."

Madam Lorelei leaned forward, her scarlet bodice dipping precariously. "If you're serious about this, you must follow the same rules as my girls."

Selena frowned, her shoulders tensing. Rules? What kind of rules? "Meaning..."

Madam Lorelei snickered. "Nothing horrible like you're imagining. You'll be free to leave whenever you wish. All my girls are."

Selena relaxed then gestured for the madam to continue. Thankfully, she was honest like her girls had said.

Madam Lorelei snickered again and straightened. "You must wear a contraceptive charm that also protects against venereal diseases."

Selena forced a nod and gripped her reticule. She'd not considered pregnancy or diseases when devising her plan. "A wise precaution, but I don't possess one."

"I provide them as part of my room and board for my girls." Madam Lorelei rooted in a desk drawer then tossed a wire bracelet at her. "Here."

Selena eyed the thin bracelet. Although contraceptive charms were harmless, this one appeared unimposing. "I can't pay for it."

Madam Lorelei smirked. "Never fear; your patron will." When Selena slid the contraceptive charm about her left wrist, Madam Lorelei continued, "Second rule, none of my patrons are rough with my girls unless they pay handsomely for it. I introduce those men as satyrs to the girls."

Her eyes widening, Selena swallowed. Dear Goddess, such a man would be almost as bad as the winner of the black witch's auction. "I don't want one of those."

Madam Lorelei flashed a sharp grin. "I didn't think you did. I shan't bring you a rough one."

Selena sighed as tension released her throat. "Good."

"And my third rule doesn't apply since I'm getting your entire fee." Madam Lorelei arched her brows. "Any other requests about your patron? A specific man, perhaps?"

A pang darted through Selena. "No one specific, but I'd like a decent gentleman if possible." 'Twould be the closest she'd get to love.

"A *decent* gentleman?" Madam Lorelei coughed a laugh. "You're aware that can be difficult at a brothel near the docks, right? Gentlemen keep to the fancier brothels unless they want a bit of rough."

Selena winced. Of course they did. "The best you can manage is fine." She couldn't wait for better.

Madam Lorelei pursed her lips. "Are you certain you wish to do this?"

Selena suppressed a shudder but set her jaw. "I must do this, so yes." What Uncle Adan and the black witch planned was so much worse.

Madam Lorelei shook her head but rose. "Come along then."

The madam led Selena back to the room where she'd met the girls. Again, Selena made herself ignore the sounds coming from the other rooms. She didn't want to hear what she'd soon experience.

When Madam Lorelei left, Selena removed her cloak then prowled about the room, keeping away from the bed. She could hardly believe she was about to surrender her virginity in this garish room. She'd always assumed she'd share that with her husband after a swift courtship, just like her parents had. But mourning that was futile.

As she waited for her patron, she paced the far side of the room, muttered prayers to the Goddess, and toyed with the vial of lymon balm scent in her reticule. She and Mother had made it two summers ago, so smelling it almost soothed her, but not as much as her sketch journal would have.

When the bedroom door finally opened and a man entered, Selena froze like a hunted moonrabbit. From the cut of his sodden clothes, he was a gentleman, likely a rich one. And he was handsome with seal-brown hair, dark-umber eyes, and strong features. What was such a gentleman doing at a brothel like *this*?

She and the gentleman stared at one another for a long moment. Her skin tingling, she forgot to breathe. He was exactly what she'd pick given a choice. She inhaled and lifted her chin. She'd better get started on her plan. She strode across the room and smashed her lips against his.

CHAPTER 4

*D*umbfounded by the spellbinding lady's rough kiss, Aragon froze.

The lady threw her arms about his neck and continued mauling his lips. She knew nothing about kissing. So why was she in a brothel near the docks? She must be more desperate than he'd realized. 'Twould be wrong to exploit her desperation, no matter how much he hungered to kiss her for real.

He wrenched his head away and rasped, "What is this?"

Her arms fast about his neck despite his dripping clothes, the lady scowled at him. "Kissing, of course."

Aragon couldn't resist a snort. "That was *not* kissing."

The lady narrowed eyes the color of black moonstone. "Teach me how to kiss then."

He scrutinized her pursed lips, his heart quickening. The adorable lady was too tempting to resist. Surely *one* kiss couldn't be considered exploitation. "Very well."

Aragon brushed a featherlight kiss against her lips until she softened with a sigh. Then tilting his head, he captured her lower lip and caressed his tongue against hers until she returned his kiss. Her refreshing lymon scent surrounding him, he raised his head and murmured, "Now *that* is kissing."

The lady blinked at him as she licked her reddened lips and wobbled a nod.

He ached for another kiss, but that *would* be exploitation. He removed her arms from his neck and stepped back to find somewhere to talk. Unfortunately, the lurid room was dominated by the crimson bed. But a small chair was tucked in the corner.

Aragon drew the lady to the bed and helped her sit. Then he snagged the chair and settled across from her, shifting his shoulders to loosen his sodden jacket. "I'm Lord Treyvan. You are?"

The lady's brow furrowed. "Lord Treyvan... Lord Treyvan... I feel as if I should know that title."

He almost smiled. Even the brothel madam had recognized his title, so the spellbinding lady must be a stranger to Ormas. And she'd responded to his kiss without knowing who he was. If only he could continue concealing his identity. "The Duke of Childes's eldest son."

The lady's eyes widened. "Oh!"

Obviously, the lady *did* know Father's title. Not surprising since Calatini only had twelve duchies. Would she fawn now that she knew who he was? Hopefully not. Aragon asked again, "And your name?"

The lady smoothed her sandy-brown hair. Her tone polite but not fawning, she asked, "What's a wealthy duke's heir doing visiting a brothel near the docks? Surely there are better establishments elsewhere."

A glow filled his chest at her forthright manner. Most ladies would have begun flirting once they knew about his influential family. He must learn more about this intriguing lady. But to do that, he must reveal why he was here. That should reassure her enough to talk.

So he coughed and gestured toward his drenched riding clothes. "My favorite tavern in Ormas, The Gold Griffin, is down the street. I was returning to the stables when the rain worsened, so I came inside to escape the deluge." He quirked a wry smile. "Paid twenty gold for the privilege too."

The lady gaped at him. "You paid *twenty* gold?"

Aragon almost winced. Perhaps he shouldn't have mentioned that. Such an amount would be staggering to a poor gentry miss. "I thought it steep, but never having visited, I was unaware that included the company of a lady." To coax her to talk, he smiled at her then added, "A genuine one, even."

A blush darkening her freckled cheeks, the lady eyed him through her lashes. "Your favorite tavern is down the street, and you've never visited here? Are you married or betrothed?"

He almost smiled. She'd not ask that unless he intrigued her too. "No, I'm unattached." Although a lady like her could change that.

She frowned and tilted her head. "I thought all unattached gentlemen in Ormas visited brothels."

Aragon tensed and straightened his soaked waistcoat. "Not all of them." He forced a shrug. "I feel lovemaking should be more than recreation."

Her eyes wide, the lady blinked at him but said nothing.

He shifted in his seat. But his opinion about lovemaking was irrelevant—they must return to her. He leaned toward her with a gentle smile. "Please, my lady, tell me your name."

The adorable lady licked her lips then replied at last, "Miss Selena Midor, from Upper Ashville in Linwick."

Aragon blinked. The mountainous Linwick duchy was across Calatini on the eastern border, and since she named herself from her village, she'd only left recently. So why was a lady fresh from the country at an Ormas brothel? Shouldn't her family be presenting her at court? He grasped her hand and kissed her fingers. "A pleasure, Miss Midor. Now, why's a genuine lady like yourself visiting a brothel near the docks?"

Selena sighed then mumbled, "Because I must dispose of my virginity, and a brothel seemed the safest place to do so."

He frowned. A brothel wasn't a safe place for a lady. Anyone could exploit her here. So what had compelled her to risk it? "Are your parents proposing an unwanted marriage?"

Selena shook her head, her voice breaking, "No, my parents died last year. Wraith flu." Most common in winter, wraith flu drained people to pale shades of themselves but was rarely fatal. The strain her parents had contracted must have been unusually virulent.

When she blinked back tears with a tremulous smile, his heart stilled at her grief. He squeezed her hands. If only he could do more. "Selena, I'm so sorry for your loss."

Selena nodded at his platitude then said, "I'm alone except for my uncle. He sold the family estate in Linwick and brought us to Ormas, but life here has been expensive." She hesitated for a breath before adding, "So he hired a black witch to generate funds. The black witch intends to auction my virginity and gather power from my rape."

Aragon clutched her hands, ice skittering across his skin. Dear Goddess. "What?!"

Selena grimaced. "Since I've no magic to foil the black witch, I decided the best way to escape being raped was to no longer be a virgin. So here I am."

He gaped at her, caressing her palms with his thumbs. Goddess, she was brave to risk such a plan, especially with a black witch involved. But surely a brothel wasn't her only option. "Why not just become a governess in another household?"

Selena shrugged. "I intend to once I'm no longer a virgin. My uncle and his black witch would hunt for me otherwise. My virginity would fetch too high a price and generate too much power for them to lose."

Aragon scowled. He should have realized that. Such greedy curs wouldn't stop pursuing her unless she was worthless to them. So she couldn't simply slip away, and she lacked the means to handle them herself. But he could. He was no witch and couldn't vanquish the black witch directly, but he could hire people to do so.

Warmth flooded his chest as he studied Selena. And such a

brave lady deserved his protection. So he must do everything he could to help her escape the black witch and her uncle. No matter the cost or potential scandal for rescuing a lady from a brothel.

Nibbling her lip, Selena slanted him a shy glance. "Now that you understand the circumstances, will you make love to me? Please? You're much better than I ever dreamt I'd find here."

He squeezed her hands again. She was more tempting than a singing siren, but he couldn't steal the gift she should bestow on the gentleman she loved. "I can't, but I'll aid you another way."

Selena sagged back with a sigh. "How?"

He studied their entwined hands. How indeed? "By ensuring your uncle and his black witch can't touch you. But the black witch is the greater threat and must be dealt with first. What do you know of him?"

Selena grimaced then shrugged. "Not much. Uncle Adan never spoke his name but mentioned the black witch possesses the reputation for generating gold from dross. The black witch's coloring is similar to yours, but his hair isn't as dark, his eyes are blacker, and his skin is pale like he rarely sees the sun. And he's lanky with a scraggly beard beginning to gray."

Aragon frowned. Too bad she hadn't a name. Finding the black witch without one would take time. But perhaps Adan Midor would lead them to him. "Not a lot to go on, but Devon has people who investigate matters for him, and he'll lend me some if I ask."

Selena's brow furrowed. "Devon?"

"King Devon," he replied without thinking. When she wrenched her hands free, he winced. He'd not meant to unnerve her. How could he explain? "We're cousins and best friends."

Selena tensed and licked her lips. "Cousins? Are you in line for the throne?"

Aragon almost shuddered. Being a duke's heir was more than enough. "Thankfully, no. My father and his mother were merely second cousins."

Stiff as a gorgon's victim turned to stone, Selena eyed him and said nothing.

He leaned toward her, his stomach tight. Would she treat him naturally again? "Devon is only two years older, and we grew up together. As children, we even spent our summers running wild on my family's country estate."

Selena still didn't speak, but the tension freezing her body softened.

Relaxing as well, Aragon captured her hands again. "We're as close now as we were as children, so Devon shan't mind lending me some of his people to unearth the black witch."

Selena sighed. "Very well. Can the king's people truly find the black witch?"

Aragon squeezed her hands. "Yes, but it may take some time considering our scant information." Unfortunately. And she couldn't return to her uncle while the black witch was free. "Is the madam here trustworthy enough to hide you?"

Selena arched her brows. "If someone paid her. Why?"

He shrugged. "You'll require a refuge from your uncle while Devon's people hunt for the black witch." He grimaced and shook his head. "I'd bring you home, but Mother wouldn't be able to resist exhibiting you to court. Plus, rumors about the lady she was presenting might start and allow your uncle and his black witch to find you."

Selena gaped at him. "You want to bring me home? To your family?"

Aragon leaned toward her with a warm smile. "Of course, but after the black witch is handled." When she continued to stare, he added, "It'll be entirely proper. Mother shall present you to court and help you find a husband. Then you can permanently escape your uncle."

Selena tilted her head. "But why would you do all that for me? We just met—in a brothel no less."

His neck heating, he shrugged. "Because you deserve help. And I admire your brave attempt to escape your uncle and his black witch." Her allure influenced him as well, but he couldn't mention that.

Silent, Selena blinked at him.

Aragon gulped a breath then stood and pulled her upright with her captured hands. "Shall we visit the madam and get your temporary lodgings arranged?"

CHAPTER 5

*S*elena stared up at Lord Treyvan. How had she gone from imminent trollop to championed maiden? He seemed determined to rescue her without taking her virginity. Her heart warmed. He was more perfect than she'd first thought.

She licked her tender lips. Yet despite her attraction, his real kiss had overwhelmed her. Clearly, she required love before she could bed anyone. She must abandon her desperate plan, so his aid was goddess-sent.

She beamed and squeezed his hands. He was the best gentleman she'd ever met. If only they'd fallen in love within moments of meeting, like her parents had. "Very well. Madam Lorelei's study is downstairs. I hope she's there rather than with a patron."

Lord Treyvan winced and smoothed back his seal-brown hair. "Me too." He threaded her arm through his. "Lead the way."

As they strode downstairs, they both kept their gazes straight ahead. She almost smiled. At least she wasn't the only one embarrassed by the explicit sounds coming from the other rooms.

When they began down the almost tasteful hall leading to Madam Lorelei's study, Lord Treyvan murmured, "Let me lead."

Selena nodded then swallowed and rapped on the carob-brown door. She sighed when Madam Lorelei replied. Hunting for the madam throughout the brothel during its busiest hours would be hideous.

Lord Treyvan winked at Selena then swept her into the madam's study.

Madam Lorelei arched her brows at them. "Done so soon? Again?"

Lord Treyvan dropped into the plush chair before the desk and drew Selena into his lap. "No, we're just beginning."

Selena stiffened for a moment then relaxed and curled an arm about his neck despite his sodden clothes. He must mean to convince Madam Lorelei they were lovers. Sensible. "Yes, we wanted to discuss terms with you."

The madam beckoned for them to continue. "Go on then."

Lord Treyvan brushed a kiss against Selena's lips. "I'm captivated by my lady here, and being a possessive gentleman, I *must* have exclusive rights."

Her lips tingling, Selena couldn't halt the blush burning her face. His declaration rang with sincerity.

Madam Lorelei glanced at her. "I believe your lady's time here was temporary."

Selena cupped Lord Treyvan's unshaven jaw with her free hand. Another tingle darted through her. "For Lord Treyvan, I'd gladly extend it."

Lord Treyvan kissed Selena's palm, his gaze never leaving hers. "State your price, madam."

Selena's heart warmed at his intense stare. He acted like a gentleman desperate to possess her. No one had ever looked at her like that. Surely it couldn't be all pretend.

Madam Lorelei's eyes gleamed. "Five gold a night."

Although that had been Selena's monthly allowance back home, Lord Treyvan merely nodded and said, "Done."

Selena tensed and bit the inside of her cheek. He could truly afford that? She'd protest, but Madam Lorelei might suspect their ruse. So she'd discuss that outrageous fee with the madam later. Perhaps she could recover some of his money.

Lord Treyvan tucked hair behind her ear, causing her skin to tingle again. "This arrangement is only until I secure a townhouse for my ladylove, but while it lasts, her presence here must remain secret. If I hear rumors about either of us, I'll expect all my gold returned."

Madam Lorelei nodded with a feline smirk. "As you like."

Lord Treyvan's eyes narrowed, but he only said, "I believe that settles everything." He turned to Selena and arched a brow.

No doubt he wanted to leave.

So she leaned against him with a coy smile. "Shall we return upstairs, my lord?"

Lord Treyvan nodded then swept her from Madam Lorelei's study. He was enthusiastic about their ruse. Hopefully, she was as convincing.

As soon as they reached her temporary room, Selena released Lord Treyvan and whirled to face him with her hands fisted on her hips. "Five gold? Really?"

Lord Treyvan shrugged. "I wanted to ensure she remained honest."

Selena swallowed. If five gold a night meant so little to him, he must be wealthier than she'd realized. And he wanted to help a penniless country miss for some reason. Shaking her head, she plopped on the bed. "For your unborn heirs' sakes, I pray you find the black witch soon, Lord Treyvan."

He sat beside her and took her hand. "Please, call me Aragon. Titles are senseless between lovers, even pretend ones."

She blushed but squeezed his hand. The strong name suited him. "Then you must call me Selena."

Aragon kissed her palm with a warm smile. "Gladly."

Her palm tingled, and her blush deepened. Goddess, he was tempting. If only she loved him. Then he could whisk her away like Father had Mother.

Aragon straightened then glanced about the garish room.

"What should we do for the next several hours? I must stay to convince the madam of our liaison."

Selena glanced about the room as well. She'd suggest a sketching game, but she'd no paper or pens, and they'd not find any here. She'd no cards either, so they couldn't play those. Conversing was their only option. Or kissing. She blushed harder.

Aragon squeezed her hand, his dark-umber eyes lambent. "What would you normally do?"

She licked her lips and willed her blush to fade. "Sketch, most likely."

Aragon leaned toward her. "What do you like to sketch?"

Selena shrugged. "Landscapes mostly." Although she'd enjoy sketching him as well. Then she could stare without appearing forward.

Aragon grinned, caressing her palm with his thumb. "I'd love to see them. I've no talent myself, so those that do amaze me."

Warmth filling her chest, she beamed back. "If I had my sketch journal, I'd gladly share them." She sighed. "But I left it at my uncle's since I only meant to be gone an evening."

Aragon squeezed her hand again. "Besides sketching, what else do you enjoy?"

Selena eyed their intertwined hands. He'd not moved to release her, even though they no longer had Madam Lorelei to convince. She smiled. He definitely felt the same attraction she did.

She returned his squeeze then replied, "Riding, although I've not gone since contracting wraith flu." Her entire life had changed then. Her throat clenched, but she forced a smile. "'Tis been so long, I may have forgotten how."

Aragon threaded his fingers through hers. "I doubt that. Once the black witch is handled, we'll go riding, and you'll remember what little you've forgotten before we leave the stables." He grinned at her. "I'll enjoy accompanying a lady who enjoys riding too. Although you must promise not to outride me."

Selena's smile softened. He must be attempting to ease her ill-disguised grief. The dear man. "I'll make no such promise." She leaned toward him—she must learn more about such a kind and chivalrous gentleman. "What's it like being a duke's heir?"

Aragon shifted beside her. "Not much different than being any gentleman's heir. Some extra duties like serving on the council, although not all dukes or their heirs serve. But my family has traditionally done so—I just assumed Father's seat today."

She stilled and eyed him. The nobles on the council were second only to the king, who was also Aragon's cousin. Clearly Aragon was both influential and dedicated, but his unease indicated he'd rather discuss something else. So she exhaled then asked, "Do you live in Ormas all year?"

Aragon relaxed, caressing her palm again. "No, only during the season. I need those months in the country to recover. I'm not sure how Devon and Mel manage to stay in Ormas the entire year."

Selena narrowed her eyes. He'd not mentioned that second name before. Who was she? "Mel?"

Aragon shrugged. "My middle brother. He's a priest at the Great Temple. A good one too. Growing up, he spent much of his time visiting poor villagers."

She relaxed, suppressing another blush. Why had she assumed Mel was a lady? Perhaps because all the ladies at court must desire Aragon. Not only was he handsome and heir to a wealthy duke, but he was amiable and modest too. "How many siblings do you have?"

Aragon flashed a wry smile. "Just two brothers." He grimaced. "When I bring you home, watch out for my youngest brother, Hawke. He's a rakehell who flirts constantly."

Her heart surged. He *must* admire her to warn her about his brother like that. "I've always wondered what having siblings would be like, but being surrounded by gentlemen must have overwhelmed your poor mother at times."

Aragon chuckled. "Not Mother. She always outwits and manages everyone."

Selena's stomach quivered. Such a formidable lady wouldn't appreciate her son forcing her to present a penniless country miss he'd met in a brothel.

Aragon winced and pulled her to her feet. "We should practice your dancing for your presentation ball."

She swallowed, glancing about the cramped room. He thought she must practice dancing? How exacting was his mother? "How? We've no space for proper dancing."

Aragon drew her into his arm and twirled her in place. "We can dance in this one spot."

Selena giggled as her tension eased. "That's not proper dancing."

Aragon grinned and twirled her faster. "Enjoyable though."

Tingling warmth suffusing her, she giggled again when she bumped into the bed. "We can't even manage dancing in one spot. Perhaps we'd better stop."

CHAPTER 6

*a*ragon drew Selena closer and continued dancing. Except he didn't want to stop. Dancing was the only proper way he could hold her in his arms. Besides, twirling in place had banished her grief about her parents that he'd provoked by mentioning Mother.

But then he stumbled into the chair beside the bed. He stilled and forced himself to release her. "Unfortunately, you're right. We must save our dancing until I bring you home."

A dimple quivered in Selena's left cheek as she sank onto the bed. "I'll look forward to that."

Warmth surging in his chest, Aragon sat beside her and took her hand. "Me too."

Selena threaded her fingers through his then glanced away. "What's court like?"

His hand tingling at her touch, he shrugged. "Like society everywhere, though fancier than you're accustomed to in Upper Ashville. Full of matchmaking parents, senseless gossip, and incessant intrigues."

Selena grimaced and blew a sigh. "Society would be much better if everyone simply treated others like they want to be treated."

Aragon's heart fluttered as he stared at her. Not many at court believed that, particularly when intent on advancing themselves. But he always had. How wonderful to meet a lady who agreed. She was nothing like Mother's candidates.

Selena blushed, glancing at him beneath her lashes. "A naive belief, I suppose."

Hunger burgeoned in his chest. "No, I believe the same." When she relaxed and dimpled at him, he forced himself not to kiss her. Goddess, she was spellbinding, but he couldn't exploit her trust. He was supposed to be protecting her, not seducing her. "I've stayed long enough. I should go."

Selena sighed. "Very well."

Aragon rose then bowed, unable to resist kissing her hand. If only he could bring her home tonight, but the black witch must be handled first. Hopefully, she'd be safe here if she took care. He frowned as he straightened. "Don't let anyone see you until morning. You don't appear like a lady who's been making love."

Selena blushed and walked him to the bedroom door. "I imagine so. I'll remain in this room as much as possible."

Good. He smiled down at her. "That's probably wise." He sighed, his chest tightening. "But if Devon's people take too long to find the black witch, I may bring you home before that, despite my mother's penchant for social display."

Selena's dark-gray eyes flickered, but she simply nodded.

Aragon squeezed her hand. Goddess, she was brave to remain in a brothel with so little complaint. "I'll visit as often as I can without drawing notice, but I doubt that shall be every night." Unfortunately.

Selena beamed and touched his arm. "I'll look forward to your visits. Thanks for helping me."

His heart warmed as he bowed again. She deserved it. "'Tis nothing. Until next time." He slipped from her bedroom but paused until the lock clicked behind him. She was as safe as she could be here.

Aragon bounded downstairs, paid Madam Lorelei for the

week, then hurried from the brothel. Fortunately, the rain had eased during the hours he'd spent with Selena. He collected his gelding from the stables and galloped home, his mind humming.

Tomorrow, he'd ask Devon to join him for a ride, so he could tell his friend about Selena without others overhearing. Then he'd visit Broad Street to purchase several sketch journals and a box of enchanted pencils that magically changed colors. Selena would need them during her sojourn at the brothel.

Aragon soon arrived home and sighed when Perkins, their longtime butler, told him Mother and Father had already left for the Campbells' ball. If he took care, he might be able to delay Mother's scold about missing dinner until after his ride with Devon.

BRIMMING WITH ENERGY, Aragon rose not long after dawn the following morning. Once dressed, he galloped to the palace and strode upstairs to the royal wing. Nodding at the two royal guards flanking Devon's door, he knocked and entered. "Morning."

Devon glanced up from his full plate of eggs, bacon, and toast. "Morning. Why are you here so early?"

Aragon ogled his friend's hearty breakfast, his stomach stirring. If only he could have risked eating breakfast at home. "I thought we could go riding before you get engrossed by royal duties."

Devon resumed eating. "That sounds enjoyable once I finish breakfast." When Aragon nodded without tearing his gaze from Devon's plate, Devon smiled and asked, "Would you care to eat as well?"

Aragon leapt into the chair across the tea table from Devon. He was ravenous as a manticore, an indomitable yet rare beast who devoured half his weight every day and never left remains behind. One that Father had teasingly called him and his brothers as boys when they devoured everything in sight. He grinned at Devon. "Yes, please."

Devon nodded at his valet, and the valet left to fetch another plate. Once they were alone, Devon arched a brow at Aragon over his cup of tea. "Still avoiding your mother?"

Aragon grimaced. "I didn't return home until late, and I didn't want to begin the day with a scold." Or to divulge Selena in a way that repelled Mother—Mother wouldn't present Selena then. And Selena needed that to permanently escape her uncle. Plus, obtaining Devon's aid with the black witch was more important than facing Mother just yet.

Devon shook his head as his valet returned with a full plate and steaming cup of kahve and placed them before Aragon. "The longer you wait, the worse it shall be."

Aragon sighed as he began his bacon. Delicious. "I know." He'd return home to face it after their ride.

He devoured his breakfast as Devon finished eating and stepped away to change. He'd just finished when Devon rejoined him. He leapt upright, then they strode down to the stables with the two guards from the door following them.

Once everyone had mounted, Aragon asked, "Shall we ride to the royal forest?" They often rode there since they couldn't be overheard—the forest was ancient with thick trees, and riding there required royal permission.

Devon grinned. "Sounds good."

As they set off, the royal guards assumed their customary positions with one riding before the king and the other riding behind, while Aragon rode beside his cousin. As usual, Aragon and Devon didn't speak while they rode through Ormas and out the eastern gate.

His chest lightening, Aragon inhaled the brisk air as they rode past several farmsteads amid the wet, soon-to-be-planted fields. Escaping the city for a time was delightful. He'd definitely take Selena riding once the black witch was captured. From their talk last night, she'd enjoy it.

Waving for his guards to ride out of earshot as they neared the royal forest, Devon glanced at Aragon. "How was The Gold Griffin?"

Aragon shrugged. "Enjoyable, as always. But the tavern wasn't the interesting part of the evening." When Devon arched his brows, Aragon grinned. "To escape the deluge, I ended up in a brothel several doors from The Gold Griffin."

Devon coughed a laugh as they entered the royal forest. "Awkward."

Aragon chuckled and steered his bay mare between the budding trees. "Especially when a lady, a genuine one not a doxy, kissed me." Tingling warmth suffused him as her kiss echoed against his lips.

Devon blinked at him. "Bold for a genuine lady."

Aragon's heart squeezed. Yes, she was. Adorable and spellbinding too. "She had to. Her uncle and his black witch had plotted to sell her virginity, so she fled to the brothel to foil them."

Devon frowned and halted his gelding. "She's involved with a black witch?"

Stiffening, Aragon glared at his friend. "No, her uncle is. Could I borrow some of your people to unearth the black witch?"

Devon started his gelding again. "Of course. Black witches must always be stopped. Just keep me informed of your progress. I don't like black witches roaming about my kingdom."

Aragon grimaced. No decent king did. Their evil spells poisoned everyone, so they were forbidden across Damensea. Yet somehow they still survived in hiding, like a pernicious disease. "Excellent. Once the black witch is captured, the lady can leave the brothel, and Mother can present her at court."

Devon frowned, slanting him a sidelong glance. "You're bringing her *home*? Is that prudent? You just met her—in a brothel, and her uncle hired a black witch."

Aragon clenched his reins to avoid scowling at Devon. King or not, he'd no right to denigrate Selena. "She deserves my help.

She's brave and sweet and..." How could he describe her allure? "...fascinating."

Devon's eyes darkened. "She must be for you to act so precipitously. I'll be interested to meet your lady when your mother presents her."

Aragon relaxed and almost grinned. All of his friend's doubts would vanish once he met Selena. "You'll like her."

Devon grunted as he urged his gelding around a fallen tree. "While the black witch is loose, your lady shall need magical protection. I'll have the royal witch create a charm for her. And feel free to call on her if my people take too long to find the black witch."

Aragon beamed at Devon. Lady Juliet was the most illustrious witch in Calatini. She'd create a spell to protect Selena, no matter how powerful the black witch. "Thanks, Devon."

Devon nodded then sighed and turned his gelding around. "We should probably return. I've a meeting midmorning with the Duchess of Wildewall about the Greysnowe-Ravenstone feud."

Aragon winced as he followed Devon. Despite the centuries-long feud, his friend had begun escorting the beauteous Lady Annalise Greysnowe while the Ravenstones had been in Wildewall mourning the old count's death last season. "Does she think the new Lord Ravenstone will retaliate your escorting Lady Annalise?"

Devon shrugged. "I'm not certain. He's never participated in the feud during the few months a year he spends at court, but perhaps she worries that may change."

Aragon suppressed a shudder. Thank the Goddess he needn't handle such matters. Selena's black witch was more than enough.

CHAPTER 7

*A*round late morning, Selena's rumbling stomach prodded her to slip from her room at the brothel. She'd missed dinner and breakfast, so she must risk leaving the dubious sanctuary of her room to find Madam Lorelei to discuss meals and other details of their arrangement.

Her skin prickled as she strode through the still brothel. Most of the girls must still be asleep. From what she'd overheard last night while locked in her room, they kept late hours entertaining the patrons. She swallowed then rapped on the madam's study door, her empty stomach tight. Please let the madam be here rather than elsewhere. She sighed when Madam Lorelei called for her to enter.

Her iris-purple dress sober compared to her racy gown from the previous evening, Madam Lorelei purred a chuckle as Selena slipped into the study. "Have an enjoyable night?"

Selena blushed as she perched on the plush chair before the desk. More enjoyable than she'd expected once she met Aragon. He was such a wonderful gentleman, so kind and dedicated with enthralling kisses—how was he still unattached? She'd been blessed when he stumbled into the brothel seeking shelter from the rain. "Yes, thank you. But we must discuss our arrangement."

Arching a brow, Madam Lorelei waved for Selena to continue. "What did you wish to discuss?"

Selena swallowed and lifted her chin. Although ravenous, she'd start with Aragon's money. 'Twould be the harder battle. "That third rule for your girls. The one involving their fee."

Madam Lorelei smirked and drawled, "I should have realized."

Selena stiffened. Doubtless she appeared only interested in money. But she must continue if she was to recover some of the madam's outrageous fee. "As we agreed before, you may keep my entire fee from last night, but I want what your girls normally receive starting today."

Madam Lorelei leaned forward. "Half your fee is mine outright then a quarter pays for your room and board. You get the remaining quarter."

Half? Selena almost snorted. The madam shouldn't keep that much of Aragon's gold for doing nothing. "I'll be much less work than your other girls. I need no patrons or wardrobe. So I keep two gold each night, and you keep three."

Madam Lorelei eyed Selena but replied, "Very well."

Energy surging in her chest, Selena suppressed a smile. She could give Aragon back almost half his gold. Surely he'd appreciate that, even though he'd not protested the price. And returning it to him would compensate for some of the hassle she was causing him.

Madam Lorelei opened a desk drawer and withdrew some coins. "Lord Treyvan paid for the rest of the week last night. Here's your portion."

Selena relaxed as she accepted the twelve gold. The madam truly was honest. Thank the Goddess for that. She cradled her full hands in her lap as her stomach rumbled again. With the money settled, she could finally address her hunger. "How do meals work?"

Madam Lorelei shrugged. "I've a cook who prepares plain meals. Grab what you want from the kitchen. 'Tis on the ground floor in the back. But if you want anything fancy, you must make it yourself."

Selena nodded with a sigh. Food would be simple then. But before she visited the kitchen, she must handle acquiring clothes. She'd only the dress she was wearing, although she could sew more. "Where's the closest shop I can purchase cloth and other necessities?"

Madam Lorelei arched her brows. "Isn't Lord Treyvan going to provide those?"

Another blush burned Selena's cheeks. Aragon paying for her clothes wasn't proper, but she'd no money of her own, so she must ask him when she returned his gold. "Yes, but gentlemen don't always remember to purchase everything a lady needs."

Madam Lorelei chuckled. "No, they don't. On Mountainglass Lane there's a miscellany shop and an apothecary after the witch shop. Head toward the tavern then turn left at the first crossing. Not the quality of shops you're used to, but they'll do."

Her chest loosening, Selena rose with Aragon's gold cradled in her palms. She'd learned everything she needed for now, so once she hid the money, she could visit the kitchen to grab luncheon. "Thanks for your time, Madam Lorelei."

She'd almost left when Madam Lorelei asked, "What's your name by the way?"

Selena turned to face the madam. Having a name would make her less remarkable. But she couldn't use her real name. Her uncle and his black witch might hear of it, and rumors about her time in a brothel might linger. "Lena."

Madam Lorelei's lips quirked. "A pleasure, *Lena*." From her emphasis, she knew 'twasn't Selena's real name.

However, Selena flashed a smile and inclined her head. Her sojourn here was too profitable for the madam to probe much. Hopefully, she'd encourage her girls to remain equally disinterested. "Likewise."

Aragon's gold concealed against her chest, she dashed upstairs to her room. She locked the door and poured the gold into her reticule. Then she slipped down to the kitchen and grabbed enough bread stuffed with cheese for luncheon and dinner.

Her skin prickling again, Selena returned to her room and locked the door behind her. As she devoured her luncheon, she perched on the crimson bed and eyed the gold filling her reticule. While living in a poor brothel, she had more money at once than ever before. She chuckled. At least until she returned it to Aragon.

She sighed and brushed the crumbs from her lap. Not that gold helped her. She couldn't pay anyone to purchase items for her without attracting notice. Madam Lorelei knowing about the gold was bad enough. And she couldn't risk visiting shops until she knew when the brothel's patrons weren't around.

Selena swallowed. Her situation at the brothel was tenuous at best. Only a flimsy lock and Madam Lorelei protected her, although 'twas better than remaining at her uncle's waiting to be auctioned off and raped. She shuddered as a chill skittered up her spine.

She dabbed on her lymon balm scent to soothe her nerves. Surely Aragon would find the black witch soon. Thank the Goddess he was helping her. Once the black witch was captured, she could leave the brothel. But until then, she must remain in this cramped room as much as possible.

A sudden knock jolted Selena from her thoughts. Her heart stuttered. Who was that? Had her uncle or his black witch stumbled across the brothel? Or was it one of the brothel's patrons seeking coupling? Oh, Goddess.

A girl's voice called through the door, "Lord Treyvan's lady?"

Selena tensed. Why was someone looking for her? Then she gulped a breath. Aragon must have sent the girl. Uncle Adan and his black witch couldn't know their connection. She swallowed and unlocked the door.

Flashing a gamine grin, the ragged girl thrust a hefty package at her then darted off.

Selena eyed the package as she locked the door then drifted back to the bed. What could Aragon have sent? Her neck tingling, she opened the note attached to the package.

> Selena—
> Here are some items to keep you amused at the brothel.
> Sorry I couldn't deliver them myself, but I should visit soon.
> Aragon

Selena tore open the brown paper wrapping. When three sketch journals were revealed, she stilled, and tears pricked her eyes. Exactly what she needed to settle her nerves while hiding at the brothel. Goddess, he was perfect.

Caressing the leather-bound journals, she eyed the small case beside them. Pencils, no doubt. She flipped open the case and stared. But like none she'd ever seen. They had transparent lead with a peculiar shimmer. Enchanted, clearly. She smiled as she read the instructions beside the three pencils. She could change their color by imagining a particular shade and saying "vario."

Her heart leapt. Had Aragon given her a faegift? Gentlemen only gave magical gifts to family, wives, or ladies they were courting. She blushed and shook her head. Surely not. He'd sent the enchanted pencils because they were more practical than sending her an entire set of colored pencils.

She curled on the crimson bed with a sigh. Aragon deserved a gift in return. She'd make him a sketch of her favorite view from home. 'Twasn't enough, but she hadn't more to give. Humming, she began his sketch. She'd sketched the outline when a vaguely familiar voice grumbled outside her door.

Selena stilled, her pulse pounding. Who was that? Not her uncle; she'd have recognized him. But someone she knew. Could it be the black witch? Oh, Goddess. She crept to her door and opened it just enough to see the hall.

The footman she'd overheard mentioning the brothel had his arm draped about the dainty redhead she'd met earlier. "Don't be like that, Mags. I saved for a month to visit you. That Midor don't pay us nothing."

Her knees shaking, Selena shut the door and locked it again. Fortunately, the footman had been too distracted to notice her. She shivered. But he easily could have, and he'd inform her uncle she was here, probably for a reward so he could visit his Mags.

She glanced about the cramped room. Although he'd not noticed her, the flimsy lock wasn't enough. She wedged the chair beneath the door. 'Twas the best she could do. If only she'd a staff or dagger for protection. To distract herself, she returned to Aragon's sketch. Hopefully, her trembling hands wouldn't ruin it.

CHAPTER 8

*a*ragon sighed when he returned home for luncheon after his ride with Devon and stopping by Broad Street to purchase sketch journals and enchanted pencils for Selena. If only he could have given them to her in person. But Mother's scolding would be much worse if he continued delaying it, so he'd best face it now.

His shoulders tensed as he strode into the family dining room. Mother and Father were alone at the table. Usually, Hawke or Mel joined them for meals, although Mel's presence was more sporadic since he lived and served at the Great Temple.

Aragon gritted a smile as he sat beside Father at the head of the table. "Is Hawke visiting Wren?" Wren was the best friend Hawke refused to admit he loved. Her parents, Sir Alaric and Lady Diana Keyes, were also their parents' best friends.

Father chuckled and shook his head. "He received word from his merchant friend this morning and bolted. Goddess knows when he'll return."

Aragon nodded and served himself stuffed quail, his skin tightening as Mother set down her utensils with deliberate care. Her scolding was about to begin already. Wonderful.

Mother frowned at him. "Did you enjoy yourself last night?"

Aragon swallowed. He had, but admitting that would worsen her scolding, so he shrugged and ate his quail instead. Judicious silence interspersed with pleading glances at Father was often the best way to handle Mother.

Father sighed as Mother pursed her lips and said, "Because your guests last night didn't. Lady Elisabeth and Miss Reid waited for you for nearly *three* hours."

Aragon almost shuddered. Why had she invited those two? Thank the Goddess he'd escaped dinner with them. "I'm sorry they were inconvenienced, but I didn't invite them or know they were attending."

Mother's eyes glinted. "I invited them for you to consider as your bride. And you knew we'd guests—I cautioned you not to be late."

Aragon sipped his wine. "I was unexpectedly delayed." By an unexpectedly spellbinding lady. Tingling swept through him as Selena's forthright manner and delightful dimple flashed before his eyes. "Besides, I don't wish to wed Lady Elisabeth or Miss Reid."

Mother sighed. "You must wed some lady soon. When he was your age, your father and I had been married two years, and you were on the way."

Aragon set his jaw. Mother's candidates might actually interest him if they were more like Selena and not grasping court flirts. "If you find candidates I could love, I'd gladly consider marrying them." He'd not settle for less.

Mother began to reply when Father interjected, "Caro, leave the boy alone. Lady Elisabeth and Miss Reid only have the benefit of being available. We don't want either as our daughter-in-law."

Mother grimaced but nodded. "True enough, Eldridge, but Aragon needs a bride." She rose. "I must be off. Diana and I have fittings at Celeste's. If only I had a daughter-in-law to join me." She tsked and swept from the room.

Once she left, Aragon shook his head. Mother was nothing if not determined.

Father chuckled then asked Aragon about the council meeting. They discussed that while finishing luncheon. 'Twas strange being the one to describe the meeting rather than hearing about it.

Afterward, Aragon wrote to Devon's people about the black witch and Midor. That done, he forced himself to read instead of visiting Selena. If he disappeared again, his parents would become suspicious, but he could risk visiting her tomorrow.

THE FOLLOWING AFTERNOON, Aragon purchased some items for Selena, ate dinner at The Gold Griffin, then headed to the brothel and pounded on her bedroom door. "Open up, wench."

Selena jerked open the door and goggled at him. Other than smudges beneath her eyes, she appeared well.

Warmth filling his chest, he hustled her back inside and locked the door. "Sorry for that, but acting like the brothel's usual patrons should attract less notice. How are you?"

Selena almost smiled as she smoothed her hair. "Well enough, though I'd trouble sleeping last night."

Aragon captured her hands then drew her to the bed and sat beside her. His throat tightened. "Did something happen?"

Selena licked her lips. "Not really, but I kept fretting it might."

He squeezed her hands before releasing her to extract a jar of strengthening charm from his satchel. "I purchased this today from an alchemical witch shop. Paint the door and lock with this, and they become stronger than stone." He handed her a dagger and one of the paired communication mirrors from the satchel. "And carry these with you in case of trouble. The dagger to defend yourself, and the mirror to contact me." He grimaced. "I've nothing to protect you against magic yet, but the royal witch is creating a protection charm, so hopefully, I'll have it next time."

Her dark-gray eyes glowing, Selena gripped the jar, dagger, and mirror against her chest. "These are wonderful."

Aragon blushed as he extracted a book of verse by an obscure bard. "I also have this. Hawke swears Lantos is brilliant, so I hope you enjoy it." And although Hawke was a rakehell, the verse couldn't be too bawdy since Wren adored it too.

Selena dimpled and accepted the book. "I'm sure I will, thank you." She reached under her pillow. "Before I forget, I've some things for you too." She opened her reticule and thrust it toward him. "I bargained back almost half your gold."

He stared at her. How had she managed that? Regardless, she needed it more than he did, so he'd not accept it. "You keep it for whatever you need. Although you can't spend it here without attracting notice." He withdrew all his smaller coins and offered them to her. When she shook her head, he scowled. "Don't be prudish. I know it's not entirely proper, but you need it."

Selena sighed as she added the smaller coins to the gold in her reticle. "True, and nothing about living in a brothel is entirely proper. But your gold wasn't the only thing I have for you." Her gaze dropping, she set aside her reticle then slid a page from her sketch journal with a blush. "'Tis my favorite mountain glen from home. A thanks for those sketch journals and extraordinary pencils."

Aragon gaped at her lifelike sketch. "'Tis exquisite." The colors were bold with the dawn sun, trembling dew, and verdant trees almost appearing in motion. She must miss Upper Ashville terribly. He tucked the sketch in his satchel and glanced at her. Could they talk about her home without provoking her grief about her parents? "What's Upper Ashville like?"

Selena's gaze unfocused as a faint smile curved her lips. "Small and quiet. We'd only two minor witches, and most villagers were goat farmers or worked in the nearby copper mine. My family was the only gentry within half a day's ride, and Lord Nolan, the mine's owner, rarely visited."

He eyed her, his heart stilling. Goddess, her village was even more isolated than he'd realized. "I suppose you didn't socialize often then."

Selena shrugged. "We attended house parties a few times a year with other gentry families within a day's ride." She lifted her chin. "If your mother asks, I do know how to dance and participate in social events."

Aragon swallowed. But she probably hadn't met more than a dozen eligible gentlemen her entire life. Acting on his attraction would just be exploiting her inexperience. He must allow her to meet other gentlemen, or she might choose him by default. His chest tightened. And she deserved to feel love, not just gratitude, for her chosen husband. So he must restrain himself. He leapt up and grabbed the jar of strengthening charm. "We should paint your door."

Selena tensed, her lips flattening. "Very well."

They painted her door, and while they waited for it to dry, he moved the chair across the room from the bed then asked her to read aloud some Lantos verse. He fled as soon as her door dried, promising to return with the royal witch's charm.

Although Aragon burned to visit Selena again, he forced himself to attend a ball the following night instead. His parents would suspect something if he eschewed all court events. Yet his mind kept drifting to Selena while he danced with other ladies. How was she faring in the brothel? Was she scared? Or bored? Or lonely?

When he returned home, he eyed the communication mirror paired to Selena's. Should he call her? He picked up his mirror then dropped it. Using the mirrors would drain them, and Selena might need hers later. He'd have to wait until tomorrow evening to see how she fared.

LATE THE FOLLOWING AFTERNOON, the royal witch wrote that her protection charm was ready. Aragon was about to leave to fetch it when Mel arrived. Although he burned to see Selena, Aragon delayed his plans to remain home for dinner. 'Twould appear odd if he ate elsewhere when Mel was visiting.

However, he barely spoke during the lively conversation between his parents and his brothers, and as soon as dessert was finished, he leapt up to leave. He must get to the palace to collect the protection charm before Lady Juliet left for the evening.

His parents exchanged a glance then Father said, "Could we speak in my study for a moment?"

Aragon tensed but nodded. He followed Father into the study and settled in the chair before the desk. Hopefully, this wouldn't take long. "What did you wish to discuss?"

Father frowned and leaned toward him. "Is something wrong? You've been distracted recently."

Aragon almost winced. Yes, because he kept thinking about Selena. Of course his parents had noticed. At least Father was asking rather than Mother. He eyed Father across the desk. Perhaps he *should* explain. Although Father would tell Mother, she must learn about Selena sometime. And Father always knew how to explain matters without riling her. "Nothing is wrong, but something extraordinary happened the other day."

Father cocked his head. "Oh?"

Aragon straightened. He must edit his words with care so his parents would fully support Selena. "The night I avoided Mother's matchmaking dinner, I stumbled across a lady hiding in a brothel from her uncle and the black witch he hired."

Father frowned. "A black witch? Alarming."

Aragon grimaced but nodded. "Devon's people are hunting him, but the lady shall hide in the brothel until he's captured. We can't risk him discovering her. Although I've provided charms to protect her during her sojourn there."

Father's eyes narrowed. "Why so much effort for a lady you just met in a brothel?"

Aragon stiffened and glowered back. "Because she deserves it. When trapped, she bravely took action few ladies would have. Plus, she's genuine and sweet."

Father studied him for a long moment. "I see..." Then he arched his brows with a wry smile. "What are your plans after the black witch is captured?"

Aragon coughed and shifted in his chair. "I thought Mother could present her at court. Then she could permanently escape her uncle." When Father chuckled, he added, "Despite hiding in a brothel, she's still an innocent. And she'll interest many gentlemen, unless they require a fortune."

Father flashed a crooked grin but only said, "Your mother shall enjoy presenting her. She'll finally have a young lady to join her at Celeste's."

Aragon relaxed. With Father's support, Mother would agree to present Selena. Good.

Father leaned back in his chair. "Sounds like you've everything handled, but if you require further assistance with that black witch or your lady, please let me know."

Aragon rose, warmth suffusing his chest. "Thanks, Father. I must be off." Once he fetched the protection charm, he could see Selena again. At last.

CHAPTER 9

*W*hen Aragon pounded on her door, Selena tossed aside her sketch journal and leapt from the bed. Finally. He'd not visited yesterday, and she'd missed him even though she'd kept herself occupied sewing dresses, reading his gift, and sketching. She beamed at him as she relocked the door.

Aragon handed her a gold pendant. "Here's the royal witch's protection charm. It shall ward you against magic for the next six months."

Her stomach fluttered as she eyed the gold gargoyle. 'Twas the perfect form for a protection charm since gargoyles were renowned for their protective nature. "Such a strong spell must bear a high magical price."

Aragon shook his head. "Not from us. Lady Juliet said it draws power from the spells attempting to influence you."

Selena gulped a breath. What an ingenious spell. No wonder Lady Juliet was the royal witch. "I hope such a spell wasn't too expensive."

Aragon shrugged, a blush tinting his cheeks. "Your safety is worth the price."

Warmth filling her chest, she flung her arms about him. He was amazing. Despite love not striking her at once, his kindness was slowly winning her heart. She craned to kiss him, her body tingling.

Yet Aragon jerked away before their lips could touch then removed her arms from his neck and stepped back.

Selena stiffened. Why had he refused her kiss? Because they hadn't fallen in love within moments of meeting? Her breath hitched. Was his kindness mere charity?

She sighed and slipped the protection charm over her head. Then she gasped when the gold gargoyle and the contraceptive charm warmed as if left in the afternoon sun.

Aragon frowned and leaned toward her. "What is it?"

Selena grimaced as she slid the thin bracelet from her wrist. "The protection charm just destroyed the contraceptive charm Madam Lorelei gave me. I could sense it absorb the magic."

Aragon frowned at her door. "I hope it won't destroy the strengthening charm on your door too."

She shuddered. She'd not feel safe living here if it did. But how could they test that? Her gaze fell on her sketch journal on the bed. "If the protection charm doesn't destroy the enchanted pencils, the door should be fine."

Selena curled on the bed and began a new sketch, and the gold gargoyle remained cool, and the pencils still changed color. She relaxed with a sigh. "The enchanted pencils mustn't count as influencing me, unlike the contraceptive charm." She darted across the room to touch the doorframe, and the protection charm still didn't warm. "The door doesn't either."

As she returned to the bed, Aragon settled in the chair across the room then asked her about life in the brothel, but he kept glancing away and shifting in his seat.

Her heart squeezing, she forced a bright smile as she described her days. Her almost kiss had embarrassed him, so he left not long after. She sighed as she locked the door behind him. Hopefully, he'd return soon.

. . .

PROTECTED by the powerful charm Aragon had provided, Selena enjoyed her first decent sleep at the brothel, so she rose early, ate breakfast, then slipped out to the miscellany shop to purchase more cloth. She'd just returned when Madam Lorelei asked to see her.

Selena swallowed as she settled in the plush chair before the madam's desk. What could the madam possibly wish to discuss?

Madam Lorelei pursed her lips. "Yesterday Mags mentioned a rumor you should hear. One of her patrons said his master is hunting a niece who disappeared a few days ago."

Selena tensed. The patron must be that footman with Mags earlier. And Selena had mentioned her uncle when arranging her proposition with Madam Lorelei, so the madam must suspect she was the missing niece. "Oh?"

Madam Lorelei arched a brow. "And the niece's description was remarkably similar to you. Light brown hair, freckles, gray eyes."

Her pulse surging, Selena lifted her chin. Yes, the madam realized Selena was the missing niece. But what did she intend to do? "Surely plenty of other ladies possess the same."

Madam Lorelei's lips quirked. "Perhaps. But how many of them are also named Selena, *Lena*?"

Selena winced. If only Madam Lorelei had accepted her bluff. But no sense in crying for spilt unicorn water. She eyed the madam. "What do you intend to do?"

Madam Lorelei shrugged. "The same as I have been. Even with your portion, Lord Treyvan is paying me well to keep your presence secret. And once bought, my loyalty is steady—until the money runs out. Not that your patron must worry about that."

Selena's chest loosened. Thank the Goddess the madam was honest. And that she knew nothing of the black witch. Knowing his involvement might have altered her loyalty. Most wouldn't cross black witches for fear of curses. Selena suppressed a shudder.

Madam Lorelei tilted her head. "So I'll remain silent about your presence here, and I'll make sure my girls do the same. But I think it's best if you remain in your room as much as possible, especially when my patrons are around. I can't control what they do outside the brothel."

Selena nodded. She'd avoided being seen before, but now she must be even more cautious. So she'd only leave her room to fetch meals. No more trips to purchase cloth. Fortunately, after this morning, she'd enough for a few more dresses. She sighed then rose. "Thank you for informing me about the rumors and for your loyalty, Madam Lorelei. Lord Treyvan and I truly appreciate it."

She swept a curtsy then darted back to her room. She locked the door behind her then sank on the bed and fingered the gold gargoyle nestled between her breasts. Considering everything Aragon had provided, she should be safe as long as she remained hidden. But hopefully, his people would find the black witch soon. During his next visit, she'd ask about their progress and mention her uncle's hunt.

So when Aragon thumped on her door the following evening, Selena dropped the dress she was sewing and ran to unlock her door. Not only must they discuss matters, but she'd missed Aragon as much as before. If only he could visit every day.

Once she relocked the door behind him, Aragon extracted a deck from his pocket with an easy smile. He'd clearly forgotten her almost kiss before. "I brought cards. What would you like to play?"

A glow warming her chest, Selena tilted her head. She'd not played cards since before her parents had died. But where could they play? She glanced about the cramped room. "Ten card. There's no table, so we must use the bed."

Aragon swallowed but waved her toward the bed. "Not entirely proper, but we'll manage."

She almost chuckled as she curled by the head of the bed and Aragon settled at the foot. At least with cards he couldn't sit across the room. But before cards, they must discuss the black witch and her uncle. "How goes the hunt for the black witch?"

Aragon grimaced as he shuffled and dealt. "Slower than I'd prefer, but Devon's people have discovered some leads after following your uncle. They also mentioned Midor is hunting you, but only at nearby taverns and shops."

Selena sighed and fanned her ten cards before her face. "Uncle Adan called me sanctimonious, so I doubt he'll check a brothel. But his hunt led Madam Lorelei to discover my identity."

Aragon glanced at her as he set up the draw and discard piles. "Shall she betray us?"

Selena smiled while sorting her cards. "No, you're paying her enough not to." When Aragon merely grunted, she flashed a coy smile. If she didn't distract him, he'd worry the entire evening. And she was safe enough for now. "I'm so glad you brought cards. I've not played in ages, but back home my parents and I played ten card most evenings. 'Twas their favorite."

Aragon relaxed and grinned at her over his cards. "Should I expect defeat?"

She tilted her head. Good, he'd allowed her to distract him. "Maybe." Mother had often won back home, but she'd taught Selena well.

Aragon leaned toward her as they began playing. "What else did you and your parents do in the evenings?"

Selena took her turn, her voice softening when she replied, "If not playing cards, Father would read aloud, usually Garoile, while I sketched and Mother embroidered. Although sometimes she made me embroider too. I much preferred sketching."

Aragon chuckled as he took his turn. "Sounds delightful. Did your uncle ever join you?"

She grimaced. "Rarely, thank the Goddess. When he did, he spent most of the evening glowering at Father and leering at

Mother." She shook her head as she drew a card then discarded one. "My parents ignored that because Father had raised him and felt guilty for falling in love with the girl Uncle Adan had wanted to court."

Aragon stilled and frowned at her. "If your father was older, how could your uncle sell the family estate?"

Selena sighed with a faint shrug. Although daughters typically inherited when their parents had no sons, she hadn't thanks to an ancient scandal. "Because the Midor who acquired the estate entailed it after his wife left him for his housekeeper, and Father could never persuade Uncle Adan to break the entail. But after Father died, there weren't male heirs, so Uncle Adan could sell."

His eyes dark, Aragon reached across the card piles to touch her hand. "How heartrending."

Her chest warmed at his tenderness. He was so wonderful. "But if he hadn't, I'd never have come to Ormas and met you." She dimpled. "Now, are we going to talk or play cards?"

They returned to their game, and both managed perfect hands after two more turns, but his cards outranked hers. They began another and continued playing until he reached a hundred points to win the game, with her close behind at ninety-two. Then he gave her the cards with a warm smile and left.

Selena grinned and shuffled the cards to play patience. Despite sitting on the bed, he'd been more relaxed today and had even touched her. Perhaps he did feel more than kindness. She simply must have startled him with her almost kiss before.

THE FOLLOWING MORNING, Selena froze mid-sketch at an unexpected knock. Aragon had only visited after dinner, and he'd have spoken. So who was it? "Yes?"

Lilly, Madam Lorelei's daughter, replied through the door, "There's a gentleman asking for you, Lena."

Spots flashed before Selena's eyes. Had her uncle or his black witch found her? Oh, Goddess. She gripped the gold gargoyle nestled between her breasts. "Did he ask for me by name? What does he look like?"

Lilly chuckled. "No, he asked for Treyvan's lady. He's real handsome for an older gent. Dark hair sprinkled with gray, brown eyes, and strong features."

Selena relaxed. Her visitor must be someone Aragon trusted, so she'd be safe enough. She sidled from her room and slipped down the back stairs to avoid being seen then halted when she joined her mystery visitor. He resembled Aragon in several decades—his father, no doubt. Gritting a smile, she shut the door behind her. "Good morning, your grace."

The Duke of Childes returned her curtsy with a deft bow. "Good morning, Miss... I'm afraid I don't know your name."

She swallowed and scrutinized his dark eyes for disdain but found none, only inquiry. Surprising. She sighed. "Miss Selena Midor, formerly from Upper Ashville in Linwick."

The duke bowed again. "Greetings, Miss Midor."

Selena eyed him. A wealthy duke visiting a common brothel was even more peculiar than his heir visiting. "Why are you here, your grace? This brothel can't be your style."

The duke flashed a crooked grin. "True, but when my son mentioned you, I had to meet you. Though it took me a few days since Aragon didn't say which brothel." He chuckled and gestured toward the sofa along the wall. "Shall we sit?"

Her stomach quivering, she sat beside him but remained rigid. He *had* to meet her? Why? Because he assumed she'd be easy to seduce? Or because he wanted to protect his son?

The duke studied her. "Aragon said you're hiding from your uncle and his black witch. Why a brothel? It seems no more your style than mine."

Selena softened at his avuncular smile. Perhaps he just wanted to verify she was worthy of his son's aid. "'Tis not, but a brothel was ideal for shedding my virginity before my uncle's black witch could use it to power his spells."

The duke's brows flew upward. "Aragon didn't mention *that*."

She almost winced. Probably to avoid tarnishing his parents' opinion of her. Although how could she be anything but tarnished when she was hiding in a brothel? "Fortunately, your son found me before I managed my desperate plan."

The duke shook his grizzled head but only asked, "So, Miss Midor, formerly from Upper Ashville in Linwick, what prompted you to move to Ormas?"

A pang darted through Selena at the home she'd never see again. "My uncle sold the family estate after my parents died last year."

The duke rubbed his chin. "Your uncle is your only family?"

She sighed and nodded as her throat clenched. Unfortunately.

The duke arched a brow. "What are your plans once my son handles the black witch, Miss Midor?"

Selena tensed and held his gaze. "I'll marry if I find love with a gentleman who loves me in return." A husband was the only way to permanently escape Uncle Adan. Though she'd considered becoming a governess or companion when she'd first fled, her uncle would remain her closest male relative, so she'd still be vulnerable to his schemes. But even to escape Uncle Adan, she'd never marry a gentleman she didn't love.

The duke coughed. "So no plans to return to the brothel?"

She almost shuddered. If only her sojourn was already over. "Goddess, no."

The duke slanted her a sidelong glance. "Has my son been treating you with respect despite the irregular situation?"

A blush heated Selena's cheeks. "He's been an utter gentleman." Except for that enthralling kiss when they'd met. When would he kiss her like that again? Tingling warmth suffused her.

The duke eyed her with a wry smile. "I see." As she attempted to reply, he rose. "I must go. 'Twas a pleasure. You're as intriguing as I hoped."

She blushed again and swept a curtsy. What did he mean by *that*?

The duke bowed in return then strode from the room.

Selena returned upstairs, her mind whirling. What an extraordinary encounter. She must tell Aragon about it when he next visited. Hopefully, 'twould be soon.

CHAPTER 10

*D*espite constantly thinking about Selena, Aragon forced himself to wait a day before returning to the brothel. Visiting every other evening was often enough to avoid rousing suspicion at the brothel, and he didn't dare visit more, even though he missed her.

He couldn't risk tarnishing his parents' opinion of Selena until Mother agreed to present her. Although Father, and probably Mother, knew about Selena, continually abandoning his duties at court to visit her might alarm them.

Besides, he must keep his relationship with Selena platonic, no matter how he hungered to kiss her again. She deserved the chance to meet other gentlemen before he courted her. And feigning mere friendship was harder every time he saw her.

Even though he must restrain himself, Aragon couldn't help his grin as he pounded on Selena's door with a book for her under his arm. After enduring all the grasping flirts at court, she was as delightful as a purring angelcat. He grinned harder when her door flew open. She was eager to see him too. Although that mightn't last once she met other gentlemen.

Selena dimpled while locking the door behind him. "I'd an unexpected visitor yesterday."

His chest clenched as he sat in the chair across the room. She'd not be so blithe if it had been Midor or the black witch. "Who was it?"

Selena tilted her head and curled on the bed. "Your father."

Aragon stiffened. He'd never told Father where to find her. Father must have come to scrutinize the lady distracting his eldest son. But what had he thought? And why hadn't he mentioned his visit afterward? "How did the visit go?"

A blush darkened Selena's freckled cheeks. "Well, I think. He called me intriguing."

Aragon relaxed with a smile. Good, then Father would influence Mother to feel the same. "Father has always admired strong ladies. He'd not have wed Mother otherwise."

Selena's voice softened, "He seems a loving father."

Aragon grinned, warmth filling him. "He is. He always nurtures our independence but supports us when we need it. And he tempers Mother's plans." When Selena sighed and studied her hands, he strode across the room to give her the book he'd brought. "Speaking of fathers, this is for you."

Selena brightened as she opened the book. "Garoile's *Summer Plays*! Mother and I always giggled when Father read these. He performed voices for the comedies." She thrust the book toward him. "Could you read for me? 'Twould be like being home again. Please?"

Aragon coughed as he accepted the book. He usually allowed Hawke to read aloud at home—his youngest brother far surpassed him after performing Wren's plays for years. "If you like, although I can't promise voices."

Selena dimpled at him. "Fair enough. How about you read the first scene, and I'll read the second? Then I can show you for next time."

He swallowed. "I'd like that." He settled back in his chair across the room then began to read. His reading was simple at first, but emboldened by her glowing face, he soon lowered or lightened his voice depending on the character. Not as dramatic as Hawke, but still decent.

When he finished the first scene, Selena erupted into applause. "You were *marvelous*. I needn't show you how to perform voices, but I'd love to read anyway."

Aragon handed her the book, and she began the second scene. She was even more vivacious than when she'd watched him. Tingling warmth flooded him. Goddess, she was spellbinding. Somehow he kept his expression friendly and didn't kiss her.

They spent the next several hours reading Garoile aloud, but eventually, he made himself return the book to her and said, "I must go. Stay safe, and contact me on the communication mirror if anything goes wrong. Unfortunately, Devon's people haven't updated me on the black witch or your uncle the past few days. If I don't hear anything soon, I'll contact them."

Selena sighed as she walked him to her door. "Madam Lorelei hasn't mentioned any further rumors about my uncle, so hopefully, he and the black witch still don't know I'm here." She dimpled and squeezed his arm. "I'll see you in a day or two."

Aragon swayed toward Selena. If only he could kiss her goodbye. But a kiss would be more than friendly, and courting her must wait until after she met other gentlemen. So he jerked a nod then left the brothel.

AT BREAKFAST THE FOLLOWING MORNING, Aragon kept waiting for his parents to mention Selena now that Father had met her. But Father merely sipped his kahve as Mother spent most of breakfast asking Hawke about his recent absences.

Aragon hid a frown while devouring his bacon. Why weren't his parents asking him about Selena? From what she'd said about their meeting, he'd assumed Father had liked her, but what if he didn't, and Mother wouldn't present her? Then Selena couldn't permanently escape her uncle, and Aragon couldn't court her without exploiting her inexperience.

Once Hawke finished eating and strode out, Mother turned to Aragon and drawled, "I've decided to cancel our dinner with the Thorpes later this week."

Aragon stilled, his kahve halfway to his mouth. The Thorpes had three eligible daughters, so Mother canceling dinner was unexpected, although welcome. He glanced at Father, whose mouth was twitching, so her decision must be because of Selena. "I see."

Mother beamed at him. "I'll be busy planning with Lady Keyes."

Planning Selena's presentation, no doubt. His shoulders tense, Aragon gulped his bitter kahve to prepare himself for his parents' questions.

Yet Mother merely chuckled and rose. "Presenting your penniless country lady shall be a lark. Hopefully, you handle that black witch soon." She grinned then swept from the family dining room.

Aragon gaped after her. She wasn't going to ask him about Selena? She adored managing her sons' lives, and she was determined to see him wed, so her lack of curiosity was suspicious. What exactly was she plotting?

Father leaned back in his seat and arched a brow. "How's the hunt for the black witch going?"

Aragon eyed Father and devoured the rest of his eggs. Although not managing like Mother, shouldn't Father ask about more than the black witch? Perhaps he'd ask about Selena after discussing the black witch threatening her. "Not fast enough."

Father inclined his head. "Maybe you should request magic marshals from Lord Islaye." The count served on the council as the Minister of Magic, so he oversaw the magic marshals who policed the witches in Calatini.

Aragon sighed and drained his kahve. Except royal agents were more discreet. "I'd rather wait to involve them until after

Devon's people find the black witch. Then I needn't reveal much about Selena."

Father nodded as he rose. "You don't want rumors reaching the black witch or her uncle." He flashed a crooked grin and clapped Aragon's shoulder. "After meeting her, I understand your determination to rescue her. She's spirited and forthright. Pretty, too."

Aragon relaxed as Father strode from the family dining room. Selena must have impressed Father enough that he'd no further questions about her. Perhaps that explained Mother's lack of curiosity as well. Thank the Goddess his parents were committed to helping Selena too. Now everything was set for her presentation once the black witch was captured.

He grinned. And his parents' approval meant he could visit Selena every evening without alarming them. Surely if he took care, his relationship with Selena would remain platonic no matter how often he visited, so he could risk visiting her tonight. Although before he did, he must find another gift to amuse her during her confinement at the brothel. Giving her gifts wasn't entirely proper, but her delight made them impossible to resist.

AFTER SHARING dinner with his parents and Hawke, Aragon galloped to Mermaid Street then bounded upstairs to Selena's room. He couldn't wait to tell her about his parents' approval. That should relieve her about her upcoming presentation. As she locked the door behind him, he grinned and tucked the book for her beneath his arm. "My parents and I discussed you at breakfast this morning."

Selena whirled to face him. "Oh?"

He winked at her. "Yes, and you truly impressed Father during his visit. He told Mother all about you, so she's eager to begin your presentation. She adores managing the affairs of others."

Selena swallowed and smoothed her hair. "How exciting."

Aragon took her hand and squeezed it. "You'll enjoy it. Mother shall ensure you meet every eligible gentleman at court." His stomach hardened. "With her patronage, many will pursue you." Which he must allow so Selena could discover love and not just gratitude.

Selena lowered her eyes and slipped her hand free. "I see. So because of your mother, court gentlemen shall desire a penniless country miss much older than most unmarried ladies? And one whose disreputable uncle hired a black witch to destroy her?"

His heart fluttered, and he dropped her book to grasp her shoulders. "Any gentleman of sense would." When she stared up at him and licked her lips, he jerked back as if scalded by a furious firelizard. He'd kiss her if they continued touching. To distract them from his almost kiss, he retrieved the book he'd dropped and offered it to her. "Here."

Selena opened the book and gasped. "*The Greatest Art in Calatini...* Goddess, the color plates are exquisite. 'Tis the most beautiful book I've ever seen."

Aragon smiled, warmth suffusing his chest. "Hopefully, it shall amuse you during your sojourn here. Hiding in this cramped room must be dull."

Selena caressed the book's leather cover. "Your lovely gifts have made it bearable." She dimpled at him. "Thank you, Aragon."

His breath quickened at her bright smile, but he forced himself to stride to his usual chair rather than drawing her into his arms. "'Tis nothing. What else do you miss living here?"

Selena plopped on the crimson bed. "The outdoors, companionship, and dessert."

Aragon coughed to disguise his laugh. Dessert seemed trivial compared to the other two. "Dessert?"

Selena sighed, her gaze hazy. "They only serve sweets at dinner, which I rarely risk." She sighed again. "I could devour a vat of karamel nut sweetice. Not that they'd serve such a luxury here."

He arched a brow. Not even he could eat that much of the rich dessert. "That's a lot of sweetice."

Selena giggled. "Yes, but 'tis my favorite dessert. We never had it often, so when I was young, I'd devour mine then beg my parents for theirs. Mother would resist so I'd not get sick, but Father always gave me his last spoonful."

Aragon grinned. He couldn't have resisted her begging either. "My brothers and I devoured *everything* as boys. Mother would say 'twas fortunate the Childes duchy was wealthy enough to feed our prodigious appetites." He chuckled. "Then Father would quip growing boys were like manticores who'd not eaten in a year, and that they wouldn't have risked begetting three sons two years apart if the duchy couldn't afford it."

Selena's mouth twitched. "I didn't realize boys ate so much." She tilted her head then patted the bed beside her. "Shall we play cards?"

He stiffened as hunger flooded him. He couldn't risk sitting so close, not when he burned to kiss her. "I'd rather see your latest sketches instead."

Selena blushed. "They're nothing compared to the art in that book you gave me, but very well." She opened her journal to a vivid sketch of a mountain lake.

After she showed him her sketches, all striking despite her modesty, he forced himself to rise. "I should go, but I'll return tomorrow."

Selena sighed as she walked him to the door. "Very well. Any word on the black witch or my uncle?"

Aragon grimaced. "No. I'll write Devon's people tonight demanding an update and share what they respond tomorrow." He forced a smile then left before his resistance crumbled and he kissed her.

As soon as he returned home, he wrote Devon's people, and Perkins handed him their reply late the following morning. At last. Aragon tore open the note. His pulse surged as he read—

they'd finally located the black witch. Thank the Goddess, he could bring Selena home soon.

But first, the black witch must be captured, and to do that, someone must lure him out. Aragon set his jaw. The heir of a wealthy duke would be too tempting to resist, so he'd confront the black witch himself.

He scowled at the note. But where could he meet the black witch? Not home. Too dangerous and might cause rumors. Perhaps The Gold Griffin. No one would notice him since he was a frequent visitor, and the black witch would resemble the other patrons.

He wrote back to Devon's people asking them to arrange a meeting at the tavern. Then he wrote to Lord Islaye requesting magic marshals to capture the black witch.

Grinning, he bounded down to the kitchen and begged Cook for a karamel nut sweetice in a cold basket. He and Selena could share it to celebrate the black witch's imminent capture. Once the dessert was ready, Aragon galloped to the brothel to visit Selena even though 'twas before noon.

CHAPTER 11

When Aragon pounded on her door before luncheon, Selena dropped her sketch journal with a gasp. Why was he here so early? Was something wrong? She jerked open the door. "Aragon, by the Goddess! You startled me."

A basket on his arm, Aragon winced as he strode inside. "Sorry, I was eager to see you."

Her stomach fluttered while she locked the door behind him. Because he'd missed her like she missed him? She leaned toward him. Perhaps he would kiss her again then. "Why?"

Grinning, Aragon dropped in his chair across the room and set the basket at his feet. "Devon's people have unearthed the black witch. They're arranging a meeting at The Gold Griffin, so magic marshals can capture him."

Selena swallowed as she curled on the bed, fingering the gold gargoyle he'd given her. Did he mean to confront the black witch himself? Dear Goddess. "A meeting with you?"

Aragon chuckled and nodded. "Of course. What better bait to lure him out?"

She shivered then leaned forward with a frown. "Be careful. He's vicious." Her throat constricted. And she couldn't bear if harm befell Aragon, especially because of her.

Aragon leapt and sat beside her to squeeze her hand. "I know, but we'll be in public, and I'll have magic marshals to protect me."

Tingling darted up her arm as she threaded her fingers through his. Hopefully, 'twould be enough. She managed a smile. "Thanks again for doing all this for me."

His dark-umber eyes flickering, Aragon squeezed her hand again then slid his free. "I'm glad to help such a brave lady." He sighed. "Although after this morning, I must avoid the brothel until the black witch is captured. I can't risk leading him to you."

Her ribs clenched. Please let his meeting with the black witch be soon and go smoothly. "I understand."

Aragon grimaced with a sigh. "But I'll risk sending a note once I learn when the meeting is set, so you know our plans." He glanced down and frowned. "I hope my abrupt arrival didn't mar your sketch."

Selena blinked at the sketch journal splayed between them. "Probably not. I'd just finished it." But a visit from him was worth marring any sketch. She turned over the sketch journal then smoothed her last page. "See, 'tis fine."

Aragon gaped at her sketch of a hawk flying over mountains. "Exquisite again." He hesitated then asked, "Could I have it?"

A blush burned her cheeks. He wanted another of her simple sketches? How flattering. "If you like."

She tore out the sketch, and Aragon slipped it inside his coat. Then he grinned at her and strode to his chair to retrieve his basket. "Before I go, I brought a treat to celebrate the black witch's imminent capture."

Her heart fluttering, Selena leaned forward as he set the basket between them on the bed. Although his visits were brief, his wonderful gifts more than offset that. He *must* feel more than charity for her. Her mouth watered when he opened the basket with a flourish. "Is that *karamel nut sweetice*?"

Aragon flashed a grin and handed her a spoon. "Yes, although we must share because I couldn't explain to Cook why

I wanted two bowls. The cold basket and two spoons were hard enough."

She winked at him. "I don't mind sharing, although you'd better hurry if you want any." She ate her first spoonful, closing her eyes and almost purring when the sweet and creamy dessert melted on her tongue. Goddess, so good. She opened her eyes with a shrug. "I devour karamel nut sweetice faster than a starving sprite."

Aragon eyed her mouth, his body still. "So I see." He swallowed then ate some sweetice. "We must alternate spoonfuls then."

Selena shivered as tingling warmth suffused her. Was he eyeing her mouth because he wanted to kiss her or because her gluttony repelled him? She gulped her second spoonful with another hum, and he stilled again, his gaze hungry. Her chest lightened. He wanted to kiss her.

They devoured the sweetice, desire burgeoning with each spoonful. Heat coursing through her veins, she leaned toward him as she set her spoon down. Surely, he'd kiss her now.

Yet Aragon jerked back, his gaze skittering away. "I must be off." He snatched the cold basket then bolted from the room.

Selena drooped on the bed, her heart clenching. Like before, almost kissing her had embarrassed him. He'd not have fled otherwise. If they'd fallen in love within moments of meeting, he'd not shun kissing her.

She must stop attempting to kiss him, even though his kindness enchanted her. Despite that enthralling kiss when they'd met and his flashes of interest, he always withdrew and kept directing her to other gentlemen. He mustn't want her as more than a friend. She rubbed her aching chest.

The following afternoon, she received a note from Aragon informing her his meeting with the black witch was set for luncheon in two days. Her hands trembling, she crumpled his note in her fist. Goddess, let him remain safe.

• • •

WHILE WAITING for Aragon to return, Selena sketched madly to calm herself. Yet her nerves continually worsened. By the afternoon before his meeting with the black witch, she could barely eat, and her hand ached from sketching so much.

So consumed with distracting herself from Aragon's upcoming meeting, she sketched until early evening without fetching food from the kitchen. She only stopped sketching when her hand could no longer hold a pencil.

Tears burning her eyes, she rubbed her cramped hand as her stomach rumbled. Although she'd not left her room during evenings to avoid the brothel's patrons, she must risk fetching dinner tonight. She'd be too hungry to sleep otherwise. At least she'd have dessert, although 'twouldn't compare to the karamel nut sweetice Aragon had brought.

She slipped down the back stairs to the kitchen and gathered enough fish stew, black bread, and bread pudding to last through luncheon tomorrow. After that, Aragon would come to take her away—if he captured the black witch. She swallowed.

Selena was about to enter the hall leading to her room when she halted at the bored drawl of the blonde who occupied the room across from hers. Her mouth dried. She must wait here until the girl and her patron left the hall.

The blonde snorted. "Sure, you can call me Isabel. You're payin'."

Selena tensed. Isabel had been Mother's name. She peeked into the hall then jerked back, spots flashing before her eyes. Oh, Goddess! Uncle Adan was the blonde's patron. If she misstepped, he'd discover her, and all of Aragon's plans would become worthless.

She shivered as Uncle Adan said, "I want you to resist too."

The blonde heaved a sigh. "I can a bit, but ropes or force costs extra. Madam Lorelei's rules."

Uncle Adan snickered. "Extra is fine."

The blonde's voice faded, "Let's go settle that with Madam

Lorelei." The girl must be leading Uncle Adan back down the front stairs.

Her heart pounding, Selena waited several long moments to ensure they'd left before bolting to her room. She locked her door, her hand trembling so hard she almost couldn't set the lock. Then she dropped her food on the bed and collapsed. Goddess, she'd barely escaped.

She dug out Aragon's communication mirror from beneath the bed. Should she call him? She caressed the mirror with a sigh. No, Uncle Adan hadn't seen her, so she was safe enough. And if she called Aragon, he'd rush to the brothel, which Uncle Adan *might* notice. Aragon storming a nearby brothel would appear suspicious to the black witch when they'd a meeting tomorrow. The black witch might flee or prepare a trap for Aragon.

She shuddered and slid the communication mirror beneath her pillow. With all the magical protection Aragon had provided, she'd be fine as long as Uncle Adan didn't realize she was at the brothel. Which he wouldn't if she remained hidden. Madam Lorelei would doubtless recognize him as her uncle, but she'd never betray Aragon or his gold for a poor gentleman like Uncle Adan. No, the madam would collect her extra payment from him without mentioning his niece was across the hall.

Selena grimaced. Though she couldn't bear to imagine why Uncle Adan was paying extra. Whatever he intended, he was pretending the blonde across the hall was Mother. Her stomach heaved.

When her pulse finally slowed and nausea faded, she forced herself to eat, even though her appetite had fled. Afterward, since her hand still ached too much to sketch, she paced the room with the gold gargoyle clenched in her other hand. To soothe herself, she sniffed the vial of lymon balm scent she and Mother had made. Thank the Goddess she was leaving the brothel tomorrow.

Unable to settle, she crawled beneath the covers early but

thrashed most of the night rather than sleeping, so she didn't wake until almost luncheon. Selena rubbed her face then ate all the food she had left. No reason to save it now.

Then she donned her nicest dress, a dusty-pink linen she'd sewn with Aragon's mother in mind. Her neck prickling, she smoothed her dress. She couldn't match a wealthy duchess, but she mustn't appear shabby. Her presentation relied on the duchess's good opinion. And finding a husband to permanently escape her uncle relied on her presentation.

Once dressed, she gathered her few possessions, most gifts from Aragon, into a small bag. She caressed the leather covers of the three books as she set them on her few gowns and the gold she'd bargained back from Madam Lorelei. Each book was perfect for different reasons. Then she tucked the cards, dagger, and communication mirror beside them before adding all but her current sketch journal. She'd sketched so much during her sojourn at the brothel that she'd filled the first one, and her current was two-thirds full. The enchanted pencils would have been worn away if they didn't replenish themselves.

Ready to leave, Selena curled on the bed and began sketching. As time trickled by, her breath accelerated, and her aching hand trembled over the page. Goddess, when would Aragon arrive? Had something gone awry? She shivered. Had the black witch eluded capture? Had the black witch cursed Aragon? Please let Aragon remain unscathed today. Please.

CHAPTER 12

*A*n hour before his meeting with the black witch, Aragon yanked on the plainest clothes he owned. Although a regular at The Gold Griffin, he wanted to remain inconspicuous during their meeting, so no rumors about him and a black witch started.

Then he rode to Mermaid Street, keeping to a trot despite his swift pulse. He left his bay mare at the stables and strode to the tavern. Were the magic marshals already waiting to capture the black witch?

When he'd returned from visiting Selena three days ago, Lord Islaye had replied to his note about the black witch and requested a meeting that afternoon. The count had introduced Aragon to one of his most powerful magic marshals, Master Marshal Thurston. Then the three men had planned how to capture the black witch during the meeting Devon's people were arranging at the tavern.

Once that meeting was set the following day, Aragon had written to Selena updating her then acted assuming the black witch was spying. Nothing must forewarn the black witch and cause him to flee. Aragon had forced himself to attend court

events and never mention Selena, not even when his parents or
Devon asked about her.

So as he strode past the brothel on his way to The Gold Griffin, he ignored the nondescript building. If the black witch realized Selena was there, he might send someone to kidnap her
during their meeting. And Aragon couldn't risk that.

Like usual, he nodded at the porter as he entered the tavern,
but instead of greeting Micah at the bar, he sat at a table along
the back wall. He beckoned the barmaid and ordered, studying
the tavern with feigned disinterest.

He muffled a sigh when he spotted Thurston at the bar.
Dressed in sailor's clothes, the master marshal and three other
pretend sailors were accepting glowing tankards from Micah.
Then they drifted to tables on either side of Aragon to capture
the black witch. Hopefully, he'd arrive soon. Feigning disinterest
was too difficult to maintain for long.

Fortunately, a lanky man with dark hair, scraggly beard, and
pallid skin slinked inside the tavern just as the plump barmaid
slammed a fish pie and two glowing tankards before Aragon.
Tingling surged in his chest. The black witch had arrived, and
soon Selena would be safe.

Aragon focused on his fish pie as the black witch glanced
about the tavern then sidled toward him. Revealing recognition
might spook the black witch. His fingers clenched on his fork.
He couldn't allow the black witch to escape now.

When the black witch coughed beside him, Aragon waved to
the opposite seat despite his tense stomach. Finally. "Sit. Have a
drink."

The black witch sat but grimaced at the glowing tankard
before him. "No drink for me, my lord."

Aragon arched a brow. "I insist." Sipping his own tankard, he
tailored his words to remain truthful, "Dealings with unknowns
fare better when honesty is assured." Plus, Thurston had said the
ale's magic should prevent the black witch from noticing any
listening spells.

The black witch grimaced again but drank from his glowing tankard. "I suppose so. Your people said you wished to hire me?"

Aragon savored a bite of fish pie with a mendacious smirk. He must mimic the black witch's usual patrons to lure the black witch into revealing the truth. So he drawled, "I heard you excel at extracting thorns."

The black witch echoed his smirk. "I do, but only if my fee is met. And you mustn't care *how* I extract that thorn."

Fire flared through Aragon. Miscreant. Maintaining his smirk, he forced himself to sip his glowing tankard. "I can afford any fee you set. I simply want my thorn removed. What do you propose?"

The black witch shrugged. "That depends on the situation. I'll need more details."

Aragon shook his head. "And I need more details before I trust you with mine." The magic marshals couldn't apprehend the black witch until he incriminated himself. "Prove your reputation is real first. Describe some of your recent under-takings."

The black witch's eyes narrowed and flicked to Aragon's glowing tankard. "Fine. But no names."

A zing darting through his chest, Aragon waved for the black witch to continue. The magic marshals could extract names from the black witch after they captured him.

The black witch smoothed his scraggly beard. "Recently, I cursed a mirror to accent ugliness for a cosmetics shop."

Aragon's breath stilled. Wicked, but hardly damning. A regular witch with shadowy morals might do as much. He snorted to provoke the black witch into confessing more.

The black witch blurted, "And I aided thieves sneak inside a stronghold to steal a baby for ransom."

Aragon snorted again. Again, not enough to prove him a black witch. They needed a confession about performing an evil spell, preferably a fatal one.

The black witch gulped his glowing ale. "And last year for

the heirs of a wealthy woman, I fed her cats fish laced with faedust and mercury so they went mad and killed her."

Energy surged through Aragon as Thurston slammed down his tankard and bawled, "I need some tripe." Tripe was the code indicating the master marshal had heard enough for his people to search the black witch's quarters for additional evidence.

Ignoring Thurston, the black witch leaned toward Aragon. "So how would you like me to extract your thorn, Lord Treyvan?"

After washing down a bite of fish pie with glowing ale, Aragon drew a deep breath. He could abandon the pretense of wanting the black witch's services. "By confessing your crimes before magic marshals."

The black witch's eyes bulged, and he leapt from his seat right into Thurston's arms.

His tension easing, Aragon continued eating as the magic marshals barked binding spells to seal the black witch's powers. The miscreant could no longer harm Selena, or anyone else, again. "Well done, marshals."

The black witch struggled to squirm free, but Thurston's grip on his prisoner remained fast.

Aragon tsked, but his neck prickled. The black witch resembled a maddened orc caught in an ensorcelled net. Deadly and wild, yet thankfully impotent. "What's the punishment for a black witch convicted of the crimes he just confessed to, Master Marshal?"

"Death," Thurston grunted over his squirming captive.

Aragon drew himself upright then arched his brows at the black witch. "Perhaps the magic marshals might allow a kind death if you tell them about Adan Midor and your other patrons." Then Midor would be arrested for hiring a black witch, and Selena would be completely free. As long as court didn't learn about his arrest, although Mother could manage that.

The black witch attempted to lunge at Aragon, but Thurston

restrained him. Then the black witch snarled, "You'll rue betraying me, my lord. I'll escape and seek vengeance."

A chill skittered up Aragon's spine. Praise the Goddess the black witch's power was bound. He'd have cursed Aragon otherwise, and a black witch's curse was no trifle. However, Aragon only snorted. He'd not show weakness to the greedy cur. "Escape? The magic marshals have you well trapped." Ignoring the black witch, he nodded at the magic marshals. "Thanks for your assistance in this matter."

"Certainly, my lord. We'll contact you if we require you for the trial." Thurston hauled the black witch from the tavern.

Aragon relaxed and devoured the last of his fish pie. The black witch was captured at last, and although alarming, his threats were hollow. Only Midor endangered Selena now, but Aragon's family could easily outmaneuver a poor country gentleman with no connections. Although Aragon would continue to have Midor watched to ensure he didn't harm Selena.

Tingling suffused Aragon's chest. Finally, he could remove Selena from the brothel and bring her home. Then he could give her his welcoming gift, inspired by her exquisite sketch of a hawk soaring over misty mountains.

The hawk's exultant freedom, which Selena no doubt craved after being trapped in the brothel, shone in her sketch and deserved recognition. So he'd taken it to The Arte of Spells, the magical art gallery on Broad Street, to have their witches enchant it like their moving paintings. An enchanted sketch would make a fine welcoming gift.

He sighed and drained his tankard, his heart squeezing. But this gift must be his last. He could no longer use her confinement as an excuse. Plus, Mother might find out and scold him for giving an unconnected lady gifts.

His pulse quickened. But since Selena would be living with them, at least he could see her whenever he wished. Although he must still keep their relationship platonic—he couldn't abuse her gratitude by seducing her before she could meet other gentlemen.

As Aragon rose, Micah barreled over with a frown. "What was that scuffle about, Lord Treyvan?"

Aragon almost winced as he clapped the huge tavern keeper's shoulder. If only he could have explained earlier without possibly forewarning the black witch. "The magic marshals apprehended a black witch I discovered. I apologize for bringing it to your door, but I couldn't think of another place I could meet a black witch without attracting attention."

Micah smoothed his bristling beard. "'Tis fine. Just wish I'd known. I could of asked the owner of the witch shop around the corner to stop by. The veiled witch is a frequent visitor since she provides the magical ingredient that makes my ale glow. The black witch wouldn't of noticed her."

Aragon suppressed a grimace. Except another witch's presence might have spooked the black witch, and they couldn't have risked him escaping. "Fortunately, nothing went awry."

He clapped Micah's shoulder again then strode from the tavern and bounded down Mermaid Street to the brothel. Selena was waiting for him.

CHAPTER 13

*W*hen Aragon finally knocked, Selena dropped her sketch journal and darted across the room. Her chest loosened as she flung open the door. Thank the Goddess, he'd confronted the black witch unscathed. "Aragon, at last!"

He bounded inside and kicked the door shut. He hoisted her in his arms and twirled her in a circle. "Magic marshals have just captured the black witch, and he'll never harm anyone again."

She clutched his upper arms, her breath stilling. "Truly?"

Aragon nodded with a broad grin.

Giddiness swamping her, Selena burrowed her arms about his waist and pressed her face against his chest. Thanks to Aragon, only her uncle threatened her now, but Aragon's influential family could easily handle a poor country gentleman. Plus, Uncle Adan wouldn't realize where she was until after her presentation at least. "Thank you, thank you, thank you!"

Aragon wrapped his arms around her. "I was glad to help."

She nestled against him. His embrace felt too right to pull away. Her heart squeezed. If only he wanted her as more than a friend.

But after a moment, Aragon coughed then stepped back. "Gather your things, so I can bring you home."

She swallowed and smoothed her dusty-pink skirt. Would the duchess like her? The duke had appeared to, but from what Aragon had said, the duchess was more exacting. However, Selena managed a smile and slipped her current sketch journal and enchanted pencils into her bag then donned her concealing cloak. "I'm ready."

Aragon took her arm, and they slipped down the back stairs and left the brothel. At the nearby stables, he mounted a darling bay mare then offered her his hand.

Tingling flashing across her skin, Selena settled behind him and wrapped her arms about his waist. Her eyes widened as they rode through the crowded streets of Ormas. Upper Ashville was *nothing* like this. She swallowed when they turned onto a broad street with vast townhouses.

Aragon halted at the grandest townhouse on the street. While he helped her dismount, she gaped at the brick mansion with ornate turrets and numerous windows. Doubtless only the palace eclipsed it. How would a penniless country miss fit here?

After the august butler ushered them inside and took Selena's bag, Aragon escorted her to the drawing room then smiled at the two older ladies on the sofa. "May I present to you Miss Selena Midor, formerly from Upper Ashville in Linwick. Selena, this is my mother, the Duchess of Childes, and her best friend, Lady Keyes."

Her stomach fluttering, Selena swept a deep curtsy and studied Aragon's mother beneath her lashes. The duchess wore an exquisite, sky-blue gown with her icy-blonde hair in a sleek chignon. Goddess, her elegant perfection was daunting.

An impish smile curved the duchess's patrician lips as she scrutinized Selena. "You are precisely as Eldridge described, Miss Midor."

Selena blushed. What exactly had the duke said? The duchess appeared to approve, whatever it was. "Thank you, your grace. Please call me Selena."

Lady Keyes cocked her silvery head and rose. "I should leave so you can become better acquainted. I look forward to seeing you again."

The duchess patted the empty seat beside her once her friend left. "Come sit beside me, Selena. Aragon, go amuse yourself elsewhere."

Selena's skin prickled as she perched on the sofa. Doubtless the duchess would quiz her as soon as her son left.

His jaw firm, Aragon sat on the chair beside Selena. "I'll remain here."

Laughter flickered in the duchess's pale-blue eyes. "As you like." She turned to Selena. "I assume your ambition at court is to secure a husband to protect you from your loathsome uncle."

Selena's heart twinged. "But not just any husband. I want a gentleman I can love." Aragon would be perfect, except he didn't want her as more than a friend. Plus, the duchess probably wouldn't want him courting a penniless country miss with a disreputable uncle.

The duchess waved her hand. "Of course, of course. We'll begin with your presentation ball in two weeks. But before that, we *must* refresh your wardrobe. I'll arrange an appointment at Celeste's at once. 'Tis the best dress shop in Ormas."

Selena sighed. She didn't care for dress shopping, and the gold she'd bargained back from Madam Lorelei wouldn't last long at such a fashionable shop. "Perhaps a more modest shop would be appropriate."

The duchess's pale brows flew upward. "Nonsense, Celeste's is perfect, and don't fret about cost—we'll supply your wardrobe."

Selena stilled, her hands tightening in her lap. Aragon's family must be wealthier than she'd realized. And as determined to help her as he was. "I'm grateful for your generosity, but I don't wish to be a leech."

Aragon frowned at her. "You're no leech."

The duchess chuckled. "And since I've no daughters, I'm eager to have a young lady to outfit and present at last." She tilted her head, eyeing Selena. "You look like you could use a rest before dinner." She turned to her son. "Make yourself useful and escort Selena to her chambers. The blue room in the family hall."

Aragon blinked at his mother then rose and offered Selena his arm.

Selena beamed at Aragon's mother. The duchess had been unexpectedly welcoming with few questions. So much better than she'd feared. "Thanks for your great kindness, your grace."

The duchess smiled back as Selena rose. "'Tis my pleasure."

Aragon escorted Selena upstairs to a sumptuous bedroom with cornflower-blue wallpaper. Releasing her, he said, "I'll return in a moment."

Once he left, she gawked at her temporary chambers. She'd never lived anywhere so fine. Aragon's family must be incredibly wealthy to loan it to *her*.

Aragon soon returned bearing a package. "A welcoming gift."

Her breath quickened. What perfect gift had he purchased now? She tore open the package then gaped at the framed sketch inside. The hawk she'd drawn last week now soared across the page over the misty mountains of Linwick. Exactly as she'd imagined. Warmth filled her chest.

Aragon blurted, "I had the witches at The Arte of Spells enchant it like they do their moving paintings. I hope you don't mind."

"Mind?" Selena snorted a laugh as she caressed her enchanted sketch. "'Tis lovely. The finest faegift I've ever received. Thank you, Aragon." Her skin tingled as she leaned toward him. If only she could risk kissing him.

Yet unlike at the brothel, Aragon leaned toward her until they almost touched.

She licked her lips. Goddess, was he about to kiss her? Her heart surged.

But then Aragon jerked back. "I'll return to escort you to dinner. My chambers are the door on the left if you need me."

After he bolted, Selena hugged her enchanted sketch.

Perhaps he wanted to court her after all. He'd given her a faegift and almost kissed her. Light bubbled in her chest. Despite not falling in love at once, she'd eagerly court him. He was dedicated and kind—and his kisses enthralling.

Her mind awhirl, she unpacked her small bag the servants had left beside the massive bed. Once she arranged her lymon balm scent and other sundries on the dressing table, she fingered the gold gargoyle nestled between her breasts. With the black witch captured, she'd no need for a charm warding against magic. But the charm was lovely. Plus, Aragon had given it to her, and she enjoyed wearing a token of his interest. She smiled and released the gold necklace.

Already wearing her nicest dress, she didn't change for dinner. Instead, she curled on her bed and sketched until Aragon returned. She almost blushed when he took her arm with a warm smile. As he escorted her downstairs, she darted glances at him. When would he kiss her again? Soon, hopefully.

When they joined his brothers in the drawing room, Selena tilted her head and blinked at them. Though Aragon had mentioned they were two years apart, the three brothers appeared like triplets except for one's pale-blue eyes.

Aragon gestured toward his brother in priest robes. "Selena, this is Mel, also known as Priest Melchior Hawke. Mel, Miss Selena Midor. Mother shall be presenting her."

His smile kind, Mel bowed. "Pleasure to meet you."

Selena smiled back. She could see a boyhood Mel visiting poor villagers like Aragon had described. "Likewise."

Aragon turned to his brother with their mother's eyes. "And this is Hawke, also known as Lord Beza. He goes by our surname since he despises his given name. Hawke, Selena."

Hawke grimaced at his brother. "You would too if you were stuck with a wretched name like Beza." An impish grin replaced his grimace as his gaze flicked between Aragon and Selena. He captured her free hand and kissed her fingers. "Now, where did my stuffy brother unearth a delectable lady like you?"

Selena stiffened and extracted her hand. The younger gentleman was as flirtatious as Aragon had warned. "A brothel."

Hawke snickered. "Truly? I can't imagine that."

Aragon glared at his youngest brother. "'Tis true, although you'd better not share that with anyone other than Wren."

As Hawke snickered again, Mel slanted her a concerned frown. "Why were you in a brothel?"

Selena shrugged. "I was attempting to evade the black witch my uncle hired." She beamed at Aragon and squeezed his arm. "But Aragon handled him for me, so I could leave."

Mel and Hawke gaped at Aragon, but before they could reply, their parents swept into the drawing room, and everyone proceeded to dinner.

Once they'd began the first course, the duke flashed an avuncular smile at Selena. "Glad Aragon rescued you from that brothel at last." He grinned at his wife. "Now Caro can stop fretting ill might befall you before she could present you."

The duchess narrowed her eyes at him. "I wasn't concerned because of her presentation. A brothel is dangerous for a lady."

Her throat thickening at the duchess's concern, Selena sipped her whitekrab soup. So delicious after the brothel's plain fare. "Aragon ensured I was well protected."

The duchess beamed at her eldest son. "Of course, but 'tis good you're safe with us now."

Hawke winked at Selena over his wine. "Definitely. Mother might confine herself to meddling with you and forgo us."

As the duke chuckled and the duchess pursed her lips, Aragon snorted and served Selena seared fish and sparrow grass. "She might, if you didn't find a new lady every week."

Shaking his head at his brothers, Mel asked Selena about her interests, and a lively discussion about sketching and riding lasted through the delectable dinner. Selena laughed more than she had in ages as she devoured each course. But tears pricked her eyes at dessert—karamel nut sweetice. Aragon's family was making sure to include her. She'd not enjoyed that since her parents had died.

Beneath the table, she grasped Aragon's hand. Thank the Goddess he'd stumbled into the brothel. Not only had he rescued her from the black witch, but he'd brought her home to his family, who were as kind as he was. If he truly wanted to court her, everything would be perfect.

CHAPTER 14

*A*fter the next council meeting, Lord Islaye waited until only Aragon and Devon remained before he said, "The magic marshals unearthed decisive evidence against that black witch you discovered, Lord Treyvan. They'll interrogate him for the next month, but then he'll hang."

His chest easing, Aragon nodded from his seat beside Devon. The black witch would definitely never threaten Selena again. And if he implicated Midor, neither would her uncle. "When he does, please let me know. Thanks for your help handling him."

"Not a problem. I'm glad another black witch has been captured." The count smiled at Aragon then inclined a respectful nod at Devon before departing.

Devon arched his brows with a faint frown. "Now that she's living with you, how *is* Miss Midor?"

Tingling warmth flooded Aragon. With Selena living so close, keeping their relationship platonic was arduous. Every morning he burned to greet her with a kiss. But she'd so few opportunities that he couldn't steal her chance to meet other gentlemen. And although she appeared to enjoy his company, she simply might be grateful. So he forced himself to treat her like a sister. Except a brother didn't burn to kiss his sister. "Well. She's enjoying being part of a family again, and Mother is ecstatic to have a lady to present at last."

Devon flashed a wry smile. "I suppose she's the reason for your mother's upcoming ball."

Aragon winced. Mother's elaborate preparations were enough to send a sensible gentleman mad, but he couldn't escape them. He must support Selena. "Yes. And Mother has decreed Selena can't be seen before then, especially in her country attire. Although Mother is handling that now."

Devon's mouth twitched. "I'm surprised she waited so long."

Aragon snorted. She'd not wanted to, but sometimes even Mother couldn't control everything. "With the season underway, she couldn't get an appointment at her favorite dress shop until today. Which seemed to relieve Selena."

Devon arched a brow. "How refreshing. I'll definitely be interested in meeting your fascinating lady soon."

Aragon grinned at his friend and rose. Good, because Selena must meet Devon before being presented. Familiarity with the king would lend her cachet. "Come by for dinner sometime."

Devon rose as well, his eyes dark. "Would tonight be too soon?"

Aragon blinked as they left the council room. Devon was free already? He *must* be interested. Did he mean to court Selena? Aragon's stomach hardened, but he managed a smile. "No, that should be fine. Same time as usual."

When he returned home, Selena and Mother were still out, so he fetched a book then waited for them in the drawing room. They finally returned an hour before dinner.

His breath seizing, Aragon gaped at Selena as she sat on the sofa beside him. Her shabby country dress had been replaced by a sleek gown in a rich raspberry that made her freckled skin glow. Goddess, she'd been pretty before, but now she was stunning. How would he ever resist kissing her? "I see the dress shopping went well." Too well.

Selena blushed but inclined her head. "Thank you. My new

gowns are gorgeous—but the quantity your mother deemed essential was staggering."

Although he should stop staring, he eyed her new gown. His heart fluttered. She was more spellbinding than a siren luring a sailor. "Well, you'll be grateful for your modish attire when Devon joins us for dinner tonight."

As Selena swallowed, Mother arched her brows from her seat opposite of the sofa. "When was that decided?"

Still breathless, he yanked his gaze from Selena to face Mother. "After today's council meeting. I let Perkins know when I returned."

"Good." Mother's eyes gleamed. "Devon should join us more often. Since his father died, he overexerts himself."

Aragon suppressed a grimace. True, but Devon keenly felt his duty to Calatini. "Good kings often do."

Mother tsked. "He needs a queen to share the burden of ruling."

Aragon sighed. Why must Mother always harp on marriage? "Yes, but he must find the right lady first." Would he decide Selena was that lady? His jaw tightened.

Her gaze darting between them, Selena coughed and licked her lips. "With the king joining us, do we dine more formally?"

Mother tilted her head, blinking at Selena. "No, Devon is family."

Selena swallowed but nodded. She was clearly nervous to meet the king. Not surprising.

Aragon took her hand to reassure her, and a shiver tingled up his arm. "He enjoys the relaxed air of our family dinners." They were one of the few times he could be himself rather than the king. "Just treat him like an ordinary gentleman. He prefers that to fawning."

Selena threaded her fingers through his and almost smiled. "I'll try."

Mother eyed their intertwined hands, so he made himself release Selena then said to distract everyone, "Before I forget,

Lord Islaye mentioned the black witch has been sentenced to death."

Selena fingered the gold gargoyle still nestled between her breasts. "I'm glad he's facing justice. What about Uncle Adan?"

Aragon sighed and shook his head. Unfortunately, he'd little news about her uncle. "There's no evidence against him yet, so he's still free. But he's not left his townhouse since the black witch disappeared, and he doesn't appear to realize you're living with us."

As Selena relaxed, Mother pursed her lips then said, "And we must ensure he doesn't until after Selena's presentation ball. I don't want him interfering with my plans." She rose. "I should let your father know about Devon. Excuse me."

To divert Selena from Devon's visit, Aragon asked about her favorite part of today. Ignoring the dress shopping, she began rhapsodizing about The Arte of Spells, which was beside Mother's dress shop. She was sighing that Mother hadn't allowed her inside when Devon joined them.

As Aragon introduced her to Devon, Selena stilled then inhaled and swept a curtsey.

Devon glinted a smile as he bowed. "I've been anticipating meeting you, Miss Midor. Aragon's tales of you have been intriguing."

Selena blushed, glancing at Aragon. Then she lifted her chin and smiled. "Intriguing is *one* word for a lady hiding in a brothel. Desperate would be more apt."

As Devon blinked at her, a glow filled Aragon's chest. Like he'd suggested, she acted as if she met kings every day. "I'm thankful I discovered you rather than some other gentleman." Most wouldn't have hesitated to exploit her desperation.

Selena dimpled and touched his hand. "So am I."

His gaze narrow, Devon eyed them for a moment. Then he relaxed and smiled at Selena. "Few would be as chivalrous as Aragon."

Selena beamed at Aragon. "I know."

As Aragon shrugged, Mother swept in with Father. Since Hawke was out again, the five of them proceeded to dinner. Aragon sat beside Selena at the small table, while Devon sat between Selena and Father, and Mother sat across from Devon.

Once they began with pea soup, Devon leaned toward Selena. "Upper Ashville is about two days west of Silverdale, I believe. Do they mine copper or iron?"

Her spoon halfway to her mouth, Selena gaped at the king. "Copper."

Aragon forced a smile, his stomach clenching. Selena hadn't gaped when she'd met *him*. "Devon's mother hailed from Silverdale, so he learned everything about the vicinity."

Devon eyed Aragon, his mouth twitching. "It made up for never meeting her, I suppose."

Aragon almost winced. If Devon had noticed his resentment, his parents must have as well. He studied them, but their smiles revealed nothing. His neck prickled. What were they about?

Mother beamed at Devon as Father served her roast lamb. "Would you take Selena's first dance at her presentation ball, Devon?"

Aragon tensed and swallowed a protest. Although he must allow Selena to meet other gentlemen, he'd wanted her first dance. Of course Mother had other plans.

Devon's gaze flicked to him. "Perhaps Aragon might be more appropriate since you're presenting her?"

Selena leaned toward Aragon as she waved her forkful of creamed spinach. "Dancing with the king first shall fluster me. Aragon would be better."

Mother chuckled. "Nonsense, you're too brave for such a dance to fluster you. Besides, Devon is family, and dancing first with a king is more impressive than a mere duke's heir. Aragon can have your second dance. After that, gentleman shall *beg* to partner you."

Selena sighed and ate her spinach as servants brought dessert. "Very well, your grace."

Warmth filled Aragon. At least she'd wanted to dance with him first. But would that last after she met other gentlemen? If only courting her now wouldn't be exploiting her inexperience. He sighed and served her a slice of rhubarb pie.

Then Father asked Devon about today's council meeting, so dessert was spent discussing political affairs.

Afterward, Aragon walked Devon to the door. What did he think of Selena? Had he decided to court her himself? Aragon's chest burned, but he maintained a smile. "Well?"

Devon grinned. "She's perfect for you. I can see why you're fascinated."

Aragon flushed, but his chest eased. He *was* fascinated—Selena had consumed his thoughts since they'd met. If she felt the same after she met other gentlemen, he'd definitely court her. Hopefully, he could restrain himself long enough.

Devon clapped Aragon's shoulder. "Tell your mother if she requires further assistance when presenting your Miss Midor, I'll be glad to give it."

Once he and Devon exchanged farewells, Aragon returned to the drawing room where Selena sat sketching alone. Hunger flooded him again. Goddess, she was spellbinding. He sat beside her on the sofa. "Where are Mother and Father?"

Selena lowered her sketch journal. "They left to dress for Lady Morwynne's ball. Are you joining them?"

He grimaced. "No. I'll save my socializing until Mother presents you." There'd be countless events to attend then. He eyed her. "What did you think of Devon?"

Selena dimpled and tilted her head. "I liked him. He appears more like a country gentleman than a king."

His stomach tensing again, Aragon nodded. "People often say that—until they see him amidst a crisis. Then he reveals his natural authority."

Selena nodded. "Doubtless he makes a fine king." She glanced at him beneath her lashes. "Since your mother insisted he take my first dance, we should practice my dancing like you suggested."

He swallowed as his pulse surged. Had she asked because she wanted to dance with him or because she wanted to impress Devon? And could he resist kissing her if they danced alone?

Selena leaned toward him. "Please, Aragon. I've been looking forward to dancing with you again."

Tingling suffusing him, Aragon took her arm. He'd risk dancing with her. He escorted her to the shadowy ballroom then lit some candles. "We haven't any music."

A dimple quivered in Selena's left cheek as she glided into his arms. "We didn't need music at the brothel."

He jerked a nod, his body hardening when he inhaled her lymon scent. Goddess, she was tempting. As they twirled about the echoing ballroom, he managed to keep the proper distance despite his hunger. But he halted and released her after one dance. He'd kiss her if they continued. "Shall we go play cards or read aloud?"

Selena sighed but nodded, so Aragon whisked her back to the drawing room. Surely he could maintain control there.

CHAPTER 15

our days after their solitary dance, Selena finally managed time alone with Aragon when the duchess attended Lady Islaye's salon. She dimpled as she sat beside him on the sofa in the morning room. "What are you reading?"

Aragon tensed as he marked his place in his book. But then he relaxed with a shrug. "*The Prince and the Truth Sword.*"

She leaned toward him. If only she could hold his hand, but he'd no doubt flee. He'd been painfully proper since their dance. Her heart squeezed. Perhaps he didn't want to court her after all. She clung to her grin as she replied, "Sounds intriguing. What's it about?"

Aragon's eyes crinkled. "A prince's quest to unearth a sword that reveals the truth after his uncle frames him for murdering his father to steal the throne."

Selena chuckled and shook her head. "Hopefully, my uncle never reads it. 'Twould only inspire his schemes." Although they'd no doubt founder like always.

Aragon winced and set aside his novel to take her hands. "We'll ensure his schemes never harm you again. Not that he knows your whereabouts at the moment. Although he's finally emerged, Midor is still hunting for you near the docks."

She squeezed Aragon's hands with a soft smile. The dear man was always protecting her. "I was jesting, you know. I'd enjoy reading your novel once you finish."

Aragon eyed her lips then swallowed and dropped her hands. "I'll lend it to you then."

Selena's heart fluttered. Had he wanted to kiss her? How could she encourage him to continue? She ached for another enthralling kiss.

But before she could reply, an auburn-haired lady breezed into the morning room. She beamed at Aragon and chirped, "Morning, Aragon." She turned to Selena. "And you must be Miss Selena Midor. My mother speaks well of you."

Selena shifted closer to Aragon. Who was this overfamiliar lady? "Your mother?"

With a blithe grin, the lady alighted on the chair beside Selena. "Lady Keyes."

Selena studied her. The dainty lady did resemble the duchess's best friend, although she was young to be the daughter of Lady Keyes, who must be a decade older than the duchess.

Aragon chuckled, his smile warm. "Selena, this is Miss Wren Keyes; she's Hawke's best friend and grew up with us on an adjoining country estate."

Wren's hazel eyes flickered. "We live two doors down in Ormas too. Our parents are inseparable. But please, call me Wren."

Selena forced herself to smile at Wren. After their lifelong familiarity, did Wren consider Aragon, Mel, and Hawke her brothers, or did she feel more for one of them? If so, 'twould be Aragon. Selena's stomach cramped. "Only if you call me Selena."

"Gladly." Wren leaned forward with a grimace. "I apologize for not visiting sooner. I meant to when Mother mentioned you last week, but I was directing a play at the orphanage."

Selena frowned. "An orphanage?" Why would a wealthy baronet's daughter be there?

Wren grinned and bobbed a nod. "Waterstreet Orphanage. I volunteer there. 'Tis near the docks."

Aragon nudged Selena. "Near The Gold Griffin."

Selena gaped at Wren. *This* dainty lady visited the brothel's neighborhood? "Your parents allow you to visit that part of Ormas?"

Wren shrugged. "At first, they insisted Hawke accompany me, but after nine years, they're accustomed to my visits. I spend most of my time there."

Selena stiffened. Wren's impossible perfection made her teeth ache. Fire flared in her chest. Goddess, was *she* why Aragon wouldn't court her? "I see."

Wren tilted her head. "Are you excited for your ball next week?"

Not really. Selena folded her hands in her lap with a glittering grin. She couldn't betray weakness to such a paragon. "Of course."

Wren wrinkled her nose. "I wouldn't be. I despise court events and rarely attend them. Although I'm glad to attend yours."

Hawke strolled into the morning room. "Meaning your mother ordered you to attend."

Her face radiant, Wren beamed at Hawke as he sat beside her. "She did, but I'm pleased to support a lady in need."

"Of course you are." Hawke shook his head but smiled at Wren.

Selena studied them, the cramp in her stomach vanishing. Wren *did* feel more for one of the Hawke brothers, just not Aragon. And from his sincere smile, Hawke probably felt the same. Selena grinned at Wren. "I'll be relieved for a female friend at my ball."

Wren grinned back. "I'm sure you'll meet others too."

Hawke rose, arching a brow at Wren. "Are you ready?"

As Wren nodded and leapt upright, Aragon cocked his head. "Where are you headed?"

Hawke shrugged. "I'm showing Wren some townhouses I'm considering."

Selena blinked. Ormas townhouses were so costly even wealthy families shared one, and most only rented a townhouse for a few seasons. If their youngest son could afford to purchase one, no wonder Aragon's family had loaned her that sumptuous bedroom.

Yet Aragon frowned at Hawke. "How are you purchasing a townhouse?"

Hawke flashed a crooked grin. "Remember that investment I made last year once I received my inheritance?" When Aragon nodded, Hawke chuckled. "Well, Buford's ships returned last month to Ormas with a fortune in goods. My profits are enough to purchase a townhouse—and then some."

Selena eyed Hawke with new respect. Despite his irksome flirting, he could be shrewd. Many younger sons squandered their inheritances rather than growing them.

Aragon arched his brows. "Mother shan't like that."

Hawke shrugged. "She must become accustomed. I'm of age and free to do as I like. *I'm* not the heir who must remain tied to the family properties."

Aragon shook his head. "True enough. You'd best warn Father, so he can prepare Mother."

Hawke snickered. "Don't we always?"

Wren wrinkled her nose at him. "Hawke!"

Hawke widened his eyes until Wren sighed. He chuckled then stepped forward to capture Selena's hand. Kissing her fingers, he slanted her a smoldering look. "Perhaps you'd care to join us? I'd *love* an artist's opinion."

As Aragon and Wren both stiffened, Selena extracted her hand. At least she wasn't the only one irked by Hawke's flirting. "I'm content to remain here, thank you."

Hawke sighed. "Very well, dear lady." He offered Wren his arm. "Shall we go?"

Wren took his arm and gave Selena a tight smile. "Pleasure to meet you."

"Likewise," Selena called while Wren and Hawke strode from the morning room. Hopefully, Wren would forget his empty flirting by the ball. A female friend there would be comforting. Once they were alone again, Selena turned to Aragon. "*That* was interesting. Shall your mother truly be upset?"

Aragon's lips quirked. "She'll fuss, but I suspect she's proud of her youngest son's independence. I know Father is."

Selena cocked her head. What was he not saying? She leaned toward him. "Oh?"

Aragon shrugged and glanced away. "He once told me they were fortunate to possess three sons they could be proud of for different strengths. Hawke for his independence. Mel for his compassion. And me for my dedication." He grimaced with another shrug. "I was lowered by Father's faint praise."

Warmth suffusing her chest, she touched his knee. Again, he was too modest. "Dedication is important."

Aragon leaned toward her as his gaze jerked back to her face. "Oh?"

Selena held his gaze. "Dedication helps accomplish your goals and inspires others to trust you. And trust is the bedrock of love." Her breath stilled. Perhaps instant attraction wasn't enough to inspire lasting love—but trust could grow that attraction into love. "And you're the most trustworthy gentleman I've ever met."

Aragon's eyes turned ebony as he began bending his head.

Tingling heat flashed across her skin. He was definitely about to kiss her this time. At last. She must remember to praise dedication in the future.

"Ahem."

At the duchess's cough, Aragon jolted back.

Selena suppressed a sigh. So much for another enthralling kiss.

A faint smile curved the duchess's patrician lips. "Your father requires you in his study for estate business, Aragon."

"Very well." Aragon stiffened but rose. He held Selena's gaze for a moment before striding from the morning room.

Fighting not to blush, Selena lifted her chin to face his mother. Was the duchess going to scold her for almost kissing her son?

Yet the duchess merely beckoned her. "Come along, I've a surprise."

Selena's pulse skittered as the duchess led her upstairs to a room at the end of the guest bedrooms. What kind of surprise?

The duchess smiled and gestured for her to enter. "I had this little room prepared for you."

Prepared how? Her mouth drying, Selena stepped inside then halted. She goggled at the large windows facing north, neutral gray wallpaper, a large drawing desk, two easels, several chairs, and a bookcase of art materials. Tears pricked her eyes. The duchess had created an art room for her!

The duchess glided about the room. "Since you always have your sketch journal, I thought you might enjoy a private room for sketching or painting. I consulted artists from The Arte of Spells to design it. Does it suit?"

Selena blinked at the duchess, clutching her sketch journal to her breast. Laughter bubbled in her throat. "Does it *suit*? I've never seen a more perfect room. My deepest thanks, your grace."

The duchess flashed a grin. "I'm pleased you like it."

Selena's heart swelled as she glanced about the wonderful room again. She must find some way to thank the duchess. Perhaps a portrait? As the duchess began to leave, she called, "Would you mind being the subject of my first sketch here?"

The duchess turned with a smile. "If you like. Where do you want me?"

Her movements fluid, Selena directed the duchess to the nearest chair and set an easel into position. She swiftly sketched the outlines of the portrait then changed her enchanted pencils into shades matching the duchess. As she began filling in the duchess's blush dress, she asked, "You've been extraordinarily kind to me, your grace. Could I ask why?"

The duchess merely smiled with a shrug. "Why not?"

Selena stilled, tingling filling her chest. "Because your son discovered me in a brothel." Most ladies would have shunned her knowing that.

The duchess shrugged again. "That has no bearing on your character. Aragon thought you were worth championing, and Eldridge seconded his opinion. Plus, everything I've seen so far has only confirmed it."

Selena's throat tightened. No one had praised her like that since her parents had died. "Thank you, your grace."

The duchess studied Selena. "Could I ask *you* something?"

Her neck prickling, Selena swallowed but began coloring the sketch again. What did the duchess want to know? "Of course."

The duchess tilted her head. "You said you want to marry a gentleman you could love. What type of gentleman is that?"

Selena finished coloring the duchess's dress. Aragon would be perfect, but she couldn't tell his mother *that*. "A trustworthy gentleman is essential. Not too young, but still willing to play. Someone who demonstrates his deep feelings through his actions." She blushed then mumbled, "And an enthralling kisser."

The duchess trilled a laugh. "I believe we can manage that. I know several gentlemen that might suit."

Still blushing, Selena finished her sketch and handed it to the duchess. But would those gentlemen be as wonderful as Aragon? Probably not.

The duchess beamed. "Lovely, I'll treasure it."

As the duchess sailed from the room, Selena remained to begin another portrait—this one of Aragon. If only she were sketching him in person.

CHAPTER 16

wo days before Selena's presentation ball, Aragon halted in the doorway of the family dining room as his heart surged. Selena was alone at the table. They'd not been alone since Mother had interrupted their almost kiss. Could he restrain himself? He swallowed then sat across from her and stuffed a roll with meat and cheese. "Where's Mother?"

Selena grimaced and set down her stuffed roll. "Speaking to the musicians for my presentation ball."

He eyed her as he ate. Her voice was flat and her movements wooden. Perhaps a ride would hearten her. She'd been confined indoors for ages—first because she'd been at the brothel and later due to Mother's edicts.

He set his jaw when she sighed and toyed with her plate. She needed out. Surely he could keep a ride platonic, and Mother wasn't here to stop them. He smiled at her. "Would you care to go riding after luncheon? The weather charm in Father's study said it wouldn't rain until after dark."

Selena brightened and began eating. "A ride would be lovely." She drooped after a bite. "But shan't a ride spoil your mother's plan to conceal me until my presentation ball?"

Aragon shrugged as he finished his luncheon. Not if they took care, and she needed it. "We'll be fine if we avoid the fashionable parks or the near the docks." Court would notice them at the parks, while Midor might near the docks. "But there are plenty of other places to ride. I thought perhaps the royal forest. I've an open invitation from Devon to ride on royal lands whenever I wish."

Selena devoured her stuffed roll with a grin. "As long as your mother doesn't object."

Warmth filling him at her grin, he drew her upright. "If we use the servants' entrance, she'll not know until too late. We can always beg for her forgiveness later." 'Twas often the easiest way to handle Mother.

Selena dimpled and threaded her fingers through his. "Come on then!"

Still holding hands, they darted upstairs to change. Afterward, Aragon met Selena at her door and recaptured her hand, then they skulked out the servants' entrance like imps escaping a demon's warren. As they approached the stables, he squeezed her hand. "We've a variety of mounts available. What type would you like?" A courser no doubt.

Selena hummed and tilted her head. "Nothing too wild, but not a slug either."

He grinned, energy surging in his veins. He'd a mare she'd love. He led her straight to his extra mount. "This sweet lady is Ember. She loves a good run but waits for her rider's direction. I bought her when my Nutmeg was breeding two years ago."

Selena cooed as the sorrel mare nuzzled her hands. "She's perfect."

Aragon chuckled. He'd been right. While she cuddled her mare, he found some grooms to help saddle their mares. Then they mounted and trotted from the stables. After they passed several townhouses, he winked at Selena. "We escaped without Mother stopping us."

Selena arched her brows. "Was that because she didn't find us or because she let us escape for some reason of her own?"

He turned his wince into a shrug as he steered his bay mare onto a street headed east. "With Mother, who can say?" Only Father knew her plans most days.

They threaded through the crowded streets of Ormas and out the eastern gate. But they urged their mares to a brisk trot as they rode past the young fields.

After the first farmstead, Aragon glanced at Selena. Her face was tilted toward the warm spring sun like a daisy. She appeared almost as blissful as when engrossed in sketching. Tingling swept through him at the joy curving her lips. Would the sun strengthen her refreshing lymon scent? He could find out if he lifted her from the saddle and tumbled her into his arms then kissed her.

His pulse thundering, he forced himself to keep riding. Kissing her would be the opposite of platonic. His chest squeezed. And he couldn't exploit her inexperience—she still must meet other gentlemen. If she remained free as well as interested once she did, then he could kiss her again. To distract himself, he asked, "Shall we race the rest of the way?"

Selena shrugged. "Perhaps, but I don't know the way."

How could he have forgotten? Aragon chuckled then waved down the road before them. "The royal forest meets this road. 'Tis impossible to miss."

Selena slanted him a coy glance. "I might be persuaded to race if a wager were involved."

He swallowed as heat surged in his veins. A wager between a gentleman and a lady might involve kissing. Not that he'd much experience with such wagers. "What kind of wager?"

Selena tsked and shook her head. "A proper wager isn't discussed beforehand."

Aragon swallowed again. Goddess help him. If he won, he'd be unable to resist demanding a kiss. He should refuse to race. Yet he replied, "First one to reach the royal forest wins."

They urged their mares forward and thundered down the road. Almost tasting her kiss, he fought to win, yet the equal-size mares possessed similar endurance, and she was lighter. She led by a head when they reached the thick boughs of the royal forest.

Reining in her mare, Selena grinned at him. "I won!"

Aragon sighed. What would she demand? Doubtless not a kiss. He waved for her to continue. "Declare your prize."

Selena peeked at him from beneath lowered lashes. "I... I..."

His body hardened. But perhaps she would. She'd not hesitate otherwise. He leaned toward her in his saddle. Goddess, he needed her kiss.

Her gaze skittered away, and Selena swallowed. "I want you to take me to The Arte of Spells on the ride home."

He clenched his reins, his insides chilling. She didn't want him, after all. She just wanted to visit the fashionable shop, which Mother had prohibited until after her presentation ball. Although somewhat risky, they'd probably be fine at this hour, and she *had* won their wager. He forced a nod. "Very well. Do you wish to return to Ormas now?"

Selena licked her lips. "No, I'd like to ride here for a while."

His chest loosening, Aragon nodded again. Although she'd not demanded a kiss, she still wanted to remain with him. Hopefully, she still would once she met other gentlemen.

He studied Selena as they meandered down a forest path. She and the sorrel mare moved together like a mara riding a night-mara. Bound by the Nightmara-Calatini Treaty, the mara clans and the nightmara herds formed the best cavalry in Damensea. Some had attended Devon's coronation, and their grace together had awed Aragon, but Selena almost matched them. He smiled at her. "After our race, 'tis clear Ember is meant for you. She's yours while you stay with us."

Selena smoothed her mare's mane. "I should refuse, but I enjoy riding her too much."

His heart swelled. And he enjoyed riding with her. So despite being tempted to kiss her whenever they were alone, he grinned and said, "If you ever want to ride, let me know, and I'll be glad to accompany you. Assuming you have time after your presentation ball."

Selena beamed back. "Thank you, Aragon."

They rode through the royal forest for over two hours before returning to Ormas. As he'd promised, they headed straight to The Arte of Spells, where Selena exclaimed over the moving paintings like she had her sketch enchanted by the witches from this shop. She particularly adored the series featuring magical creatures like mermaids, firebirds, and tygrises.

Tingling swept through Aragon again at the rapture lighting her face as she studied the painting of a tygris basking in the sun. What would it be like for her to look at him like that? His throat thickened. Perhaps someday he'd know. If another gentleman didn't captivate her first.

As expected, no one from court interrupted them at the magical art gallery. But when they were leaving, a sultry voice called from the steps of Mother's favorite dress shop next door, "Aragon, is that you?"

He winced at Kit's voice. The same age as Hawke and Wren, the fashionable countess had grown up on a nearby country estate before her marriage to his mother's cousin, Lord Blaine, so he couldn't feign Selena was an old acquaintance. Damnation. He swallowed and turned to face Kit. "Afternoon."

Her gaze probing, Kit studied Selena. "And who's this?"

Aragon sighed but smiled. "Kit, this is Selena. Selena, this is the Countess of Blaine." Hopefully, his irregular introduction would prevent Midor from finding Selena before her presentation ball and wrecking Mother's plans.

A knowing smirk curved Kit's lips. "You *must* be the surprise the Duchess of Childes intends to present at her upcoming ball."

Selena shook her head with a grin. "I'm just a country miss who adores art, so when we met at a ball, Lord Treyvan offered to escort me to the finest gallery in Ormas."

Before Kit could ask anything further, Aragon nodded at the countess. "I must return Selena to her family, so I can return in time for dinner. Until later." *Please let Kit believe Selena's excuse.*

His stomach tense, he propelled Selena to their mares, and they leapt into their saddles.

Once they turned from Broad Street, Selena glanced at him. "I assume from your reticence that Lady Blaine is a great gossip."

He grimaced with a shrug. Kit was when it served her. "She adores being fashionable, and revealing the Duchess of Childes's plans shall impress court."

Selena winced. "I shouldn't have asked you to bring me to The Arte of Spells."

Aragon sighed and shook his head. Although he'd assumed the risk was trivial, he should have refused to bring her until after her presentation ball. Hopefully, his lapse wouldn't allow Midor to discover her whereabouts. "'Twas more my fault than yours, but there's no sense in crying for spilt unicorn water. Instead, we must concentrate on sneaking home without Mother catching us."

Selena nodded. "Yes, please."

So they returned using the servants' entrance, but when they were about to slip upstairs, Mother drawled from behind them, "And *where* were you two?"

His pulse skittering, Aragon faced Mother but kept Selena's hand. Since their riding clothes betrayed them, he replied, "Riding in the royal forest."

Mother's eyes narrowed. "I suppose that's fine as long as no one saw you."

Aragon and Selena said nothing, and he gritted a smile. Did their faces betray their guilt? Mother was too perceptive to miss any they revealed.

But they must have looked innocent because, after a moment, she shooed them upstairs. "Go change for dinner."

Their hands still intertwined, Aragon and Selena fled up the stairs before Mother could reconsider. He sighed. Although they'd avoided a scold for now, they'd earn one when Mother learned about Kit.

CHAPTER 17

*T*he following morning at breakfast, the duchess eyed Selena and Aragon over her teacup. "At Lady Osteen's card party last night, I heard some interesting rumors about Aragon and his art-loving country miss. I thought you went riding in the royal forest."

Selena winced and swallowed her toast. How had the duchess heard about their encounter with Lady Blaine already?

She was about to reply when Aragon shrugged and said, "We did, but afterward we visited The Arte of Spells."

The duchess tsked. "Fortunately, with Selena's presentation ball tomorrow, the rumors shall only tantalize court." She tilted her head. "But to further enhance that, we shan't present Selena in the usual receiving line. Eldridge shall fetch her when the dancing begins."

So the following evening, Selena paced alone about an anteroom while the guests arrived. Her stomach quivering, she fingered the gold gargoyle from Aragon to hearten herself. Would court gentlemen really pursue her simply due to his mother's patronage like he'd claimed? Did she even want them to?

At last, the duke entered the anteroom and rescued her from

her whirling thoughts. The ballroom hushed then murmured as
he escorted her to the center where the king and Aragon waited.

When King Devon offered his hand, Selena swallowed and
swept a formal curtsy. The eyes of court oppressive, she accepted
his hand. She wouldn't have noticed that if Aragon had partnered her.

King Devon rumbled a chuckle as they began dancing.
"Smile, Miss Midor. Our dance shall end soon, and you'll be free
to dance with Aragon."

A blush warming her cheeks, she nibbled her lip. "I've been
churlish, haven't I?" Had she offended him?

King Devon smiled. "Not at all. Just clear in your preference
for my cousin. I find it refreshing."

Her blush scorched her skin. Was she that transparent? Did
Aragon—or his parents—know too? She almost winced but
smiled at the king. "Thank you, your majesty."

King Devon's green eyes gleamed. "I ensured Aragon was
occupied during our dance so he couldn't brood."

Selena followed his nod and stiffened. Aragon was dancing
with the most beautiful lady she'd ever seen. Her stomach hardened as she gaped at the lady's white-blonde hair and exquisite
figure. "Who is *that*?"

King Devon chuckled as he twirled Selena. "Lady Annalise
Greysnowe. I escorted her tonight, so she required a partner for
the first dance."

Selena scowled. Greysnowe sounded familiar, but why?
Aragon or the duchess hadn't mentioned Lady Annalise.
"Greysnowe?"

King Devon shook his head. "The family feuding with the
Ravenstones."

Her eyes widened as she curtsied and King Devon bowed at
the end of the first song. The two Wildewall families were infamous for that centuries-long feud. Yet the king was escorting a
Greysnowe? Wouldn't that exacerbate the feud between the two
families?

"The feud notwithstanding, Lady Annalise is a fine lady. I'll introduce you." King Devon led Selena to Aragon and Lady Annalise.

Selena tensed as she and Lady Annalise exchanged greetings. Although wearing a raspberry ballgown from Celeste's, she still felt an utter country drab beside the icy beauty. Then she glanced at Aragon. Despite Lady Annalise, his gaze was riveted on Selena. She almost grinned. He definitely wanted her, even when beside such an extraordinary beauty.

The music soon resumed, and Aragon whisked Selena back onto the floor. Her chest lightened. Much better than dancing with King Devon. If only he'd hold her closer, like when they'd danced at the brothel. Tingling warmth suffusing her skin, she eased closer.

His dark-umber eyes ebony, Aragon swallowed and shifted back to the proper distance. "Your ballgown is lovely. Gentlemen shall duel over your dances."

Her breath froze. Just her ballgown? She licked her lips with a coy smile. "Would you?"

Aragon tensed, his gaze skittering away. "Mother would murder me if I did."

Selena sighed. For him to withdraw again, when tempted by her alluring ballgown, must mean he didn't want to court her despite their attraction. Echoing him, she finished their dance with utter propriety.

Aragon inclined a polite bow afterward. "Have fun tonight."

She lifted her chin as she rose from her curtsy. Again, he was shoving her at other gentlemen. Her heart clenched. "I will."

Wren on his arm, Hawke strode over and pressed a flute of sparkling wine into Selena's hand. "You'll have more fun if you drink this." He waggled his brows at his brother. "*You* can fetch your own."

Selena tossed back her sparkling wine in one draft. Hopefully, 'twould lighten her heavy chest. Although one flute probably wasn't enough.

Aragon frowned at her. "Be careful with that."

Her fingers clenched about her flute. *He* should be careful almost courting ladies he didn't actually want. Fortunately for him, the next song deterred her reply.

Lobbing her empty flute at Aragon, Hawke swept Selena onto the floor and flirted outrageously until she snorted with laughter. Then he handed her to Mel for the next dance. She blinked when they began twirling about the floor. Mel danced with more verve than she'd have expected for a priest.

Mel and Selena were at the refreshments table when a black-haired gentleman joined them. Unlike most gentlemen at court, he'd a short beard, and his shoulder-length hair was tied in a neat queue. The gentleman smiled at Mel. "Good evening, Priest Melchior. Could you introduce me to your companion?"

Mel nodded while handing Selena a flute of sparkling wine. "Certainly. Lord Ravenstone, this is Miss Selena Midor. Selena, this is the Count of Ravenstone."

She tilted her head, her eyes widening. Ravenstone? As in the family feuding with the Greysnowes? She glanced across the ballroom where Lady Annalise was talking with King Devon and Aragon. Why had the duchess invited them both?

Lord Ravenstone bowed over her free hand, his gaze lingering on her gold gargoyle. "A pleasure, Miss Midor. Where-abouts are you from?"

Selena sipped her sparkling wine, a lump clogging her throat. "Eastern Linwick." How she missed the mountains of home.

"Another easterner!" A genial smile creased Lord Raven-stone's rugged face. "I'm from Wildewall."

She nodded as her pulse stirred. Mountainous like Linwick, Wildewall was just south of the Walle separating Calatini from kingdoms ruled by magical creatures since the Stone Wars. The northern duchy was rumored to be brimming with wild magic. She'd never visited, but the tales were fascinating. She was about to ask about his home when another song began.

Lord Ravenstone offered his arm. "Shall we?"

Selena handed her sparkling wine to Mel and accepted Lord Ravenstone's arm. As they began dancing, she leaned toward him. "Tell me, is Wildewall as full of magical glens, enchanted lakes, and vision summits as they say?"

Lord Ravenstone chuckled. "Yes, it is. Many witches relish Wildewall's wild magic. Especially nature witches."

She sighed. If only she could visit one day. "I'd love to sketch some of those magical places."

Lord Ravenstone's amber eyes brightened. "You're an artist then?"

Selena shrugged with a blush. "A passionate dabbler really, but I adore sketching scenes from nature." Particularly mountainous ones.

"You'd find plenty of those in Wildewall." As their song ended, Lord Ravenstone bowed. "Do you enjoy riding?"

Her chest warming, she straightened from her curtsy. "I do."

Lord Ravenstone beamed at her. "Would you care to go riding one day soon?"

Selena smiled back and nodded. He wasn't Aragon, but the count seemed nice enough. And he was actually interested. "I'd enjoy that."

"Splendid." Lord Ravenstone turned and introduced her to the next gentleman.

She danced with that gentleman and then several others, and although all were pleasant, none were memorable until Lord Edouard Gernand drawled, "I believe you met my dear stepmother several days ago."

Selena frowned as her stomach quivered. Before tonight's ball, she'd only met the Hawkes, the Keyes, the king—and Aragon's gossiping cousin. "Lady Blaine is your *stepmother*?"

Lord Edouard inclined a wry nod. "For the past four years."

She cocked her head. Lady Blaine appeared around their age. How uncomfortable to have a stepmother that young. Poor Lord Edouard.

Lord Edouard studied her, his pale-blue eyes sharp. "Step-

mother told me and Elise *all* about your encounter. Along with
the rest of court."

Selena blushed and almost winced. No wonder the duchess
had heard so quickly. "Elise?"

"My twin." Lord Edouard nodded across the ballroom. "She's
dancing with her betrothed, Lord Farson."

Her blush fading, Selena followed his nod. Lady Elise was
giggling with her bearded partner. Considering the twins' blond
hair and Lord Edouard's eyes, they must be related to the
duchess.

Lord Edouard spun her in a deft turn. "Stepmother said you
adore art." When she nodded, he said, "My father has a fine
collection of masters from the previous century, if you'd care to
see them."

She grinned as her pulse quickened. Who wouldn't love to
see artwork by masters in person? "I would!"

Lord Edouard chuckled. "We'll arrange a time next week
then."

The music drew to a stop, and Selena curtsied at Lord
Edouard's bow.

She stiffened in her curtsy when an unwelcome voice
drawled, "Selena, there you are, my dear."

Selena rose, forcing a smile. "Good evening, Uncle Adan."
The rumors about Aragon's art-loving country miss must have
led her uncle here. But how had he gotten past Perkins and the
usher? And what scheme was he plotting now? Her stomach
knotted. She turned and beamed at Aragon's cousin. He
shouldn't overhear her conversation with her disreputable uncle.
"Thank you for the dance."

After Lord Edouard left and another song began, Uncle Adan
offered his arm. "Shall we?"

A chill skittered across her skin. "I'd rather not." She
narrowed her eyes at him. "What are you doing here? The
duchess didn't send you an invitation." And had instructed
Perkins to refuse him.

Her uncle smirked back and lowered his arm. "Shouldn't an uncle witness his niece's triumphant presentation at court?"

Selena snorted, bitterness flooding her mouth. Not one who plotted his niece's destruction. "That depends on whether the uncle sold his niece to a black witch or not."

Uncle Adan's eyes glinted. "How else could I rid myself of the burdensome dross my *dear* brother left me?" He sighed. "I'd have earned a fortune and influence at court if Lord Treyvan hadn't interfered. A pity."

She shuddered. Thank the Goddess Aragon had. She jerked her head toward the door. "Please leave, Uncle Adan. I've powerful friends now; you can't touch me."

"Can't I?" Color suffused Uncle Adan's face as he gripped her arm like a striking wyvern.

Spots flashing before her eyes, Selena winced and struggled to free herself. "Release me!"

CHAPTER 18

*a*s Aragon handed Mother a flute of sparkling wine, he refused to glance across the ballroom where Selena was no doubt still flirting with his cousin Edouard. His stomach twisted. Goddess, allowing Selena to meet other gentlemen was more miserable than he'd expected. But she deserved this chance, and he couldn't steal it from her. No matter how much he burned to monopolize her attention.

Mother's eyes narrowed as she sipped her sparkling wine. "Who is *that*? I'm certain I didn't invite him."

Aragon jerked around, his gaze flying to Selena. He stiffened. Edouard was no longer with her. Instead, a sneering gentleman with graying dark hair in shabby clothes gripped her upper arm. Her uncle, no doubt. Escorting Selena to The Arte of Spells the other day must have allowed Midor to find her. Damnation. Why hadn't the people watching Midor notified him the rumors had reached the docks?

He set his jaw and strode through the dancing couples to rescue Selena. He'd not allow Midor to terrorize her or wreck her presentation ball. As he approached, Selena kept struggling to free herself. How dare Midor maul her? Fire flashing through him, he seized Midor's wrist. "Release Selena at once."

Midor grunted but didn't move.

Aragon strengthened his grip until Midor winced. But the obstinate cretin still didn't release Selena. He clenched harder. "Now!"

With another wince, Midor dropped Selena's arm.

His gaze locked on the older gentleman, Aragon drew Selena to his side then released her. His heart squeezed. If he pulled her into his arms like he wanted, he'd scandalize court and steal her chance to consider other suitors. "Adan Midor, I presume."

Midor flashed an obsequious smile. "Yes, my lord, just so."

Aragon almost glared. Did Midor think fawning would excuse his abhorrent treatment of Selena? "You weren't invited. Leave."

Midor's smile faded to a frown. "Why should I?"

Selena sighed and pursed her lips. "Your lack of invitation, perhaps?"

Midor leaned toward Aragon with a smirk. "I'm sure 'twas inadvertent."

Aragon kept his face blank despite the bile burning his throat. How could such a sycophant be related to Selena? "No, your exclusion was deliberate. We don't associate with patrons of black witches. In fact, I should have Lord Islaye, the Minister of Magic and fellow councilor, summon magic marshals to arrest you."

Midor stiffened, his smirk vanishing. "'Twould cause a scene."

Aragon shrugged and arched a brow. "Perhaps, but it'll make Mother's ball the most thrilling of the season. She'll be ecstatic." Or vexed at her upset plans.

Midor's jaw twitched as he glared at Selena. "My arrest would ruin my dear niece. No gentleman would have her then."

Aragon forced another shrug. "I would." A scandal wouldn't alter his interest in Selena, although it would steal her choice of husband. But at least then he'd never need feign indifference to her dancing with other gentlemen.

Selena whirled to goggle at him.

Midor snorted. "Fool." He glowered at Selena again. "I'll leave, but you and I aren't finished."

His brow furrowed, Aragon kept watching Midor until the greedy cur left. Then he turned to Selena, and warmth flooded him. "Are you all right?"

Selena's dark-gray eyes glowed. "Yes. Thank you for rescuing me again. Would you truly marry me if Uncle Adan ruined me?"

His heart fluttered. Without hesitation. "Mother would never allow your uncle to ruin you." He coughed and turned to study the dancers. "This dance is almost over. We must find you an illustrious partner to distract court from your uncle."

Selena dimpled at him and lowered her lashes. "You're illustrious."

Aragon shook his head despite the heat surging through him. He couldn't trust himself to dance with her. During their last one, he'd struggled to not yank her against him. He'd be the one to ruin her and steal her choice of husband if they danced again. "We danced earlier."

Selena frowned at him. "Only once. We can dance again without concerning even the strictest chaperone."

He swallowed. True, but his hunger would concern them. A decent chaperone would keep Selena far away from him. "Another gentleman would be better."

Selena paled but lifted her chin. "I see."

Aragon winced. He'd been churlish. He was about to soften his refusal when Mother sailed over with Winston in tow.

Mother beamed at Selena. "Selena, this is Mr. Herrick Winston. He requested your next dance."

Aragon's stomach hardened as Selena grinned and said, "I'd be delighted."

Once Selena and Winston swept off, Aragon frowned at Mother. "Why did you encourage Selena to dance with *Winston*? He's a cad." And a fortune hunter. Despite being a future baron, not even the most desperate mothers wanted their daughters to marry him.

Mother shrugged. "True, but he was the closest available gentleman."

Aragon tensed, allowing his gaze to follow Selena as the next dance began. "Surely you could have found someone else." Anyone else.

Mother arched a brow. "*You* could have said Selena's next dance was yours if you were so concerned."

He shifted, a blush burning his neck. Except he couldn't trust himself with her. Her allure tempted him too much.

Mother shook her head. "Stop fretting about Selena and Mr. Winston. He'll not attempt anything in public. And once he learns she has no dowry, he shan't pester her again."

Aragon grunted. But until then, she was vulnerable. "I suppose."

Mother threaded her arm through his and drew him across the ballroom. "Speaking of Mr. Winston reminds me, his sister hasn't danced the last several songs. Go find her and request a dance."

He nodded without hesitation. Although she wasn't spellbinding like Selena, Miss Winston was pleasant and nothing like her brother.

Mother tsked. "Poor Miss Winston. 'Tis a shame about her deplorable brother and lack of funds. Not that you must regard such impediments."

Aragon tensed, his skin prickling. Why was Mother so insistent? "Miss Winston doesn't seem fond of court, so she'd be ill-suited for a councilor."

Mother slanted him a flat glance. "Aragon, find the lady and dance."

He sagged with a sigh. When Mother used that tone, arguing was futile. "Of course, Mother."

He found Miss Winston sipping sparkling wine in a chair near the chaperones and dowagers. When he asked her to dance, her eyes widened, but she accepted, and they talked while he escorted her toward the dancers.

Yet Aragon kept glancing at Selena and Winston. So far, the cad had remained entirely proper, but how long would that last?

As the current song ended, Miss Winston glanced between him and her brother. "Tell me, Lord Treyvan, does Miss Midor possess a fortune?"

He winced and turned back to Miss Winston. He'd been rude, and Miss Winston didn't deserve it. "No."

Miss Winston quirked a wry smile. "Then she'll be safe with Herrick."

Aragon almost blushed as he led Miss Winston onto the floor. "I apologize for neglecting you." She was remarkably calm about his inconsideration. Most ladies wouldn't be.

Miss Winston shrugged. "I'm accustomed to it."

He stiffened. That made it worse. He'd keep his attention on her during their dance—no matter how much he hungered to watch Selena. So he asked Miss Winston about her favorite country pursuits.

While they danced, Aragon and Miss Winston discussed living in the country then methods of agriculture. She brightened as she compared several new substances for increasing harvest yields. He was about to quiz her on her unexpected knowledge when he glanced across the ballroom. Selena was beaming as she danced with Lord Ravenstone for the second time.

His chest burning, Aragon twirled Miss Winston closer. Lord Ravenstone had always seemed a decent sort despite his family's absurd feud with the Greysnowes, but was the rugged count as genial as he seemed? His smile was practically a leer, and he held Selena too close. Aragon forced his gaze back to his partner. "Would you care to meet Selena? You two have a great deal in common."

Miss Winston cocked her head. "Do we?"

His gaze returning to Selena, he inclined a nod. "You're both from Linwick. And—" He almost winced as he faced Miss

Winston again. Mentioning their nonexistent dowries would be insensitive.

Miss Winston narrowly eyed him but agreed. Once he led her to Selena and made the introductions, Miss Winston drawled, "I'm told we have a great deal in common, Miss Midor."

Aragon suppressed another wince. From her tone, Miss Winston knew what he'd almost said. He was a boor.

Still beside Lord Ravenstone, Selena glanced at Aragon. "Oh?"

Miss Winston nodded. "We're both country ladies from Linwick."

Selena returned her nod. "Your brother mentioned your father is Lord Winston. I'm from Upper Ashville, a village two days northeast of your father's estate."

Miss Winston pursed her lips. "Upper Ashville has a rich underground deposit of yellow copper ore."

Aragon frowned at her. Miss Winston knowing that was just as unusual as her knowing about increasing harvest yields.

As Selena blinked at Miss Winston, Lord Ravenstone grinned and asked, "How did you know that?"

Miss Winston shrugged. "The local alchemist mentioned it."

"Ah..." Lord Ravenstone offered Miss Winston his arm as another song began. "Shall we?"

While they glided away, Selena arched her brows at Aragon.

He swallowed. He couldn't refuse her a second time. Yet his control was tenuous, so how could he avoid titillating court when he slipped? Perhaps if they were out of sight. "Except for when speaking with your uncle, you've danced every dance. Perhaps you'd care for a respite on the balcony?"

A dimple quivered in Selena's left cheek. "A respite would be most welcome."

As he escorted her to the balcony, heat suffused him at her touch on his arm. Not even the cool night air on the balcony assuaged it.

Selena sighed as she stared out into the moonlit garden. "This view makes my fingers itch for a pencil."

Aragon dropped her arm, his heart pounding. He must stop touching her, or he'd kiss her again. And she was trusting him to behave like a gentleman, not a rakehell. "Fortunately, you can return another evening to sketch it."

Selena whirled to face him and leaned against the parapet. "If your mother permits me any free evenings, I shall."

He winced, his stomach sinking. Free evenings would be few with the many events Mother had accepted. And all those events would be as miserable as tonight because he must feign indifference when other gentlemen courted Selena. But he'd restrain himself—he couldn't steal her chance to find love.

CHAPTER 19

*H*er heart squeezing, Selena eyed Aragon as she leaned against the parapet. Did he want her or not? Every time he appeared interested, he withdrew not long after. He rescued her from Uncle Adan like a griffin protecting his lifelong mate but pretended 'twas insignificant. He shoved her at other gentlemen but watched her the entire night. He refused to dance with her but brought her onto the balcony—the perfect place to sneak a kiss.

She almost sighed. He surpassed every gentleman she'd ever met. He was dedicated and kind and brave, and although they'd not fallen in love within moments like her parents, they'd been instantly attracted. She'd not experienced that with anyone else.

Her jaw tightened. She must find out if he truly wanted to court her. Surely she'd know if he kissed her again. But how could she tempt him into acting on their attraction? Perhaps if she drew him close. She shivered even though the spring night was pleasant after the sweltering ballroom.

Aragon frowned. "Are you cold?"

No, but Selena shivered again and rubbed her arms to feign a chill. "A little."

Aragon yanked off his evening coat and wrapped it about her shoulders.

Warmth filled her chest. He'd not surrender his coat so swiftly unless he was interested. She caressed his upper arm with a coy smile. "Thank you for your solicitude."

Aragon swallowed, his gaze riveted on her mouth. "'Twas nothing."

Selena lifted her chin. Why hadn't he kissed her yet? She must be bolder. Her heart pounding, she craned to brush a kiss against his lips then stepped back. "'Tis much more than nothing."

Aragon rasped, "You're making it arduous to remain a gentleman."

She licked her lips and eyed him through her lashes. "I never asked you to be a gentleman." Especially if that meant he'd never kiss her again.

With a groan, Aragon lunged forward and kissed her.

Selena clutched his shirt and parted her lips to return his kiss with equal fervor. Tingling heat swamped her as they devoured each other. Definitely as enthralling as last time—she never wanted to stop.

But then the duchess called, "Selena, are you and Aragon hiding from your guests?"

Aragon and Selena leapt apart like startled naiads when a traveler approached their lake. As the duchess glided onto the balcony, crimson scorched Selena's face. Goddess, 'twas mortifying for his mother to discover them kissing.

Yet the duchess beamed at her. "Edouard wants another dance."

Selena blinked, her head swirling. Wasn't the duchess going to scold them? Maybe she hadn't seen them kissing. "Does he?"

Aragon pursed a tight smile. "My younger cousin did appear to enjoy your dance together."

Selena licked her lips and scrutinized his stiff face. Her

stomach fluttered. Was he jealous? When he said nothing further, she deflated and nodded at the duchess. "Very well." Although she'd rather dance with Aragon.

The duchess beckoned her. "Return Aragon's coat and come along."

Aragon muttered as he accepted his evening coat, "I apologize for mauling you. I'll show better restraint henceforth."

Selena gaped at him. After that kiss, he still withdrew? Why did he deny their attraction? Her chest seized. Perhaps he assumed, like she had, that lasting love would be instantaneous.

She forced herself to follow the duchess inside and accept Lord Edouard's arm with a smile. As she danced with him then many others during the rest of the ball, Aragon again watched her, but he remained across the ballroom. He definitely didn't want to court her.

Tears heated her eyes as she prepared for bed. Despite preferring Aragon, she must forget him and turn her attention to others who appeared interested. She'd never permanently escape Uncle Adan's schemes without a husband. She sighed. Both Lord Ravenstone and Lord Edouard had danced with her twice, and each had proposed outings in the next week. She must give their courtships a fair due.

OVER THE NEXT FEW DAYS, Selena endured garden parties, tea receptions, card parties, and more balls. The duchess escorted her to multiple events each day, and Aragon always accompanied them but watched from afar. If only he would pursue her.

During the countless court events, all her new acquaintances blurred into a welter of recognizable faces, but she met too many people to make close friends. Each night, she collapsed into her bed and sank into slumber. She almost wanted to wed someone to escape the duchess's intense social rounds.

So when Lord Ravenstone arrived to take her riding, she

closed her sketch journal with a smile. At last, a quiet event with no introductions. And she'd further her courtship with the count.

Lord Ravenstone bowed to the duchess then Selena before nodding at Aragon beside Selena. "Afternoon, everyone." He grinned at Selena. "Are you ready?"

Selena leapt from the sofa. She'd not ridden since Aragon had taken her last week. And she couldn't wait to ride the sweet mare he'd loaned her. If only his kindness was more than charity. "Very much so."

When Aragon set aside his book and rose, the duchess eyed him over her goldwork embroidery. "Lord Ravenstone can escort Selena alone, except for a groom, of course."

Aragon opened his mouth then paused and returned to the sofa. "Very well, Mother." He slashed the count a narrow glance. "Where do you plan to take Selena?"

Selena sighed as Lord Ravenstone took her arm. Doubtless Aragon's interest was only because Uncle Adan knew her whereabouts now. Too bad it wasn't because he wanted to ride with her himself.

Lord Ravenstone smiled at Aragon. "I thought the royal bay and back."

Aragon nodded. "If you don't return an hour before dinner, I'll ride after you."

Selena blushed as the count's brows flew skyward. Lord Ravenstone must assume Aragon was jealous, but he wasn't. If he wanted her, he wouldn't have apologized for kissing her on the balcony. He would have kissed her again instead.

Instead of replying, Lord Ravenstone merely returned Aragon's nod and swept Selena from the room. Once they were riding down the street with a groom trailing them, he glanced at her. "Lord Treyvan seems protective of you."

She blushed harder but shrugged. If only Aragon was protective because he wanted her. "The Hawkes are shielding me from my uncle, so Aragon worries he'll attempt something." Until she knew the count better, she'd not reveal Uncle Adan's involvement with a black witch.

Lord Ravenstone's amber eyes narrowed, darting to the gold gargoyle nestled between her breasts. "I suppose that explains your powerful protection charm."

She blinked and fingered the protection charm. He'd noticed 'twas enchanted? No one else had. Was he a witch or just more perceptive since he was from Wildewall? No doubt he often saw magic there.

Before she could ask, Lord Ravenstone smiled at her. "Have you ever visited the royal bay?"

Selena sighed. She didn't know Lord Ravenstone well enough to ask about magic when he was clearly diverting the conversation. So instead, she replied, "No, I've not seen much outside of the city walls since I moved to Ormas." And she probably wouldn't while the duchess managed her social rounds. She suppressed a grimace.

Lord Ravenstone grinned as they threaded through the crowded streets. "Then, as a lover of nature, you'll enjoy today. The king's private bay is just north of Ormas and quite picturesque."

She tilted her head with a frown. Although King Devon was Aragon's best friend, she and the count couldn't trespass on the king's private lands. But surely Aragon would have objected if 'twas forbidden. "Private?"

Lord Ravenstone nodded. "The royal bay and the royal forest both require permission from King Devon. But they're the closest natural areas, so I wrote him after your presentation ball."

A pang darted through Selena. She'd loved riding in the royal forest with Aragon. She'd believed he wanted her then. She sighed and forced herself back to today's ride. "Why the bay rather than the forest?"

Lord Ravenstone urged his stallion to a trot after they rode through the northern gate. "The bay is half an hour closer, and the king prefers the royal forest."

Matching his pace, her chest lightened as she inhaled the balmy spring air. A refreshing ride was the perfect escape from intense social rounds, a disreputable uncle, and Aragon's lack of interest. "Thanks for arranging this."

Lord Ravenstone chuckled. "'Twas nothing. When I reside in Ormas, I request permission to ride on the royal lands at least twice a month. The scenery is tame compared to Wildewall's mountains but better than nothing."

Selena eyed the rugged count. He was grinning like a relaxed tygris in the sun. Native to the Tsarkan Empire south of Calatini, the massive feline ruled torrid grasslands and was rumored to bask in the blazing sun for hours. The moving paintings of them at The Arte of Spells had been stunning. She'd adored seeing them with Aragon. Forcing her mind back to the count, she smiled and shook her head. "You sound like you despise Ormas."

Lord Ravenstone shrugged. "No, although I don't enjoy it much. I come to the season every year, but I've yet to last the entire six months. When I can no longer stand town life, I return to Wildewall."

She pursed her lips. "Why do you come at all?" He'd be happier back home.

Lord Ravenstone flashed a wry smile. "Because I need a wife. And no one back home appeals."

Her chest warming, Selena echoed his wry smile. She knew all about *that*. "Once you marry, I assume you'll return to Wildewall and rarely return to Ormas."

"Most likely." Lord Ravenstone stilled his stallion at the edge of a cliff. "We're here."

She halted her mare beside his and gaped at the large bay. Goddess, she'd never seen anything like it! The cerulean ocean stretched out to the horizon, and frothy waves crashed against the golden sand at the foot of verdant cliffs. Gulls swooped in the angel-blue sky, but she, the count, and the groom were the only humans. She breathed, "I should have brought my sketch journal."

Lord Ravenstone smiled at her. "We must return then." He waved toward a narrow path. "Do you want to ride down to the beach? We must go one at a time."

Selena beamed. "Yes, please." So they rode down the winding path and spent a delightful hour riding on the beach. On the return ride to Ormas, she said, "Thank you for bringing me to the royal bay, Lord Ravenstone." His kindness almost equaled Aragon's.

Lord Ravenstone grinned. "I'm pleased you enjoyed it. I recall when my father brought me here for the first time." His grin dimmed. "My father died just before last season."

Her throat tightened. "So did mine. My mother too." She rubbed her throat. "A virulent strain of wraith flu killed half my village."

Lord Ravenstone shuddered and urged his stallion to a trot. "How horrid. My father died in a hunting accident, but my mother is still living."

Selena blinked. "I don't think I've met her." Why hadn't she? The duchess had introduced her to *everyone* in Ormas. Was something wrong with Lady Ravenstone, or was she not interested in meeting Selena? If so, that didn't bode well for her son's courtship.

Lord Ravenstone shrugged. "She rarely leaves Wildewall. We've paired communication mirrors so we can talk during the season. Much easier than letters."

Selena inclined her head. So nothing was wrong with Lady Ravenstone except disliking Ormas as much as her son. But when would Selena meet her to see if they could get along? Gripping her reins, she shoved that aside and asked the count about his home.

She and Lord Ravenstone continued talking the rest of the ride, and she agreed to ride with him again next week. She managed a smile as he helped her dismount. He didn't enthrall her like Aragon, but she and the count had similar preferences, and she might learn to love him.

CHAPTER 20

*H*aving spent the afternoon pacing and picturing Lord Ravenstone kissing Selena, Aragon burst from his chambers as soon as she returned. He stiffened at her glowing smile. "How was your ride?"

Her hand on her doorknob, Selena dimpled at him. "Glorious! I've never seen the sea before. I wish I'd brought my sketch journal."

His ribs squeezed. He'd missed her joy at seeing the sea for the first time. He should have taken her to the royal bay when they went riding last week. Damn Lord Ravenstone for stealing that from him.

And had her joy inspired the count to tumble Selena from her saddle and devour her lips? Heat surged through Aragon. He wouldn't have been able to resist. Not again, especially after their kiss at her presentation ball. He slitted his eyes. "Did Ravenstone attempt anything?"

Selena frowned and tilted her head. "What could he have attempted? We were on separate horses the entire time."

His jaw tightened. She was so innocent. A clear sign of her inexperience. "A gentleman with lechery in mind can manage a great deal when assisting a lady from her horse."

Selena's lips parted in a ragged breath. "I see. I must remember that the next time I go riding with a gentleman."

Burning to capture her parted lips, he glared at her. Goddess, must she be so tempting? She was as impossible to resist as a siren's song. "Yes, do that."

Selena smoothed her hair. "I must change for dinner. Excuse me."

As she slipped inside her chambers, Aragon shuddered with hunger. He should follow her and demonstrate how creative a lustful gentleman could be. But seducing her would be exploiting her inexperience, and 'twould be wrong to steal her choice of husband. He gulped a breath then retreated to his chambers and yanked on his evening clothes.

He'd just finished tying his cravat when someone knocked on his door. He opened it and gaped—Selena was waiting with a bright smile. Hadn't his ill-temper flustered her?

Selena tilted her head then threaded her arm through his. "Ready for dinner?"

His jealousy softening, Aragon nodded and squeezed her arm. "I'm hungry as a manticore." Perhaps that could excuse his earlier behavior.

Selena tsked as they strolled downstairs. "Try not to gorge at dinner. Else you'll have difficulty dancing tonight at Lady Staghorn's ball."

Aragon tensed, his skin tightening. Winston was sure to attend his great-aunt's ball, but Selena should avoid the cad. Even though she'd no dowry to tempt the future baron, he still might attempt to seduce her as a lark. So during dinner, he asked, "Must we attend Lady Staghorn's ball?"

Mother shrugged as she cut her stuffed capon. "Her ball was the best court event tonight."

He grimaced and sipped his wine. Remaining home would be preferable, but Mother would never permit Selena to do so during her debut season. And he'd not allow Selena to attend alone.

Mother narrowed her eyes at Aragon. "The Winstons shall doubtless be there, and I expect you to dance with Miss Winston at least once tonight." She turned to Hawke. "You too."

Hawke flashed a crooked grin. "Unfortunately, I'm attending a wyvern fight instead." Although owning wyverns hadn't been fashionable at court since the previous century, wilder gentlemen still patronized wyvern fights held in poorer neighborhoods. Yet Hawke never attended blood sports, so he must be desperate to avoid Lady Staghorn's ball.

Aragon's jaw tightened even though he also avoided blood sports. As the heir, he hadn't the freedom to disregard Mother's plans like Hawke did. Not that he'd abandon Selena.

"Lucky lad," Father drawled, his tone revealing he'd also prefer to join his youngest son rather than attend Lady Staghorn's ball.

Mother shook her head as she buttered a roll. "Very well, you scamp. You do recall we're having dinner at Blaine House in a few days? Since they're family, I expect you to attend."

Hawke chuckled. "Of course, Mother."

After dinner, everyone except Hawke headed to Staghorn House. As soon as they arrived, Mother glanced at Aragon then nodded at Miss Winston.

He sighed but asked Miss Winston for her first dance. Mother would harp until he did. Soon the music began, and he led Miss Winston onto the floor. As at Selena's presentation ball, he endeavored to keep his attention on Miss Winston during their dance.

Yet he was distracted by Selena dancing with the Duke of Oakmoor. His chest clenched. Why had Mother allowed Selena to dance with *him*? Although a wealthy councilor, the unwed duke was also twenty years Selena's senior and a worse rakehell than Hawke.

During the first dance, Aragon managed polite conversation with Miss Winston while eyeing Selena and the rakish duke. Although the duke flirted the entire dance, she deflected him with tepid smiles. Nothing like the one she'd given Aragon before dinner. His pulse quickened. Although still inexperienced with lechery, perhaps she'd now met enough gentlemen to know whom she preferred. If so, he could begin courting her. At last.

So once the dance ended, Aragon fetched Miss Winston sparkling wine then strode over to Selena. "Is your next dance free?"

Selena dimpled at Lord Ravenstone to her right. "Lord Ravenstone has already spoken for my next dance." She turned her smile to Edouard on her left. "And Lord Edouard has requested the following one. But I'm free after that."

Aragon's heart stuttered. Naturally, she already had partners. And her smiles for them were brighter than the one she'd given him earlier. She knew whom she preferred, and 'twasn't him. He forced a nod. "Then I'll take the dance after Edouard's." Unable to remain while suitors flanked her, he marched across the ball-room to Mother.

Mother arched her brows at him. "Who's Selena dancing with next?"

He kept his expression bland despite his burning stomach. "Lord Ravenstone." Damn the count for stealing that from him too.

Mother grinned like a puckish pixie, clearly pleased with her successful matchmaking. "Excellent." She chuckled. "You'd better find Lady Annalise and dance with her. We can't have the Greysnowes believing we favor the Ravenstones."

Aragon sighed but nodded. He might as well since he couldn't dance with Selena. His hands fisted behind his back, he approached Lady Annalise. "Could I request a dance?"

Lady Annalise inclined her white-blonde head with a cool smile. "The Duke of Oakmoor has bespoken my next dance, but the following one is free."

Not bothering to hunt for another lady, Aragon waited by the refreshments table during the next dance. He sipped a flute of sparkling wine, his ribs tight as he pretended not to watch Selena dance with Lord Ravenstone.

After that dance, Aragon partnered Lady Annalise but barely spoke because he kept eyeing Selena with Edouard. Yet the icy beauty, dubbed Lady Snow by some at court, continued murmuring idle pleasantries. No wonder Devon had risked inflaming the Greysnowe-Ravenstone feud to begin escorting her last season—her steadfast serenity would be invaluable when state affairs intruded.

Aragon ended his dance with Lady Annalise beside Selena. As their former partners glided to the refreshments table, he turned to Selena and gritted a wry smile. "You're most popular tonight."

Selena shrugged, smoothing her periwinkle skirt. "All your mother's doing, I assure you. I swear, she'd be the most effective general ever promoted if she put her hand to it."

Warmth flooding his chest, he shook his head. Mother wasn't why Lord Ravenstone and Edouard pursued Selena. Her wholesome beauty and cordial charm no doubt spellbound them too. Yet he couldn't explain that without sounding ardent, and she was no longer interested.

As the music began again, Aragon drew Selena into his arms. Heat flared in his veins as they glided about the ballroom. If only he could hold her closer without titillating court. Although if she was still interested, he'd have ignored court to dance closer. But his hunger cooled when they passed Winston and Lady Annalise. "Has Winston requested a dance yet?"

Selena grinned. "No, thank the Goddess. He lost interest as soon as he learned I've no dowry."

He drew her slightly closer and examined her face with a frown. "You sound too gleeful. Did he take liberties?" The cad.

Selena shrugged. "No, but his eyes held a predatory gleam. If *he* had found me in a brothel, he would have happily taken me."

Aragon almost snorted. Again, she showed her inexperience

with lechery. "So would many of your other dance partners. Like your first tonight—the Duke of Oakmoor patronizes brothels when he's between mistresses. He's not particular either."

Selena pursed her lips. "No, you misunderstand. Mr. Winston possesses an edge of cruelty the duke doesn't. I could see him as a buyer the black witch would contact—if he'd any money."

Aragon slashed Winston a narrow glance and drew her closer. "So could I."

A faint smile curved Selena's lips. "Now, the Duke of Oakmoor is assuredly a rakehell, but he's suave about it." Despite her disinterest earlier, she sounded almost admiring.

His stomach hardening, Aragon twirled her in a complicated turn. 'Twould give her something to consider other than the duke. When she blanched and gasped midway through the turn, he tensed and ceased twirling her. He must have alarmed her. "My apologies."

Her dark-gray eyes shaded, Selena blinked at him. "What?"

His throat clenched. Goddess, he was a churl. "For twirling you without warning."

Selena swallowed. "No, 'twas fine. But I saw my uncle."

Fire flashed through Aragon. "What? Where?!"

Selena nodded toward the back. "Over by the musicians." She grimaced. "He's clearly plotting another scheme. If only I knew what."

He followed her nod with a scowl. Midor lurked beneath the musicians' balcony, his gaze trailing them as they danced. After a moment, Midor smirked and saluted them with his flute of sparkling wine.

Aragon suppressed a growl. How dare Midor smirk like that? And what was he doing at Lady Staghorn's ball? The people watching him hadn't mentioned him knowing anyone at court. He must have managed to sneak in like he had Selena's presentation ball. Aragon set his jaw. But he'd not allow Midor to harass her. "I'll handle him once our dance is over." By dragging him from the ballroom.

Selena clutched his shoulder. "No, 'twould engender gossip."

His heart softening, he drew her close enough her periwinkle skirt brushed his legs. Who cared about titillating court when her uncle threatened her? "I can't allow your uncle to pester you."

CHAPTER 21

*H*er heart surging at Aragon's declaration, Selena swayed toward him. Goddess, if only his protectiveness was due to love rather than chivalry. She swallowed and forced herself to retreat to the proper dancing distance. "I should be fine as long as I avoid him."

Aragon's eyes narrowed. "Are you certain?"

She straightened to her full height despite her prickling shoulders. "Although I wish I knew his latest scheme, whatever he's plotting can't touch me thanks to your family's protection. The worst he can do is start rumors, and your mother can easily squash those."

Aragon sighed, his jaw firming. "Very well, but I'll stay close while your uncle remains."

Selena's chest fluttered. He truly was the best of gentlemen. If only he wanted to court her. Then she needn't consider others. She forced a smile as their dance ended.

Aragon relinquished her to a nearby gentleman and partnered that gentleman's erstwhile partner. But as he promised, he and his new partner remained close. He repeated that through her following dances, especially when she danced with Lord Ravenstone and Edouard again.

While she danced, Uncle Adan lurked beneath the musicians' balcony, his gaze never leaving her, even when he talked to other guests. His incessant scrutiny chilled her despite her earlier words. *What* could he be plotting? Her destruction again?

After an hour enduring his scrutiny, Selena ached to relax with a pot of tea and her sketch journal. So when another gentleman requested a dance, she said Aragon had already claimed it then turned to him with wide eyes. "Could we tell your mother I've a headache and want to leave?"

Aragon frowned and leaned toward her. "You've a headache?"

Selena grimaced. She'd worse—a disreputable uncle who kept staring. "No, but I want to leave. Please, Aragon."

He nodded then escorted her to the duchess. "Mother, Selena has a headache. I'm taking her home."

The duchess waved them toward the door. "Of course." She smiled at Selena. "Go rest; I'll see you in the morning."

Aragon whisked Selena out to the carriage, and she relaxed as she sank onto the forward seat. But when he began sitting across from her, she tugged him beside her, warmth suffusing her chest. Although 'twasn't proper, she threaded her fingers through his and nestled against him. "Thank you."

Aragon tensed, but his thumb caressed her palm. "You're welcome."

Tingling skittered up her arm, and her breath quickened. If he wanted her, she'd attempt a kiss. Her heart clenched. But he didn't, so she'd best release him before she kissed him anyway. So when the carriage turned, she sighed and began releasing him.

Aragon gripped her hand for a moment then dropped it like a firelizard heated by embers. He swallowed but didn't stop her as she slid to the carriage window.

Her chest tight, Selena remained silent the rest of the ride. If only he'd pulled her into his arms rather than releasing her. Goddess, why did he keep denying their attraction?

. . .

THE DISAPPOINTING CARRIAGE ride was the last Selena was alone with Aragon over the next few days. The duchess began taking her to events for ladies, so he remained home. Although she missed him, she finally made friends at court during an afternoon salon about art.

Selena was eyeing a smooth painting by a recent artist when Miss Madeleine Thorpe joined her. The other lady leaned toward the painting and murmured, "What invisible brushstrokes. Mine are blobs compared to these."

Selena smiled at Madeleine. "Mine too. That's why I sketch instead." Plus, pencils were much more affordable than oils.

Madeleine arched her brows at Selena. "Are you also an artist?" When Selena nodded, Madeleine chuckled and beckoned her. "Come, you must join me and my friends. So few ladies are artists."

Selena grinned as they settled in the chairs beside Lady Cecilia Cassell and Miss Rosamund Blakeley. She'd met all three ladies before, but she'd not realized they were artists.

Madeleine beamed at her friends. "Selena just mentioned she sketches, so I invited her to join us." She turned to Selena. "Cecilia is a mosaicist, and Rosamund a sculptor."

Selena gaped at the other ladies. What unique talents. If only she was as gifted. "I'd love to see your work. Paintings, mosaics, and sculptures are so interesting compared to sketches."

Cecilia winked at her. "Only if you bring your sketches. We could have luncheon and make an afternoon of it. We love nothing more than discussing art."

Rosamund snickered. "Which our mothers continually bemoan. They say we'll never find husbands if we keep chattering about art."

Selena's chest lightened. How wonderful to meet ladies who loved art as much as she did. And thanks to her time at the brothel and the enchanted pencils Aragon had given her, she'd plenty of sketches to show them. "Luncheon and an afternoon discussing our art sounds perfect."

Rosamund heaved a sigh. "You know what doesn't sound perfect? The Landrys' ball tomorrow. Their parties are always dull, and their refreshments ghastly." As the others grimaced, she turned to Selena. "After a few obligatory dances, we always sneak away to talk."

Selena tilted her head. Although that sounded interesting, she couldn't. "I would, except the Hawkes and I are attending a family dinner at Blaine House. Lord Edouard asked his father to invite us to see his art collection."

Madeleine leaned toward her with a heavy sigh. "'Tis said the Count of Blaine's collection of tenth-century masters is the finest in all Calatini. I'd love to see it."

Energy darted through Selena. And she—a penniless country miss—was going to see such an extraordinary collection.

Cecilia flashed a waggish smile. "Perhaps Selena could bring us as her guests."

Raising her eyes skyward, Rosamund drawled, "*Or* she could just smuggle us in her reticule."

Selena suppressed her grin. She mustn't inflame her new friends' envy. "Once I meet Lord Blaine, perhaps I could convince him to show the artwork to you another time."

Rosamund snorted. "Not if Lady Blaine has any say. Ladies more interested in art than court are of no use to the fashionable countess."

Selena almost winced. Which she definitely was, so 'twas fortunate the duchess was Lord Blaine's cousin. She'd never see his collection otherwise.

Madeleine shook her head. "How about we have luncheon at my family's townhouse the following day instead? Selena can at least tell us about Lord Blaine's collection. Then we can show each other our recent work."

Selena dimpled at her new friends. "I'll look forward to it."
She'd bring the hawk sketch Aragon had enchanted for her. The
moving sketch should impress them. But she mustn't mention
he'd paid for it—they'd assume he was courting her, which he
sadly wasn't.

THE FOLLOWING EVENING, Selena yanked on her teal gown then
flew downstairs to visit Blaine House. But only Aragon and his
parents were there, so she asked once the carriage rumbled
down the street, "Where's Hawke?" How had he managed to
evade the duchess's earlier edict?

Aragon shrugged. "He's riding with Wren and her parents."

The duchess nodded with a grin. "The carriages are more
comfortable that way."

Selena blinked. The carriage could comfortably hold two
more, but with Hawke elsewhere, at least she needn't endure his
flirting. As the others began discussing the upcoming dinner, she
clenched her hands to keep them still. Soon she'd see tenth-
century masterpieces in person.

After they arrived at Blaine House and the duchess introduced Selena, Lord Blaine's pale-blue eyes studied her. "So you're
the lady who adores art that Edouard begged me to invite."

A blush warmed her cheeks. Lord Edouard had begged? He
must want to court her—unlike Aragon. "Yes, my lord. Thank
you for inviting me."

The count chuckled. "Edouard can show you my collection
after dinner. He's almost as well-versed as I. And he's a more
rousing escort for a young lady."

Lady Blaine sashayed over and slipped her arm through her
husband's. "You're rousing enough for any young lady."

His silvery hair aged by her sable locks, Lord Blaine smiled at
her. "Thank you, my dear." He arched a brow. "Shall we proceed
to dinner?"

Selena swallowed as Lord Edouard captured her arm with a warm smile then escorted her to a seat beside his twin Lady Elise. While she sat, she glanced about the table for Aragon. He was several places down with Wren and Hawke. Her chest tight, she turned her attention back to her neighbors.

As the gentlemen served the first course, Lady Elise grinned at Selena. "We've not officially met. I'm Lady Elise." She waved to the bearded gentleman beside her. "And this is my betrothed Seanian, Lord Farson." She cocked her head. "How are you enjoying the season so far?"

Selena sipped her fish chowder with a wry smile. "It's been interesting. Much busier than I had imagined." So much busier.

Lady Elise chuckled. "That's because the duchess is managing it."

Selena nodded. True, but she'd not disparage Aragon's mother after her generosity. "When are you and Lord Farson getting married?"

"Next week." Lady Elise cast her betrothed an ardent look. "I'm eager for that day."

Lord Farson returned her look and purred, "Me too."

Selena blushed and glanced away as her chest tightened. What would it be like to feel such passionate devotion and have it returned?

Lord Edouard winked at Selena as he served her slices of beefsteak. "Ignore Elise and her besotted swain. They can't recall appropriate dinner behavior."

Lady Elise huffed. "Just wait until you're in love. Then you'll act the same."

Lord Edouard arched a brow and snorted.

When Lady Elise scowled, Selena interjected to distract her, "How did you and Lord Farson meet?"

Lady Elise chattered about that for the rest of dinner with Lord Farson adding notes and Lord Edouard interjecting quips. Selena chuckled at their banter, and dinner passed swiftly but not swift enough. Once dinner was over, she could finally see Lord Blaine's collection.

As the ladies rose to withdraw, Lord Blaine glanced at his son. "Edouard, take Miss Midor to the collection. No doubt she's anxious to see it."

Although her pulse surged, Selena forced herself not to beam. 'Twould be impolite to her dinner companions.

Lord Edouard chuckled and took Selena's arm. "Of course, Father."

Aragon began to rise, but the duchess waved him back. "Stay here and enjoy the company of the gentlemen, Aragon. Edouard is well-equipped to show Selena his father's collection."

Aragon's mouth tautened, but he nodded and returned to his seat.

Lord Edouard glanced between the duchess and her son before escorting Selena from the dining room. When they were alone, he drawled, "Aragon is protective of you."

Her heart squeezing, Selena fought a blush and shrugged. "He feels responsible for me." If only he felt more.

Lord Edouard hummed as they turned left. "The duchess approves of you, doesn't she?"

Selena tilted her head. "I believe so." Besides zealously presenting her, the duchess had given her that wonderful art room. Warmth filled her chest.

A wry smile curved Lord Edouard's lips. "I see." He halted as they reached an open room lined with paintings and containing sculptures in the middle. "We're here."

She gaped at the tenth-century masterpieces, energy coursing through her. Vibrant and bucolic, the paintings depicted a variety of outdoor scenes, while the sculptures were movement captured in marble. She'd never seen anything like them. "Exquisite!"

Lord Edouard released her arm then explained the significance and meaning of each piece, his passion for art shining in his face. Yet his interest in her had waned, for he no longer interjected flirtatious banter or slanted her heated glances. He treated her as a brother would.

Selena muffled a sigh as Lord Edouard escorted her to the drawing room after the tour. Having lost his interest, she must focus on Lord Ravenstone. She swallowed, her stomach tensing. She'd encourage the count to kiss her when they went riding in a few days.

CHAPTER 22

*a*t breakfast the following morning, Aragon eyed Selena across the table. Since her presentation ball, they'd barely been alone. His heart squeezed. "Would you care to go riding? The royal bay, perhaps? We could bring luncheon, and you can sketch the bay."

Selena sighed as she sipped her tea. "I can't. I'm meeting some friends for luncheon. They insisted I tell them about Lord Blaine's collection. They're jealous they couldn't see it themselves."

Aragon swallowed. Her friends were probably ladies she'd met at an art salon Mother had taken her recently. At least she wasn't spending the day with Edouard or Lord Ravenstone.

Mother smiled over her toast. "Art enthusiasts always covet my cousin's invitations."

Father chuckled while finishing his eggs. "Too bad for them, he doesn't care to entertain. Too bad for his young wife too."

Ignoring Father, Aragon leaned toward Selena. Despite her preference for other gentlemen, he missed spending time alone with her. "We could ride tomorrow instead."

Selena glanced away, adjusting her teacup. "You needn't bother. Lord Ravenstone intends to take me riding again soon."

Aragon crumbled his bacon. Of course she'd rather spend time alone with one of her suitors. If only she still wanted him. "I should have realized."

Father rose and arched a brow at Aragon. "You could join me and Alaric on our ride instead."

Aragon suppressed a grimace. And subject himself to Sir Alaric's ubiquitous teasing? The baronet was worse than Hawke. "Thank you, but I'll see if Devon wishes to ride. He rarely makes time unless I invite him."

Mother tsked and rose as well. "He *really* must find a queen to help him relax."

Father took her arm with a crooked grin. "Most gentlemen don't find their wives relaxing, Caro. Quite the opposite."

Mother pursed her lips. "Most gentlemen are unenlightened then."

Once his parents' left, Aragon forced himself to eat his last few bites. Then he glanced at Selena, who was nibbling her toast and frowning at her plate. Their flowing conversation from the brothel was lost. He coughed then said, "I finally heard why your uncle was at Lady Staghorn's ball."

Selena blinked at him. "Oh?"

He grimaced. "Apparently, he and Lord Winston met at the brothel not long after your presentation ball. They bonded over their taste in girls and lack of funds. So the baron invited Midor to join them."

Selena sighed and set down her half-eaten toast. "Then doubtless we can expect Uncle Adan to appear at more court events. Wonderful."

Aching to pull Selena into his arms to comfort her, Aragon clenched his hands to remain still. If he held her, he'd be unable to resist kissing her. And she was no longer interested. "I'll make sure to protect you."

Selena rose with an almost smile. "I know."

As she glided from the breakfast room, he gulped a shuddering breath. If only he could do more than offer his protection. He set his jaw then headed to the palace.

Devon eagerly agreed to a ride, so with the royal guards, they rode through Ormas and out the eastern gate. Devon ordered his guards to fall back once they reached the royal forest. He turned to Aragon. "I've not seen much of you the past two weeks."

Aragon's stomach tensed, and he shifted in his saddle. "You saw me at the council meeting three days ago."

Devon slanted him a flat glance. "You know that's not what I meant."

"I know." Aragon grimaced as he urged his mare around a fallen tree. "Mother's presentation of Selena," and watching her with her suitors, "has occupied my time."

Devon's eyes gleamed. "I suspected as much. How is your Miss Midor?"

Aragon stiffened. "Selena isn't *mine*." If only she was. He forced a shrug. "Mother has taken Selena to countless court events, and Selena has been popular at every one. At balls she rarely sits out a dance, and at meals she never lacks partners."

Devon arched his brows as he turned his gelding onto a game path. "Any serious suitors?"

Aragon inclined his head. "Lord Ravenstone and Edouard." He scowled. "Mother has encouraged Selena to spend time alone with them, which I'm uncertain is wise." Who knew what improprieties they might attempt?

Devon's mouth twitched. "You don't count yourself a serious suitor?"

Aragon swallowed and studied his reins. "I would be, except she's not interested." Not since she'd met other gentlemen.

Devon halted his gelding to stare at Aragon. "Nonsense. Miss Midor made her preference for you clear."

Aragon sighed, his ribs squeezing. "Before her presentation, perhaps. Now she won't even go riding with me."

Devon arched a brow. "You rescued her from a brothel and a black witch but allowed her to meet other gentlemen without protest. Perhaps she assumed your riding invitation was charity rather than interest."

Aragon gaped at Devon. Charity? He'd only restrained himself to avoid exploiting her inexperience. Tingling warmth flooded him. Goddess, he couldn't imagine not wanting her. She was spellbinding.

Devon held Aragon's gaze. "If you truly want her, continue courting her to prove your interest."

His mind whirling, Aragon remained silent as they resumed riding. Could Devon be right? Could Selena not realize he wanted her? If she did, no wonder she'd turned to other suitors. Perhaps if he continued courting her like Devon suggested, eventually she'd realize his interest was sincere.

He set his jaw. Yet he couldn't rush her. She was under his protection, and she might feel compelled to accept him if he was too forceful. So he must still restrain his hunger for her. If he ensured their outings involved others, he might manage it. He could start by escorting her and her friends to places she'd enjoy. Then once she reciprocated his interest for a while, he could arrange private outings, and eventually, even kiss her again.

So when they dismounted at the palace, he asked Devon, "Could I show Selena and her friends the royal portrait gallery later this week?" A lover of art like Selena would enjoy that.

Devon grinned. "How about the day after tomorrow in the afternoon? I've nothing planned yet."

Aragon echoed his grin and clapped his shoulder. Devon was the perfect friend. "Thanks, I'll see you then."

At dinner that night, Aragon's stomach fluttered as he asked Selena, "Would you like a tour of the royal portrait gallery? Your friends should come too." His breath stilled. Would she refuse him like she had at breakfast?

However, Selena dimpled at him over her vegetable bisque. "'Twould be lovely."

His heart lightened, and he couldn't resist grinning in return.

She'd accepted, thank the Goddess. Hopefully, she'd enjoy herself, and he could arrange further outings to court her.

AFTER LUNCHEON TWO DAYS LATER, Aragon escorted Selena and her friends to the palace. Warmth filled him as he slid beside her in the carriage. If only he could hold her hand without scandalizing her friends.

To distract himself, he asked her friends about their art. Like Selena, they glowed when they described their favorites. As the carriage slowed to a stop, he smiled at Selena. "Perhaps you should set up a gallery for charity. If your work is as fine as Selena's, you'd raise a lot of funds." And many causes always needed money, like the orphanage Wren and Hawke supported.

Selena blushed as he helped her friends alight. "My sketches aren't that wonderful."

Aragon squeezed her hand while assisting her down. Her modesty was adorable. "Yes, they are." He threaded his arm through hers and led the ladies up to the royal portrait gallery. He smiled seeing the two royal guards beside the doorway. "Excellent, Devon is already here."

Miss Thorpe squeaked, "King Devon is joining us?"

Aragon blinked with a faint frown. "Of course." How else could they have visited?

Miss Blakeley smirked at her friend. "The gallery *is* his, after all."

Lady Cecilia smoothed her hair. "But King Devon joining us is a great honor."

Selena tsked, shaking her head. "Cease twittering. The king is Aragon's cousin and best friend, so he's doubtless pleased to show Aragon's guests the royal portrait gallery."

Aragon grinned when Devon chuckled from the doorway and said, "So I am." Once the ladies darted curtsies, Devon beckoned them inside. "We'll start with the oldest portrait—Calator."

Aragon muffled a laugh when Selena blinked then glanced

between the portrait of Calatini's first king and Devon several times. The strong resemblance between Devon and his ancestor from a millennium ago *was* astounding.

When they continued to the portrait of Calator's wife Annalise, Aragon studied Selena. Was she enjoying the tour? Her face glowing, she gripped his arm as she and her friends chattered about the paintings and pelted Devon with discerning questions. Aragon grinned. Selena and her friends were definitely enjoying themselves. The tour was a success.

Afterward, Aragon escorted the ladies back to the carriage then dropped Selena's friends at their homes. When he and Selena were finally alone, he threaded his fingers through hers, tingling sweeping up his arm. "How did you like the royal portraits?"

Selena dimpled. "They were all exquisite. And the king's anecdotes about his ancestors made them even more enjoyable."

He chuckled and caressed her palm with his thumb. "Devon doubtless enjoyed showing them to people more interested in the portraits than in fawning."

Selena blushed then shrugged. "I'm grateful we got to see them." She smiled at him. "'Twas kind of you to arrange the tour. Thank you."

Aragon tensed. If she assumed his courtship was mere kindness, he must arrange better outings. But he returned her smile and replied, "I'm pleased you enjoyed it. Now that you've attended court events for over a week, what have been your favorites?"

Selena tilted her head, tendrils of sandy-brown hair caressing her cheek. "Most have been interesting, even though your mother's intense social rounds were overwhelming at first. They're more bearable now that I'm acquainted with most of court and have made some friends, but I'd prefer a quieter schedule."

He squeezed her hand. So did he. "If Mother's socializing becomes too much, let me know, and I'll speak to her."

Selena giggled, arching a brow. "Shall that succeed?"

Aragon shrugged with a wry smile. "Perhaps not, but I can attempt it at least." Selena was worth confronting Mother.

Her face softening, Selena leaned toward him and touched his knee. "Thank you, Aragon."

Heat surged in his veins at her touch. He swallowed and tucked her loose hair behind her ear. "'Tis nothing." Goddess, he burned to kiss her again. His body hardening, he began bending his head.

But then the carriage halted, and he jerked back. Selena might simply be grateful for the tour and not truly interested. And kissing her now would *definitely* be rushing their courtship. He couldn't pressure her into returning his interest. He could risk kissing her after a few more outings. Until then, he must control himself. He forced a smile and gestured toward the door. "Shall we?"

CHAPTER 23

*S*elena froze and gaped at Aragon. Why hadn't he kissed her? He'd not released her during the tour and held her hand once they were alone, so he definitely wanted her. But he'd withdrawn yet again—he mustn't want her enough to actually court her. If only he did.

Her throat aching, she gritted a smile then accepted his escort inside. Although she'd rather kiss Aragon, she still must proceed with encouraging Lord Ravenstone to kiss her during their next ride. Otherwise, she'd never permanently escape Uncle Adan. Now that he had friends at court, she must act before one of his schemes stole her chance to find a husband.

Over the next two days, Selena avoided being alone with Aragon. He drew like a lodestone, and she forgot all her careful plans when they were alone. She kept almost kissing him, which was wrong while courting Lord Ravenstone.

The afternoon of her ride with the count, her hands trembled as she yanked on her burgundy riding habit. Goddess, was she ready to kiss him? She didn't know Lord Ravenstone well, and he didn't draw her like Aragon. She set her jaw. Somehow she had to be. She darted down to the drawing room, clutching her sketch journal and enchanted pencils.

When she perched beside him, Aragon glanced up from the stack of papers he was reading. His eyes narrowed while he scrutinized her. "Is today your ride with Lord Ravenstone?"

Selena tensed as she straightened her sketch journal and enchanted pencils to distract herself. "Yes."

Aragon's jaw tightened. "I can accompany you if you like."

She swallowed, weight compressing her chest. If only he could, but 'twould prevent the count from kissing her, and she couldn't miss this chance. She must secure a husband before Uncle Adan interfered. She shook her head. "You needn't bother. I'll bring a groom."

Aragon stiffened but nodded. "Very well."

Selena muffled a sigh as he turned his attention back to his papers. He appeared jealous, but not enough to stop her outing with another. If only he would. Her fingers tingled to touch his knee and recapture his interest. She began reaching toward him.

But before she touched Aragon, Lord Ravenstone joined them and smiled at her. "All ready for our ride, I see."

She dropped her wayward hand and leapt upright. Her mouth dried as she returned the count's smile. Time to tempt Lord Ravenstone. Oh, Goddess.

His eyes narrow, Aragon glanced up from his papers as she accepted the count's arm. "The royal bay again?"

Lord Ravenstone nodded. "Yes. I'll return Miss Midor an hour before dinner."

Selena and the count strode down to the stables. She slid her sketch journal and enchanted pencils into her satchel before mounting her mare. Her mind on her plan, she said little as they rode through the crowded streets of Ormas with the groom.

But once they passed the northern gate, she roused herself. She'd never get Lord Ravenstone to kiss her if she ignored him. She dimpled at him even though her pulse pounded in her ears. "I'm eager to see the royal bay again."

The count urged his stallion to a trot. "And sketch it too, I imagine. I saw you brought your sketch journal."

Selena forced herself to match his eager pace. "I hope you don't mind." If they married, he'd need to become accustomed to that.

Lord Ravenstone chuckled. "Not at all. I brought a blanket for us to sit on while you sketch."

They continued to talk as they trotted to the royal bay. Her nerves eased when she saw it again. The bay was as glorious as before, and she couldn't wait to sketch it. She glanced at Lord Ravenstone and stiffened again. But she mustn't neglect the count.

Selena and Lord Ravenstone rode by the frothy waves as the groom spread the blanket. Once the groom finished, the count leapt from the saddle to help her down.

She gulped a breath. Aragon had mentioned a lecherous gentleman could exploit helping a lady from her horse. So she allowed herself to fall into Lord Ravenstone's arms. "Oops."

The count stilled, his amber gaze on her upturned lips. A heartbeat later, he stepped back. "I apologize for my clumsiness."

Selena blinked at him. Why hadn't the genial count kissed her? She managed a smile. "No, the clumsiness was all mine."

Lord Ravenstone waved toward their blanket. "Shall we sit?"

She swallowed then nodded before retrieving her sketch journal and enchanted pencils. When she sat, she eased close enough her riding habit brushed the count's legs. Then she began sketching him. Surely her proximity and scrutiny would tempt him. When she finished his likeness, she turned her sketch journal toward him. "Look."

Lord Ravenstone arched his brows. "I thought you brought your sketch journal to capture the natural glories of the royal bay."

Selena slanted him a coy glance despite her quivering stomach. "I did, but I wanted to capture my handsome escort first."

Lord Ravenstone smiled. "I'm flattered."

Over the next hour, she sketched and flirted with the count.

She flashed warm smiles, touched his arm, and asked about his life. Yet with each flirtatious act, her stomach quivered more.

Lord Ravenstone leaned toward her as she finished her third sketch of the bay. "Did you enjoy visiting the royal bay again?"

Selena's heart stuttered. Not particularly. But she nodded and leaned toward him too. Goddess, she needed this kiss done. Then they could return home.

Lord Ravenstone murmured, "May I kiss you, Miss Midor?"

She swallowed then jerked another nod. Please let her be ready for this.

The count bent his head and kissed her. His kiss began gentle but soon turned torrid. Physically, he was as deft a kisser as Aragon.

Yet her stomach churned, and Selena had to force herself to remain still. Was it his beard? She continued allowing his kiss. No, his beard was ticklish but not the difficulty. The difficulty was he wasn't the gentleman she loved—Aragon was. Goddess, how could she have been so blind?

She jerked back, her chest tight. What should she say? The entire afternoon she'd teased the count like a starving venus seducing her prey while he slept, but now that she'd won his kiss, she burned to leave. She swallowed and eyed her hands. "Shall we return to Ormas?"

Lord Ravenstone studied her for a long moment then nodded. "If you like."

Selena darted to her feet with a sigh. "Shall we ride on the beach while the groom stows the blanket?"

Lord Ravenstone nodded again and followed her over to their mounts.

She shoved her sketch journal and enchanted pencils into her satchel then leapt on her mare without the count's aid. She mustn't encourage another kiss. Remaining silent on the return ride, she glowered at her reins. How could she end her courtship with Lord Ravenstone after all her brazen flirting?

As she brooded, Lord Ravenstone slanted her frequents glances but didn't interrupt.

Selena set her jaw when they rode through the northern gate. She'd best confess. "Lord Ravenstone?"

The count arched his brows. "Yes, Miss Midor?"

She gulped a breath, rubbing the gold gargoyle Aragon had given her for courage. Hopefully, Lord Ravenstone wouldn't be too upset. "I've enjoyed our dances and rides over the past two weeks, but I can't continue courting you. I'm truly sorry, my lord."

A wry smile glinted in the count's black beard. "Lord Treyvan, I assume." When she winced, he chuckled. "I'd suspected as much from his suppressed glares, but I allowed your explanation about your uncle to persuade me otherwise."

Selena winced again as they reached Aragon's neighborhood. "Again, my sincere apologies." She'd not meant to mislead him.

Lord Ravenstone smiled and shook his head. "Don't apologize for preferring another." When she slid from the saddle, he added, "I wish you and Lord Treyvan well."

She swept a deep curtsy in the stable yard, her heart warming. The count was exceedingly gracious—a true gentleman, just not the one she loved. "Thank you, my lord."

After her erstwhile suitor rode off, Selena retreated to her chambers. Her throat burned as she changed into a turquoise evening gown. Why hadn't she realized she loved Aragon sooner? Because her assumption love should strike within moments had blinded her. But no wonder he drew her like a lodestone, and she kept almost kissing him. She licked her lips as she strolled down to the drawing room.

Aragon halted his conversation with Hawke to drawl, "How was your ride?"

She fought not to blush, and her chest fluttered. "Illuminating."

Aragon frowned, but his parents' arrival quelled his reply.

Then Hawke bounded forward and stole her arm. Disregarding Aragon's glower, he slanted her a fervent grin as he led her to dinner. "How is it you appear more lovely each time we meet?"

Selena pursed her lips. "How is it your words grow more farcical," and irritating, "each time we speak?"

Hawke chuckled and continued flirting outrageously, but she ignored him to glance at Aragon throughout dinner. Courting others would be futile since she loved him, yet she still must marry to escape Uncle Adan. So how could she convince Aragon to cease withdrawing?

After dinner, everyone attended a new sirenic play. Although she'd never seen one, sirenic plays were supposedly spectacular because the ethereal yet seductive sirens performed flying sword fights, glass-shattering melodies, and bewitching love scenes. Yet she'd rather remain home with only Aragon.

Fortunately, when Wren joined them at the theater, Hawke abandoned Selena, so Aragon escorted her at last. A blush warming her cheeks, she squeezed his arm. "Thank the Goddess Wren attended tonight. I couldn't have withstood your brother's flirting much longer."

The tightness around Aragon's eyes relaxed. "Most ladies find it charming."

She shrugged, her heart leaping at his smile. "I might if he meant any of it. I prefer sincerity to blandishment." No doubt why she'd grown to love Aragon. He was the most sincere gentleman she'd ever met.

Aragon threaded his fingers through hers as they took their seats. "So do I."

Warmth flooding her, Selena forced herself to scan the other boxes. If only they were alone so she could kiss him like she had at her presentation ball. Perhaps he'd cease withdrawing if she kept kissing him.

Her gaze halted at Lady Staghorn's box where Uncle Adan smirked at Selena while speaking with his new friend Lord Winston. What was her uncle plotting now? She grimaced then nudged Aragon and nodded at her uncle. She relaxed when Aragon glared until her uncle quit staring. Then the sirenic play began, and 'twas as spectacular as promised, and she forgot about her uncle.

Until he strolled into their box with an unctuous grin during intermission. Her neck prickling, Selena tensed and gripped Aragon's arm to prevent him from leaping to his feet. Court would gossip if he attacked her uncle.

The duchess flashed a glittering smile. "We don't associate with churls who hire black witches, Mr. Midor."

Uncle Adan stiffened as a flush stained his cheeks.

His eyes narrow, the duke drawled, "Leave, or I'll force you to."

Uncle Adan clenched his hands then glared at Selena before storming from the box. Goddess, he was acting like a crazed chimera. And the three-headed hybrid of a lion, goat, and snake always left disaster in its wake. During the Stone Wars, a chimera crazed by his injuries had razed the Goddess's Great Temple in Oress.

Selena fingered the gold gargoyle as she returned her unseeing gaze to the sirenic play. Fortunately, unlike an actual chimera, Uncle Adan had little power, so whatever disaster his latest scheme created, Aragon and his family would protect her. She relaxed and eased closer to Aragon. So she must only worry about their courtship.

CHAPTER 24

wo mornings after the sirenic play, Aragon paused before the door of Selena's art room and gulped a breath. She was stunning in her elegant mauve gown. When Edouard and Lord Ravenstone saw her, they'd burn to kiss her too. If only he and Selena could remain home instead of attending Elise's wedding. He sighed and knocked on the door-frame. "Are you ready?"

Selena dimpled at him then set her pencil on her easel. "Time to leave already?"

His pulse surging at that dimple, he forced a wry smile while taking her arm. "Not anticipating Elise's wedding?"

Selena squeezed his arm as they began downstairs. "No, I was sketching and forgot the time. Shall her wedding be lavish, do you think?"

He grimaced. "Probably. The wedding is being held in the nave of the Great Temple." Which an art lover like Selena would adore. "Plus, Lord Farson is a councilor, and Elise is well-off."

Once they settled on the backward seat across from his parents, Selena smiled at Mother. "Are Hawke and Mel meeting us at the temple?"

"Yes. Hawke is attending with the Keyes." Mother beamed,

proud as a mama roc when her townhouse-sized nestling fledged. "And Mel is officiating the wedding ceremony, his first. Elise insisted despite Kit's attempts to have the high priest officiate."

Mother continued discussing the upcoming ceremony for the rest of the ride, so Aragon only half listened. Would Selena glow when she first saw the Great Temple? After his parents exited the carriage, he leapt out and helped Selena alight with a smile.

Selena gripped his arm, her eyes widening at the three-story temple of white limestone. "No wonder 'tis called the Great Temple."

He chuckled as he led her past the pillars toward the central door. "The inside is even more magnificent." And he couldn't wait to see her expression.

Selena's freckled face glowed when they entered the nave. "'Tis like entering a pearl. And the stained glass and appointments are *stunning*."

Aragon suppressed a grin while escorting her through the crowd. Her excitement was delightful. If only they were alone so he needn't hide his echoed fascination. "We should return for Sext sometime then tour the temple." If they ate an early luncheon, they could spend the afternoon there.

Selena squeezed his arm as they sat beside his parents in the row behind Elise's father and Kit. "I'd enjoy that. Perhaps Mel could show us."

Warmth surged in his chest. He'd his next courtship outing. How soon would Mel be free? Not that he could ask until after the wedding. To distract himself, he scanned the groom's side for Devon then waved to catch his friend's eye.

Devon waved back before everyone turned to the altar as Mel strode up the aisle.

While Mel began the ceremony with a prayer to the Goddess, Selena took Aragon's hand.

Tingling skittering up his arm, Aragon glanced at his parents beside him, but neither seemed to notice, so he twined his fingers through hers as the prelude began. Her overture couldn't be gratitude this time, so she was definitely interested—perhaps he could kiss her again soon.

The resplendent Elise and Lord Farson processed to the altar with their four witnesses behind them. How had they managed only four?

Selena murmured in his ear, "I'm astonished Lady Blaine allowed Lord Edouard to act as the first bride witness."

He smiled and rubbed his thumb against her palm as Mel continued the ceremony. "No doubt she protested, but Elise is close to her twin." She wouldn't have allowed tradition to exclude Edouard from her wedding.

Elise's wedding was lavish enough for the Great Temple but concise, thank the Goddess. The witnesses merely read some liturgies the priest usually did before Mel gave a sermon about marriage and began the vows. Crowned by tied garlands of sweet peas, Elise and Lord Farson spoke their vows then exchanged gold spiral armlets as wedding tokens. They beamed at each other as Mel announced them. With their hands joined, Elise and Lord Farson left with Mel and their witnesses to sign the matrimony certificate.

Aragon sighed and released Selena's hand. His parents would notice now that the ceremony had ended. Too bad.

As his parents conversed with Elise's father and Kit, Devon met them in the aisle, and the three talked as they drifted from the temple. Devon asked them to join him in his carriage, but once at the reception, he reluctantly excused himself to greet other guests.

Aragon and Selena remained near the refreshments, and soon Elise, Lord Farson, and their witnesses arrived amid cheers. Aragon's stomach hardened. His duty done, Edouard would head for Selena. Yet his cousin didn't, so he forced himself to ask, "Do you wish me to escort you to Edouard?"

Selena's fingers tightened about her flute of sparkling wine.

"No, he appears busy. But I'll be fine alone if you wish to socialize."

Aragon almost smiled. Had her interest in his cousin waned? "I'm content to remain here." If only he could hold Selena the way Lord Farson was holding Elise.

When the radiant bride and groom visited the refreshments table, Aragon and Selena grinned and offered their felicitations. His throat thickened. Might he and Selena look the same one day?

Mother joined them once Elise and Lord Farson left. "Why are you two loitering on the outskirts? Selena, come along. Aragon, go congratulate Mel."

A pang darted through Aragon at losing Selena, but he nodded and found Mel. After congratulating his brother, he arranged a tour of the Great Temple next week. He couldn't help a grin. Soon he could enjoy Selena's excitement at the beautiful temple without all of court watching.

When Hawke and Wren joined Mel, Aragon began circulating but watched Selena to see if Edouard or Lord Ravenstone approached. His tension eased when neither did. She spent most of the reception with her three art friends. As he escorted her to the carriage afterward, he asked, "Did you prefer the wedding or the reception?" He'd preferred the wedding since they'd held hands.

A dimple quivered in Selena's left cheek. "The wedding was lovely, but the reception was inspirational."

Aragon blinked. "Inspirational?" What did that mean?

Selena's smile turned coy. "Yes."

He swallowed and eyed her. What could she be planning? Hopefully, 'twouldn't involve Edouard or Lord Ravenstone. Her pursuing other suitors made his stomach ache.

. . .

ARAGON WATCHED Selena to find out her plans, but she revealed nothing until she joined him in the morning room an hour before luncheon three days later.

Selena leaned toward him with a warm smile. "Today promises to be lovely. We should go riding and share a picnic."

He brightened and closed his book. That sounded wonderful. If only they could go alone. But doubtless she'd already invited some of her art friends or another suitor. "Who shall be joining us?"

Selena's smile burgeoned into a coy grin. "No one."

His pulse surged as he stared at her. Last week she'd declined his offer to go riding alone. What had changed? Her grin told him nothing. He inhaled. Goddess, they'd finally be alone again. But then he froze—he'd plans this evening. "I can't. I must meet Devon after dinner to discuss agricultural reports."

Selena arched a brow. "We'll return well before then."

Aragon swallowed as heat flared in his chest. They would if he controlled himself. But would he be able to? He mustn't risk kissing her to ensure he did. Once he kissed her, his control would vanish like kindling in dragon flame.

Selena dimpled and grasped his hand. "I had Cook pack your favorite foods. And you can pick where we eat."

He grinned then allowed her to pull him upright. They needed another courtship outing before their tour of the Great Temple next week anyway. "Very well."

Aragon was quiet during the ride through Ormas. Where should he take her? It must be as breathtaking as the royal bay. He grinned while they rode through the eastern gate. The heart of the royal forest was otherworldly, and most had never seen it. "I know the perfect spot in the royal forest."

Selena dimpled at him as they trotted past the verdant fields. "Lead on."

They talked the entire ride about her favorite art in Ormas then several novels they both loved. Soon they rode into the royal forest, still talking. When the buzzing was within earshot, he waved her to silence with a grin. "Quietly now. And no galloping."

Selena tilted her head. "What's that buzzing?"

Aragon chuckled. "You'll see." She'd not believe it until then. They rode into the small clearing at the heart of the royal forest, and he halted his mare. "This is close enough."

Selena peered at the ancient cottage in the center of the clearing surrounded by bees as large as songbirds. Her mouth gaped. "Are those *melissae*?"

Tingling darting through him, he nodded and helped her alight. He forced himself to release her rather than tumbling her into his arms. "Yes, descendants of the ones kept by Calator's mentor Esme the Great. They're the reason the royal forest was created."

Her eyes wide, Selena crept toward the cottage. "Their stings are deadly—are we safe so close?"

Aragon smiled at her adorable bravery. "As long as we don't alarm them or attempt to harvest their ambrosia. Devon and I have picnicked here on occasion."

Selena shook her head as he laid out the blanket. "I never imagined I'd see melissae in person. 'Tis an experience I'll never forget. Thank you, Aragon."

Warmth infused his chest. He'd picked well. Certainly more impressive than the royal bay. He grinned as he unpacked their picnic.

Selena extracted her sketch journal and enchanted pencils from her satchel. "I must sketch them before they disappear!"

As she sketched, he chuckled while fixing her a plate and pouring her a flute of sparkling wine. Engrossed by her sketch journal, she was spellbinding. Would she look the same if he kissed her? He devoured his luncheon to distract himself.

Selena soon finished sketching then ate her food and showed him her sketch. After he complimented it, she grinned. "Now I must sketch you with the melissae."

Aragon suppressed a wince, his stomach tensing. He was

unremarkable compared to the magical melissae. "Is that necessary?"

Selena dimpled at him. "Definitely."

He sipped his sparkling wine to hide his sigh. She was too spellbinding to resist. "Very well."

Selena leaned forward and nudged him to the left. "Move over here." Then she ran her hands over his shoulders and down his chest with a faint smile. "There, no more crumbs."

Aragon swallowed as heat flared beneath his skin and his body tightened. Although she appeared interested, she was still courting other suitors, and he must allow her time to choose among them. He mustn't seize her like a lusty satyr—with his control so tenuous, he might not stop at kisses.

CHAPTER 25

*H*er heart pounding, Selena suppressed her smile as she brushed imaginary crumbs off Aragon. Sketching him gave her an excuse to touch. And considering his avid gaze, he enjoyed her touch too. Perhaps he'd kiss her if she continued. Lady Blaine's reminiscences during the reception about the Hawkes' childhood picnics had been the perfect inspiration.

She began sketching him, pausing often to readjust him or his clothes. Each time she did, Aragon stiffened further but made no move to kiss her. She must kiss him instead. She tensed as she turned her finished sketch to show him. "What do you think?"

Aragon inclined his head. "Very nice." His approval of her sketch was more tepid than usual, probably because he was the subject.

After setting aside her sketch journal with a coy smile, Selena studied him beneath her lashes. How could she initiate a kiss? "Thanks for sitting so patiently. It must have been hard."

Aragon swallowed, his eyes turning ebony. "I suppose."

"Well, thank you again." Her pulse surged as she leaned forward to brush a kiss against his lips. When he stilled, she wrapped her arms about his neck and kissed him again.

Aragon shuddered but yanked her into his lap and deepened their kiss.

Selena pressed against him and parted her lips, tingling heat consuming her. Goddess, she'd never tire of his enthralling kisses. 'Twere surely sweeter than the ambrosia inside the nearby melissae hive, although they'd not cure any ill.

As they devoured each other's mouths, Aragon began bending them toward the blanket. Then he halted and wrenched back his head.

Burning for more kisses, she whimpered and threaded her fingers in his seal-brown hair and attempted to capture his lips again.

Aragon groaned, keeping his head beyond her reach. "We must stop, Selena."

She licked her swollen lips. Her body throbbed with hunger, so stopping was painful. Only more kisses would soothe her. "Why?"

Aragon shut his eyes and swallowed. "Because we might go beyond kisses. And we must return before we're missed."

Selena shivered as heat flared in her veins. She'd not mind going beyond kisses with Aragon. And from his hungry expression, he burned as she did. Yet he still withdrew, not because he didn't want her, but to protect her. Her heart swelled as she caressed his face. "Your mother knows we're out riding. I consulted her about which day was best."

Aragon winced then lifted her from his lap and set her on the blanket. "Mother knows?"

Her body aching without his, Selena sighed and smoothed her rumpled riding habit. "Yes." And the duchess hadn't protested either, so she either approved or trusted he'd act like a brother. Which he *definitely* hadn't. Tingling suffused her skin.

Aragon began tossing food back into the basket. "Then we'd better return posthaste."

She grimaced but helped him pack their picnic. Although she'd rather stay here, he was right. Even if the duchess did approve of their courtship, she'd not approve of them missing dinner. After they finished, Aragon hoisted her into her saddle without even sneaking a kiss. Her chest squeezed as he swung onto his mare. Surely they'd time for a brief kiss.

Unlike the ride out, they didn't speak as they rode through the royal forest. Selena stiffened and eyed him when he urged his mare to a trot outside the clearing. His face was tight, and his eyes black. Although their kisses hadn't been entirely proper, why would he appear guilty if he wanted to court her? Her throat clenched. Despite their attraction, he mustn't love her as she loved him. He'd only kissed her because she teased him until his resistance crumbled.

When they left the royal forest, Aragon finally spoke, his mouth grim, "We should race back to Ormas."

She winced but nodded. They mightn't arrive in time for dinner otherwise. Tears burning her eyes, she bent forward and thundered past the green fields, reaching the eastern gate well before him. She gritted a grin and drawled as he joined her, "I won our race... again. Did I win another boon?"

Aragon shifted in his saddle as they rode into Ormas. "I suppose. What did you want?"

Clinging to her grin, Selena licked her lips. She wanted *him*, but what boon could inspire his love? "I'm not certain. I'll save it until I decide."

Aragon nodded, and they hurried back to the townhouse and changed for dinner then headed downstairs.

The duchess beamed when they strode into the drawing room. "How was your ride?"

Selena's heart quivered as they sat on the sofa. Wonderful until Aragon had withdrawn yet again. She forced a smile. "Thrilling. Aragon showed me the melissae in the royal forest."

An impish light glint flickered in the duchess's eyes. "Much more thrilling than tea at the Campbells', I'm sure."

Hawke breezed into the drawing room. "What could be more thrilling than tea at the Campbells'?"

The duchess slanted her youngest son a flat glance. "Nearly anything, according to you this afternoon."

Hawke chuckled. "True enough." He turned to Selena with a smoldering smile. "You were *greatly* missed at tea today."

Selena stiffened and arched a scornful brow, but the duke and Mel arrived before she could reply, and everyone proceeded to dinner. Despite not truly wanting her, Aragon kept her arm, although Hawke sat on her other side.

As always, Hawke flirted outrageously throughout dinner, ignoring her retorts and Aragon's scowls. During dessert, he said, "Since you've nothing special tonight, Mother, I'll bring Selena with me to the Westons' musical evening."

The duchess inclined her head. "That sounds fine. Your father and I are joining the Keyes for cards."

Selena tensed. She couldn't withstand an evening of Hawke's flirting. Surely Aragon would protect her. She flicked him a pleading glance over her cherry tart. "Shall you join us?"

Aragon frowned and shook his head. "Remember, I'm meeting Devon tonight."

Selena's throat cramped as she set down her spoon. She'd forgotten that after his heartrending withdrawal during their ride. But she couldn't refuse Hawke's invitation without appearing brusque. If only she could feign illness without worrying Aragon or his family.

Once Hawke escorted her to the carriage and sat on the backward seat across from her, she folded her hands then lifted her chin. "Is Wren accompanying us?" That might moderate his flirting.

His tone no longer flirtatious, Hawke replied, "She intended to, but she sent her regrets this afternoon since she's writing a new play for the orphanage. I thought you might like to attend in her stead."

Selena pursed her lips and almost snorted. "How flattering." She eyed him for a moment. "Why do you bother with your farcical flirting?" He clearly wasn't interested if he only thought to invite her because his best friend wasn't free.

Hawke flashed a crooked grin. "To torment Aragon, of course. Big brother is *smitten*."

She blushed, and her heart quickened. If Aragon was smitten, then why did he keep withdrawing? Could his chivalry be restraining him? Please, Goddess, let that be why. She narrowed her eyes at Hawke. "I want you to stop. Both Aragon and Wren dislike it."

"Wren?" Hawke chuckled. "She doesn't mind. I tell her about all my dalliances, although most have more substance."

Selena goggled at him. A lady who beamed at him like Wren did couldn't want to hear about his dalliances. Was he blind? As he helped her alight from the carriage, she shook her head. "Regardless, I want you to stop flirting with me."

Hawke shrugged. "As you like. 'Twas becoming dull, anyhow." He escorted her inside and warmly greeted their hosts. The only people he was that cordial with were Wren and his family.

Once they settled in their seats, she quirked a wry brow. "You must attend the Westons' musical evenings often."

Hawke chuckled. "Yes, their musical taste is always superb, and they never permit talking during the performances."

Selena smiled. Not surprising he appreciated that since he was a dedicated violinist who played most days. She'd been impressed when she'd first overheard him in the music room last month.

Soon a string quartet entered and began playing once the room hushed. Although she preferred art to music, she enjoyed their vivid performance until Uncle Adan, appearing more disreputable than ever, slipped into a nearby seat. She tensed. Lord Winston wasn't with him, so he'd gained entry on his own. How did her uncle know an elegant couple like the Westons? When the quartet left for a break, she murmured in Hawke's ear, "My uncle is here."

Hawke frowned at Uncle Adan. "Do you wish to leave? Or I could ask him to leave."

Selena winced but sighed. "No, we should stay, and he'd quarrel if asked to leave." He'd enjoy the chance to tarnish her reputation. 'Twas the worst he could manage while the Hawkes protected her. Although the duchess would doubtless squash any rumors by the following morning.

Hawke nodded as the quartet returned.

Her stomach quivering, she couldn't help slanting glances at Uncle Adan throughout the rest of the performance. Why was he here? He didn't care for music. Back home, he'd never listened to the occasional bard traveling through Upper Ashville, attended musical evenings during house parties, or joined in caroling at Longnight.

Hawke attempted to whisk her out after the final song, but her uncle waylaid them.

Uncle Adan smirked at her. "Where's Lord Treyvan, niece?"

Selena forced a serene smile to disguise her unease. "Meeting with the king, so his younger brother, Lord Beza, offered to escort me instead. Why are you here?"

Uncle Adan's eyes glinted. "To check on you. I told you we weren't finished—you'll earn me a fortune yet."

She swallowed, a chill dousing her skin. What did he mean by that? And how had he known she'd be here? She hadn't even known she was attending until dinner. Did he have someone spying on her?

Hawke scowled at Uncle Adan. "You informed the Westons you're Selena's estranged uncle."

Uncle Adan sneered. "Yes, and because of their missing daughter, they were *eager* to facilitate a reunion." He smirked at Selena again. "Any suitors yet?"

She raised her chin with a glittering grin. Only Aragon— maybe. "That's none of your concern, uncle. I'm of age, and you no longer support me."

Uncle Adan snickered. "So no, then."

Hawke arched a brow and drawled, "My family shall announce happy tidings soon. You'll read it in the newspaper." With that jab, he swept her outside and into the carriage.

As the carriage rumbled down the street, Selena stared out the window and fingered the gold gargoyle Aragon had given her to reassure herself. What could Uncle Adan be plotting? She shivered. His smirk had been too gleeful. She must tell Aragon as soon as he returned from the palace.

CHAPTER 26

$\mathcal{A}$s Aragon discussed agricultural reports with Devon, he glanced at the clock on the mantel every few minutes, his jaw tensing. What were Selena and Hawke doing now? Despite his repressed love for Wren, Hawke flirted with Selena too much—what would he attempt when they were alone?

After an hour, Devon waved a hand before Aragon's eyes. "Hello? Has your mind wandered again?"

Aragon winced and jerked his gaze back to the agricultural reports. "Yes. Sorry for my preoccupation." Damn Hawke for escorting Selena tonight.

Devon arched his brows. "Did Miss Midor rebuff your attempts to court her?"

Aragon fought not to blush. Their passionate kisses at today's picnic had been the opposite of rebuffing. His chest tightened. Despite warning himself not to kiss her, he'd almost made love to her and stolen her choice of husband. "No, and she even invited me on a picnic this afternoon."

Devon tapped a finger against his desk. "Did her other suitors supplant you since?"

Aragon's chest eased. "Neither Edouard nor Lord Ravenstone have approached in recent days." Goddess knew why.

Devon frowned. "Then what's vexing you?"

Aragon tensed and shifted in his seat then admitted, "Hawke is escorting Selena to the Westons' musical evening tonight. Alone." The flirt.

"Jealous, are you?" Devon chuckled. "Your brother shan't take his flirting too far."

Aragon grunted and clenched his hands. "I'm not certain of that. His flirting is outrageous whenever he sees her." Although so far, Selena hadn't seemed to enjoy it.

Devon's eyes gleamed. "Miss Midor is nothing like his ordinary dalliances—she's looking for a husband. No doubt he only flirts with her to torment you."

Aragon sighed and relaxed his fists. He'd suspected the same. Then his stomach hardened. "But what if Selena begins to take his flirting seriously?"

Devon leaned back in his seat. "You're fretting over nothing."

Aragon grimaced and rubbed his brow. "Probably, but I can't seem to help it." Just like he couldn't help kissing her this afternoon, even though he'd known his control was too tenuous to risk it.

Devon tsked then shook his head. "Shall we return to the agricultural reports? The better you concentrate, the sooner you can check on your Miss Midor."

Aragon straightened. True, although he must avoid spending time alone with her unless she chose him over her other suitors. His hunger for her was too strong to resist. He nodded and redoubled his focus, and they finished reviewing the reports. He was about to leave when a knock shook the door.

He and Devon exchanged a narrow glance, then Devon called, "Enter."

His face flushed, Lord Islaye burst inside the king's study. "Your majesty, Lord Treyvan, I've some disturbing news."

Devon's brow furrowed as he eyed the count. "What is it?"

Lord Islaye blurted, "That black witch Lord Treyvan discovered. He escaped."

Aragon leapt upright as his pulse surged. "What? How?!"

Lord Islaye shook his head. "The magic marshals aren't certain yet."

Aragon's fists tightened, but he forced himself to remain still despite his racing pulse. "When did the black witch escape?"

Lord Islaye grimaced again. "Shortly before midnight last night."

"What?" Fire flaring through him, Aragon glared at the other councilor. They should have been informed as soon as the black witch escaped. "Why are we only learning of this *now*?"

Lord Islaye shifted with a cough. "Because the black witch created a golem to take his place." Made of mud infused with magic, golems could imitate humans or act as warriors, so they were favorite constructs of ambitious witches. "The magical construct fooled his guards until it vanished several hours ago."

Aragon slammed a hand on Devon's desk, blood rushing in his ears. "Damnation! The black witch could be *anywhere*." And was probably hunting Selena. She was too tempting a prize for him to forget.

Lord Islaye looked past Aragon to slant Devon an apologetic grimace. "The magic marshals are hunting the black witch now. They know his magical signature and expect to find him soon."

Devon inclined his head and rumbled, "Make sure they do. Have the royal witch assist them."

"I'll visit Lady Juliet's wing next. Thanks, your majesty." Lord Islaye snapped a bow and left.

Aragon bolted to the door. "I must find Selena at once." His stomach clenched. Please, Goddess, let her be safely back home.

Devon called after him, "Let me know she's safe as soon as you find her."

Aragon waved an acknowledgment as he rushed from the king's study. Ignoring the eyes following him, he hurtled down to his carriage and ordered his driver to race home. What if Selena wasn't home because the black witch had already found her? Would he be able to rescue her in time?

As soon as the carriage slowed, he leapt out and bounded up the front steps. When the door swung open, he barked, "Perkins, has Selena returned yet?"

The butler nodded. "Miss Midor and Lord Beza returned an hour ago. She went up to her chambers, I believe."

His muscles and stomach easing, Aragon nodded at Perkins in thanks then swept inside. But once he passed the butler, he paused and turned around. "Has Father returned from the Keyes's yet?"

Perkins arched his brows. "Not yet."

Aragon quirked a wry smile. Not surprising. His parents often stayed at the Keyes's until well after midnight. But since Father wasn't home, he'd arrange increasing their magical defenses without informing Father first. Unlike before, Selena wasn't hidden from the black witch, and he'd follow if they attempted to hide her elsewhere, so defense was their only option until the black witch was found.

He leaned toward the butler. "The black witch hunting Selena has escaped. Please alert the other servants to be vigilant. Also, send word to our usual witch to bolster the house wards within the hour. And see if she has people who can guard the townhouse as well. If not, contact Master Marshal Thurston about magic marshals available for private duty."

Perkins stiffened but nodded. "Yes, my lord."

Aragon smiled at him. Their longtime butler would ensure everything was handled swiftly. "Thank you, Perkins." He turned and strode upstairs to rap on Selena's door. With their defenses arranged, he must inform her about the black witch.

Selena flung open her door and dimpled at him. "You're back. At last. I must talk to you about my uncle."

He frowned as he stepped inside her chambers. Midor was trivial compared to the black witch. And the people watching Midor hadn't sent word of unusual behavior. "Your uncle?"

Selena pursed her lips and shut the door behind him. "Yes, he wheedled into the Westons' musical evening. And he kept smirking at me—he's plotting something."

Aragon stiffened then grasped her shoulders and drew her close. "He must have known the black witch escaped late last night." But how had the black witch contacted Midor without alerting the people watching? Aragon must write them at once.

Selena clenched the gold gargoyle nestled between her breasts, her face turning ashen. "What?"

His heart squeezed at her distress, but he nodded. "Yes, the black witch created a golem to take his place. The magic marshals are hunting him, and Devon ordered the royal witch to help."

Selena dropped the gold gargoyle to clutch his waistcoat. "When shall they find him?"

Aragon managed a soothing smile. "They hope soon." If only he could offer more reassurance.

Selena shuddered. "I pray to the Goddess they do." She worried her lip. "So what should we do until they capture the black witch?"

Warmth welling in his chest, he wrapped his arms about her shoulders to comfort her. "You must remain confined here. No more court events." They weren't safe for her with the black witch free.

Selena sighed as she hugged his waist. "Your mother shan't allow that. She has events chosen for days."

Aragon snorted and set his jaw. He'd not allow Mother's penchant for social display to endanger Selena. "She shall once she knows about the black witch."

Selena studied his face with a frown. "Shall avoiding court be enough? The black witch knows where I am now. Uncle Adan would have told him."

Aragon scowled. Doubtless within moments of the black witch contacting him. Greedy cur. "I arranged to increase our magical defenses, and the protection charm from the royal witch should guard you against the black witch's spells. So if you stay inside the townhouse, he can't touch you."

Selena shuddered and buried her face in his chest. "I apologize for inspiring such hassle."

His heart fluttering, Aragon lifted her chin to brush a kiss against her lips. "You're no hassle. We'll keep you safe from the black witch, I swear it."

Selena's dark-gray eyes shimmered as she kissed him in return. "Thank you, Aragon. You've been a dedicated protector since we met."

He sighed and forced himself to release her. If only he could hold her forever, but his control wouldn't last much longer. "I'll leave now. Try to get some rest."

Selena nodded, then he slipped out her door. After writing Devon and the people watching Midor, Aragon paced about his chambers. He must help further the hunt for the black witch. He'd visit Master Marshal Thurston tomorrow straight after breakfast to discover how. Hopefully, the people watching Midor would have written back by then, and they or the magic marshals would have a lead on the black witch.

He made himself stop pacing and crawled into bed, yet nightmares about the black witch finding Selena permeated his sleep. His eyes burning and body sluggish, he rose shortly after dawn the following morning.

He'd just finished dressing when someone knocked on his door. He opened it and blinked at Selena. Why was she here so early? "Ready for breakfast?"

Selena shook her head. "Not yet. Could I come in for a moment?"

Although he shouldn't allow her inside his chambers, Aragon nodded and stepped back, his heart quickening. He shut the door once she glided inside, so no one would see her. "What did you wish to discuss?"

Selena drew a deep breath and began pacing before him. "The increased magical defenses and the royal witch's protection charm aren't enough to protect me. The black witch escaped from the custody of *countless* magic marshals. He'll evade the defenses and protection charm somehow."

Aragon frowned and captured her elbows to draw her close. "If bolstered house wards, magical guards, and Lady Juliet's powerful spell aren't enough, how else can we protect you?"

Selena glanced away and licked her lips. "There's another option we didn't discuss yesterday."

His gaze drawn to her mouth, he swallowed as tingling flooded him. Goddess, even skittish and in peril, she was spell-binding. "What?"

Selena inhaled another deep breath. "A husband."

Aragon gripped her elbows. Had she accepted a proposal from Edouard or Lord Ravenstone? Neither deserved her. His stomach burned. *They* hadn't rescued her from the black witch the first time. And neither had pursued her for days.

His jaw clenched. Was she accepting simply to escape the black witch? She should only wed a gentleman she loved. Or did she love one of her other suitors?

His stomach lurched again. If she loved another, how could she have kissed him so passionately yesterday? Passion like that must be genuine. He couldn't lose Selena now. She'd only lived here for a month. And he'd barely courted her to avoid rushing her choice of husband. But now she appeared to have chosen another to escape the black witch. What was he to do?

CHAPTER 27

a fter declaring she needed a husband, Selena inhaled and eyed Aragon beneath her lashes. If he truly wanted her, surely 'twould inspire him to propose. Then he could make love to her and permanently rescue her from the black witch. And considering their ravenous kisses yesterday, they'd both enjoy it.

Yet Aragon merely gripped her elbows and stared at her, his eyes narrow and jaw tight.

She swallowed as her throat clenched. Goddess, he wasn't going to propose. He desired her, just not enough to marry her. But she still needed him to make love to her to escape the black witch. She didn't want anyone else. So how could she persuade him? He *had* hovered when others courted her, so perhaps jealousy would motivate him. "I need your help convincing one of my suitors to propose—perhaps kissing them would serve. I thought we could practice like we did at yesterday's picnic."

His nostrils flared, Aragon rasped, "Was that all yesterday was? *Practice?*"

Selena lifted her chin and forced a smile despite her aching chest. No, she'd kissed him because she loved him, but his jealousy would vanish if he realized that. "You're not courting me, so what else could it be?"

Aragon paled and dropped her elbows then stepped back. "I see."

Her breath froze. She must recapture his waning interest. So she dimpled and smoothed the raspberry gown she'd worn with him in mind. 'Twas the one he'd goggled at when she'd returned from Celeste's. "But practicing is the only way for me to perfect my kissing."

Aragon stiffened with a grunt. "Your kisses are fine."

As Selena stepped forward to caress his arm, her stomach fluttered, but she maintained her coy smile. "Fine isn't enough to persuade one of my suitors to propose." Or enough to incite Aragon into making love to her. "I need more practice."

Aragon's jaw twitched as he removed her hand. "Practice with one of your *suitors*."

Her heart squeezed. Only if he was the suitor. She tilted her head and licked her lips. "I can't trust them to not take too many liberties."

His eyes ebony, Aragon gritted a tight smile. "Are you certain you can trust me?"

Selena beamed and caressed his arm again. She'd trust him with everything. "Why wouldn't I? You rescued a penniless country miss you just met from a brothel." And she loved him.

Still eyeing her lips, Aragon jerked back. "Enough of this. I'm too famished to quarrel. I'm going down to breakfast."

She muffled her sigh then lifted her chin. She'd lost for now, but she'd try again after he appeased his hunger. "I'll join you."

Aragon offered his arm, and they strode downstairs to the breakfast room. They dined in silence until Perkins handed Aragon a note.

A forkful of eggs halfway to her mouth, Selena stilled when Aragon growled. "What is it?" Bad news about the black witch?

Aragon grimaced as he crushed the note. "Word from the

people watching your uncle. Apparently, a beggar visited your uncle's kitchen yesterday morning, and Midor gave him some food."

She shuddered and set down her fork. "The black witch, no doubt. Uncle Adan wouldn't involve himself with an ordinary beggar." The miser refused to feed his own servants enough, so he'd never feed a random beggar.

Aragon nodded. "But since no one realized the black witch had escaped, the people watching Midor disregarded the beggar's visit. And Midor behaved normally the rest of the day, until his watchers lost him at the Westons'. He's not returned to his townhouse since."

Selena swallowed then forced herself to finish her eggs. "He must be with the black witch. Wherever that is." Goddess, let the magic marshals discover the black witch soon. Who knew what scheme he and Uncle Adan would spawn together? But doubtless something plotting her destruction.

Before Aragon could reply, his parents swept into the breakfast room.

As they sat, the duke arched his brows. "Any word on the black witch?"

Aragon sighed, crumbling his bacon instead of devouring it like normal. "No, although we've just learned Midor has vanished."

The duchess pursed her lips as she buttered her toast. "That's suspicious."

Selena grimaced over her tea, bitterness flooding her mouth. As suspicious as the time Uncle Adan had disappeared after Father had said they couldn't afford to hire brownies. Her uncle had returned a week later with a spell to bind them, which wrecked the kitchen when they'd broken the spell and escaped. "Definitely."

The duchess glanced at Selena. "I'll make your excuses today at the Campbells' garden party then Lady Nolan's ball. But hopefully, the magic marshals shall recapture the black witch by tomorrow. Rumors shall start if you miss too many court events."

Aragon slammed down his teacup and glared at his mother. "Who cares about rumors at court when the black witch is free?"

The duke narrowed his eyes at Aragon. "We all realize the black witch is more grievous, but rumors shall matter once he's captured, so we must address them now."

When Aragon stiffened, Selena ached to touch his knee and comfort him. He was just concerned for her and didn't deserve to be scolded.

She was about to defend him when the duke shook his head and added, "Besides, all the precautions you arranged shall protect Selena from the black witch until the magic marshals recapture him, so we can concentrate on rumors at court instead of the black witch."

Aragon inclined his head. "I'll allow you and Mother to handle any rumors." He finished his breakfast and rose. "I'm off to visit the magic marshals to check their progress hunting the black witch and update them about Midor. I'll return soon."

Downing the last of her tea, Selena leapt and hastened after him. She must persuade him to make love to her. 'Twas the only way to permanently escape the black witch. "Aragon, wait!"

Aragon halted in the entrance hall and arched his brows.

She flashed a coy smile despite her quivering stomach. "Now that we've eaten, we should continue our discussion upstairs."

Aragon scowled at her. "I'm not discussing that again."

Selena's breath stilled. He'd never been so disobliging before. Why now when 'twas imperative? She licked her lips. "But, Aragon..."

Aragon jerked around and bolted toward the door. "I must go."

Her heart twisting, she stared after him as he left. Provoking his jealousy had driven him to flee. But how else could she induce him to make love to her? Perhaps she should try kissing him first? That had almost succeeded at yesterday's picnic. She retreated to her art room and spent the next couple hours sketching. She'd just finished her third sketch when Aragon knocked and entered.

Selena dropped her sketch journal and darted over to him. Her chest lightened. He'd returned at last. "How was your visit to the magic marshals?"

Aragon grunted. "Unproductive. Master Marshal Thurston and his people have been unable to find the black witch. When the black witch escaped, he destroyed any physical remnants, like hair or blood, that could be used to trace him. And although the magic marshals recognize his magical signature now, he's not used magic strong enough to trace."

She shivered as a chill prickled her skin. If the black witch had vanished so completely, how would the magic marshals ever manage to discover him? "Have they attempted tracing Uncle Adan instead?"

Aragon grimaced and grasped her hand. "Once I mentioned Midor had also vanished, Thurston sent people to fetch physical remnants from your uncle's townhouse, but Midor also left none behind to trace."

Selena tensed. Doubtless the black witch had told Uncle Adan exactly what to destroy. And her uncle wasn't a witch, so he'd no magic to trace.

His jaw taut, Aragon drew her into his arms. "But I told Thurston to use me to lure the black witch from hiding if they don't unearth him by today. The black witch swore to seek vengeance when I helped capture him, so he shan't be able to resist."

Her heart swelled as she stared up at Aragon. Goddess, he was so dedicated and brave—the finest gentleman she'd ever known. She flung her arms about him and kissed him.

Aragon returned her kiss for a moment then wrenched back his head. "Practicing kissing again?"

Dazed, Selena blinked at Aragon. No, she'd kissed him because she loved him more than a griffin loved her lifelong mate. However, she forced a coy smile and replied, "More practice is always beneficial."

Aragon snorted and strode from the room.

She whisked after him into his chambers. Heat surged in her veins. She must convince him to make love to her. He was the only gentleman she wanted, and she must lose her virginity to escape the black witch.

Aragon frowned at her, his hands twitching. "Selena, you shouldn't be here."

Selena licked her tingling lips. "But where else can we discuss kissing that your mother shan't overhear?" And that was so near a bed?

Aragon crossed his arms. "Fine. Say your piece. Then leave."

She gulped a breath and smoothed her raspberry gown. "There's only one way I can escape the black witch."

His jaw twitching, Aragon drawled, "Disposing of your virginity. So you said at the brothel."

Selena swallowed and nodded. "And since I've abandoned the brothel scheme, I need a husband, or at least a betrothed, for that. But none of my suitors have proposed." Not that she wanted them to when she loved Aragon. "Perhaps they might if I kissed them the right way." She tilted her head. "I need you to teach me. Like you taught me about kissing at the brothel."

Aragon snorted. "You were a remarkably quick pupil. After that lesson, your kisses have been fine. Surely your other suitors haven't complained."

Her chest squeezed at his calm reference to her other suitors. "Well, no, but Lord Edouard never bothered to kiss me, and Lord Ravenstone only kissed me once." But more importantly, Aragon kept denying their attraction. "I must be doing it wrong."

Aragon's jaw tightened. "Trust me, you aren't."

Warmth supplanted the ache in her chest. Their kisses must

enthrall him too. So how could she tempt him to kiss her again? "I can't be. I must learn more about kissing."

Aragon blew a sigh. "Fine. I'll fetch a book about the erotic arts that gentlemen pass amongst themselves. I believe Hawke has one."

Selena gaped at him. There were books about that? Astonishing. She made herself shrug. "Books are very well, but kissing is a physical skill and requires manual instruction."

Aragon grunted. "This book shall instruct you plenty."

She tilted her head to feign considering it. After a moment, she pursed her lips. "I doubt it. Although since Hawke has the book, perhaps you should fetch him instead." Would mentioning his brother finally goad him into acting?

Aragon stiffened as a flush stained his face. He didn't like that idea. But he didn't move to kiss her.

Selena sighed. She'd failed again. And she couldn't even maintain the pretense of kissing Hawke—he felt too much like a younger brother. "Or perhaps not. I'd feel guilty kissing Hawke when Wren is so clearly in love with him."

Aragon relaxed, and his flush faded. "I'll fetch the book then."

"Don't bother." She studied Aragon through her lashes, her heart fluttering. "I want manual instruction, and you're the only gentleman I trust." Or wanted kissing her.

Aragon glared at her. "I'm no kissing tutor."

Selena tensed. Why was he being so obstinate? Another gentleman would have already kissed her. But she'd one more trick to play. She licked her lips. "I've decided what I want as my boon from our race yesterday."

Aragon's eyes darkened as they dropped to her lips. "Oh?"

Her pulse leapt at his obvious fascination. She licked her lips again to tempt him further. "I want you to practice kissing with me. And more. I don't want to be surprised when one of my suitors goes beyond kissing."

His eyes narrow, Aragon strode over and jerked her into his arms. "Fine. But you don't know what you're asking."

Her heart galloped as she lifted her chin to meet his gaze. He'd succumbed at last! Thank the Goddess. "I know enough." And wanted to know more.

Aragon snorted then swooped like a hunting roc and seized her lips in a fierce kiss.

CHAPTER 28

*H*is pulse pounding, Aragon seized Selena's lips in a punishing kiss. He'd show her not to torment a suitor by compelling him to teach her how to kiss others.

Selena flung her arms about his neck and parted her lips to return his kiss with equal hunger.

For the first time, he dropped his gentlemanly restraint and unfettered his hunger for Selena. Tingling warmth swamping him, he devoured her lips as he steered her toward his bed. How convenient she insisted he kiss her in his chambers. Still kissing her, he tumbled her onto his bed and sprawled atop her.

Yet Selena didn't stiffen or attempt to push him away. Instead, she wrenched off his cravat and yanked on his waistcoat.

Aragon shoved her hands aside to tear open his waistcoat. Then he began unlacing her gown, although with much more care than he'd taken with his own clothes.

Selena sighed and burrowed her hands beneath his shirt.

He shuddered as fire blazed where her hands caressed his bare skin. He groaned and reared back to shrug out of his coat, waistcoat, and shirt all at once.

Her hair tousled, eyes black with passion, and freckled skin rosy, Selena breathed, "Oh my."

The fire inside Aragon flared at her dazed yet wanton appearance. After he finished removing her gown and his clothes, he'd make love to her and ruin her for anyone else. *Then* she'd never speak of other suitors again.

He stiffened at his feral thoughts. What was he *doing*? 'Twas wrong to ruin Selena and steal her choice of husband. He'd allowed his hunger and jealousy blind him to her feelings— again. She deserved to love her chosen husband, and she'd never said she loved him. She just wanted to escape the black witch. He lurched off her and stumbled across his chambers.

Selena blinked and licked her lips. "Aragon?" She sat up and clutched her gown as it slid off her shoulders. "What are you doing?"

His body painfully hard, Aragon shut his eyes. His restraint wasn't strong enough to resist the spellbinding picture she made. "I was just asking myself that."

Selena sighed. "Come back here so we can discuss it."

He shook his head, his eyes still squeezed shut. "No, I can't trust myself near you." He kept acting like a degenerate rakehell. Not even Hawke would seduce an innocent lady seeking a husband.

Selena's skirt rustled as she slid from the bed. "I trust you."

When her refreshing lymon scent reached him, Aragon tensed, and his pulse surged. Goddess, she was tempting. He retreated until his back touched the wardrobe. "You shouldn't."

Selena rustled closer. "But you were finally showing me more."

He clenched his closed eyes, his breath quickening. And he burned to show her even more. Which was why he'd halted. "If I continued, I'd be unable to stop. I'm a mere man, not a god."

Selena caressed his bare chest. "Would not stopping be so bad?"

Her touch fanning his hunger, Aragon shuddered and

shoved her hand away. 'Twould be glorious, but wrong. "I'm not making love to you so you can learn how to seduce your other suitors."

Selena inhaled a sharp breath. "Aragon..."

"No," he growled while blood pounded in his ears. "Get out!"

Selena rustled away, and the chair before the bed creaked as she sat. "What if I said I care nothing about other suitors?"

Aragon's eyes sprang open as his stomach spasmed. "What?!"

Her shoulders hunched in her half-undone gown, Selena nibbled her lip. "Neither Lord Edouard nor Lord Ravenstone are still courting me, and I was relieved when they ceased."

Tingling surged in his chest, but his head swirled. She no longer had other suitors? Since when and why? And *why* had she pretended she did moments ago? He swallowed and crossed his arms. "Then what was all of this about?"

Selena smoothed her sandy-brown hair. "Because I wanted *you* to make love to me."

Aragon shut his eyes again and sighed. "To escape the black witch." She didn't truly want him. Not the way he wanted her.

Selena's chair squeaked. "No... Yes... Maybe..."

He opened his eyes and glared at her. Couldn't she answer?

Selena swallowed. "Fine. I pushed for you to make love to me now because the black witch escaped. But I needed it to be you because you're the only gentleman I want."

Aragon studied her, his stomach twisting. Could he believe her after everything she'd said since the black witch had escaped? Or was her admission just another ploy?

Selena lifted her chin. "Say something, will you?"

He choked back a strangled laugh. "What would you have me say? Thank you for tormenting and deceiving me because you want me?"

Selena winced, her gaze darting away. "I shouldn't have done that. But you always withdraw after you kiss me, and I was desperate. This was the only way I could think of to goad you past your sense of chivalry."

Aragon swallowed as heat skittered across his skin. And she almost had. Fortunately, his jealous thoughts had halted him. Jealousy was no reason to make love to someone. He sighed and shook his head. "You'd best return to your chambers and repair your disheveled appearance."

Selena leapt upright and began toward him. "But Aragon..."

He clenched his jaw and flung out a hand to halt her. "Selena, please. I need some time alone." He couldn't think with her near.

Halfway toward him, Selena drooped. "Very well." She turned and drifted to the door. She glanced over her bare shoulder and murmured, "I'm sorry."

After she left, Aragon stumbled over to the chair she'd vacated. His body aching, he ran his fingers through his hair. 'Twould be so easy to follow her and continue making love. Selena wouldn't stop him. But that didn't mean 'twas right.

He sighed and rubbed his face. He needed time to consider everything. A brisk ride would clear his head and keep him away from Selena. So he stripped off his trousers and donned riding clothes then strode downstairs.

Mother intercepted him in the entrance hall. "Aragon, where are you going?"

Aragon shrugged despite his prickling shoulders. Hopefully, his perturbation wasn't obvious to his perceptive mother. She'd attempt to help if she knew, and he didn't need her interfering in his relationship with Selena. "Riding."

Mother's brows arched. "What about Selena?"

His temples tightened as he suppressed a wince. He mustn't reveal his perturbation involved Selena. Or Mother would *definitely* interfere. He scowled at her. "Selena must remain here while the black witch is free."

Mother tsked and pursed her lips. "Obviously. But aren't you going to stay to help protect her?"

Aragon shrugged, struggling not to blush. Except he must escape Selena. If he stayed to protect her, he might seduce her instead. Especially if she kept goading him. "As Father said, my precautions shall protect Selena if she stays inside the town-house. My presence shan't provide further protection."

Mother narrowed her eyes with a long hum.

He forced a shrug. "And I require some physical exertion to relax. I'll not be gone long." So Mother didn't decipher more than she already had, he turned and strode outside.

Energy burning in his veins, Aragon saddled his bay mare and trotted through Ormas then urged his mare to a gallop after the eastern gate. The fields passed in a green blur, and he was soon riding amid the thick boughs of the royal forest.

He slowed his winded mare to a walk, his chest twinging as he patted her shoulder. "Sorry for the strenuous ride. Escaping dangerous desires. You know all about those when you go into season. We'll keep to a more sedate pace for the rest of the ride."

As Aragon rode through the royal forest, he frowned and clenched the reins. How could he have allowed jealousy to goad him into almost making love to Selena? His uncontrollable desire made rational thought arduous around her.

He sighed, warmth suffusing him. Since the night Selena had smashed her lips against his, he'd desired and wanted to court her, but what else did he feel besides desire and jealousy? Her bravery, candor, and sketching impressed him. And her love of country life and beliefs about lovemaking and society echoed his own. He enjoyed giving her gifts to elicit her adorable dimple. He yearned to protect her from all threats, and he longed to hold her and never let go. And he hungered to do the same for the rest of their lives.

Tingling flooding his chest, Aragon grinned and halted his mare before the clearing at the heart of the royal forest. By the Goddess, he loved Selena. And as soon as he returned home, he'd tell her. Unlike seducing her, confessing his love couldn't be deemed stealing her choice of husband.

His stomach fluttered as he drummed his fingers against his thigh, staring at the melissae and their cottage. Despite loving Selena, he'd repeatedly withdrawn to avoid exploiting or rushing her. So she'd not believe him if he simply told her he loved her, especially after their quarrel earlier. He must prove his love, but how?

A sudden gust flooded Aragon with Selena's lymon scent. His heart quickened. But the refreshing scent was from an herb beside the melissae's cottage, not Selena. He tied his mare to a tree and eyed the bushy herb with wrinkled leaves and white flowers. Selena would adore having one, and a melissa plant would be the perfect gift to prove his love.

Moving cautiously and watching the melissae, he found a digging stick and flat rock then dug up a lymon-smelling herb. His pulse skittered as he worked—'twould be deadly to anger the melissae. He only relaxed once he wrapped the herb's roots in his pocketcloth and mounted his mare.

Aragon grinned as he inhaled the fragrant herb on the ride back. He couldn't wait to give Selena her gift, confess his love, then beg her to marry him. If she accepted, he could make love to her like she wanted. Unlike jealousy, love *was* the right reason. Plus, she'd be useless to the black witch afterward, so he'd cease hunting her.

Aragon swallowed as he emerged from the royal forest. Would Selena accept him? She'd said she wanted him to make love to her, but she'd never admitted she loved him. But neither had he, and his fury might have kept her from confessing her feelings. His heart squeezing, he patted his mare. "Up for another gallop?"

When she tossed her mane, he chuckled and urged her faster. He rode as swiftly as possible without crushing the melissa plant. Selena was waiting for him.

CHAPTER 29

*H*er face buried in her pillows, Selena winced at a knock on her locked door. If anyone saw her half-undone gown, disheveled hair, and ravaged face, they'd know she'd attempted to seduce Aragon. His tight expression during their quarrel blazed in her mind again. Using jealousy to goad him into making love had hurt him. She'd allowed her fear of the black witch to blind her and leapt without thinking. Tears burning her eyes, she remained silent. Perhaps whoever knocked would leave her alone if she didn't respond.

Unfortunately, the duchess called after a second knock, "Selena, are you in there?"

Selena sighed and lifted her face, her temples tightening. But she didn't move or unlock the door. "Yes, your grace."

After a pause, the duchess said, "'Tis time for luncheon."

Selena slid from bed despite her knotted stomach. Food sounded less than appealing, but the duchess would realize something was wrong if she didn't come. "I'll be down in a few moments."

A lump clogging her throat, Selena undid the final laces on her raspberry gown and flung it aside. Her seduction attempt had been both reckless and heartless. No matter her reason, she *never* should have deceived Aragon like that. She'd abandoned her principle to treat others like she wanted to be treated. And would he forgive her deceit? If he'd done the same, she'd be furious and might never trust him again. She couldn't expect him to be more tolerant.

Her stomach spasmed as she yanked on an ash-gray dress and tidied her hair. Had she wrecked her chance to win Aragon's love? Loving him as she did, she couldn't bear to lose him forever. Yet she might have with her reckless deceit. Dear Goddess, what was she to do?

Selena swallowed and studied herself in the mirror. She appeared somewhat wan but otherwise normal, so hopefully, the duchess would detect nothing amiss. But how could she face Aragon without blushing or crying?

When she entered the family dining room, he hadn't arrived, so no blush or tears betrayed her—yet. She flashed a bright smile at the duke and duchess. Was it enough to mask her distress? "I'm sorry for making you wait."

The duke chuckled from the head of the table. "Don't fret; we just arrived as well."

Selena blinked when the duke began serving her and the duchess, even though Aragon still hadn't joined them. "Aren't we waiting for Aragon or Hawke?"

The duchess shook her head. "Aragon went riding an hour ago—he looked as if he needed it. And Goddess knows where Hawke is; he's been out since before breakfast."

Selena tensed then sipped her wine to hide her grimace. No doubt Aragon had gone riding to escape her. Her heart squeezed. She must apologize again as soon as she saw him. But at least she wouldn't blush or cry throughout luncheon and betray herself.

The duchess slanted her a probing glance. "Are you well? You appear peaked."

Selena shrugged and forced herself to begin her spinach soup. She must offer a believable explanation, so the duchess didn't connect her distress to Aragon's. "As well as can be expected. I'd trouble sleeping last night due to the black witch's escape. I tried taking a nap before luncheon, with little success."

The duchess nodded. "I was concerned 'twas more serious when you weren't sketching in your art room."

Selena swallowed as warmth filled her at the duchess's concern. Goading Aragon into almost seducing her and possibly losing him forever was definitely more serious. But she couldn't admit that. If Aragon's loving mother learned of their quarrel, she'd attempt to mend their relationship, and 'twas best if she didn't.

The duke grinned while serving her and his wife broiled salmon. "Given your fatigue, I suppose you're glad to escape the whirl of court."

Despite her distress, Selena almost smiled. And Aragon's father was always ready with a quip to cheer everyone. She leaned toward him and whispered, "Don't tell your wife, but yes. All those court events are too much for a country miss." She winked at the duchess.

The duchess tsked, her lips twitching. "You've done well until now. Everyone extols your graciousness. And you've attracted several suitors."

Selena almost winced. Suitors who were no longer pursuing her, much to her relief. But she couldn't explain why to the duchess without revealing her love for Aragon.

The duchess arched a brow as she finished her salmon. "Have you decided if you prefer Edouard or Lord Ravenstone?"

Selena sighed and studied her empty plate. No, she preferred Aragon and always had. She made herself meet the duchess's gaze with a serene smile. "Both are fine gentlemen."

The duchess narrowed her eyes with a long hum as the duke served them cherry flummery.

Her mouth drying, Selena swallowed and gripped her spoon. Had she revealed too much? To distract the duchess, she asked, "How soon after luncheon do you leave for the Campbells' garden party?"

The duchess continued scrutinizing Selena. "Straight after. Shall you be fine alone?"

Selena nodded as her pulse settled. 'Twould be a relief to quit feigning blithe serenity. "I'll amuse myself in my art room until everyone returns."

So once Aragon's parents left, she retreated upstairs, but every time she lifted her pencil, his tight expression flashed before her eyes, and her hand stilled. Goddess, how could she have been so heartless?

After multiple attempts, Selena threw down her pencil and rose. Attempting to sketch was futile. She must talk to someone, but she was confined to the townhouse, and none of her friends knew she loved Aragon. Even if they did, she couldn't admit her shameful seduction attempt to them.

But the mare Aragon had loaned her would be a fine confidant. She'd listen and offer affection without judgment. Surely the house wards extended to the stables, so visiting them wouldn't count as leaving the townhouse. Plus, she'd see Aragon as soon as he returned.

Selena skulked down to the stables through the servants' entrance to avoid Perkins. The exacting butler would protest her visiting the stables, and she needed the respite. When she slipped inside, she relaxed then nodded at the grooms and requested a currycomb before entering Ember's stall.

The sorrel mare nuzzled her as she murmured compliments and began brushing.

Selena's heart softened. Once the grooms couldn't overhear, she murmured, "Do you think Aragon shall ever forgive me? He's so generous—he loaned me you, after all—but 'tis a lot to forgive."

The mare leaned into her brushstrokes with a nicker.

Selena nibbled her lip as she continued brushing. "Perhaps if I revealed *why* I want him when I apologize again. I never did explain I loved him. Maybe he'd forgive me if I told him. But what if he doesn't love me in return? I couldn't bear his pity."

The mare nudged her when her hands slowed.

Selena chuckled, warmth surging in her chest. "Such a glutton for attention. 'Tis fortunate you're so beautiful and a delight to ride. Alas, we can't go riding today. Although 'twould help untangle my mind, it *would* be too risky."

She sighed and finished grooming the mare. After a final pat, she left to return the currycomb to a groom. Yet none were there. Her skin prickled at the hush blanketing the stables. When had it gotten so quiet? She'd waited to confess to Ember until the grooms had drifted away, but when had they disappeared?

A rustle drifted from the saddle room. Selena sighed then strode across the stables. But then she halted, her stomach tensing. Two rough men were dragging a groom across the saddle room floor. Spots flickering before her eyes, she blurted, "Who are you, and what have you done to the grooms?"

The fairer man smirked. "Same that we're 'bout to do to you."

Her throat tightened, and her pulse surged. Why had she recklessly confronted the intruders? Her uncle or the black witch must have hired them. And the black witch must have helped them evade the house wards. What other evil spells had he provided?

Rushing filling her ears, she flung the currycomb at the fairer man's head then whirled to flee, not wasting breath screaming. She could do that when someone was awake to hear.

The men thundered after her. She'd almost reached the stable door when one grabbed the back of her dress and yanked her into his rough embrace.

Selena thrashed. Goddess, she must escape! Like before, whatever the black witch or her uncle planned would be horrifying. And 'twould probably start with an auction for her virginity.

Dizziness darkening her vision, she attempted to kick her captor and scratch his face, but his grip never loosened.

He cackled instead. "Spirited one, ain't she?"

The darker man grabbed her chin. "Best make sure she's the one."

Her chest burning, she jerked her chin free and attempted to bite him. Perhaps then he'd release her.

The darker man slapped her and grabbed her chin again.

The tang of blood filling her mouth, Selena glared at him but remained still. "Release me."

The darker man snickered. "When we went to such trouble to catch you?" He peered at her face. "Freckles, gray eyes, and brown hair, just like requested. She's the one."

Her captor chuckled. "Good. Dose her."

Despite her galloping pulse, she widened her eyes with a smile. She couldn't escape the intruders, so she must convince them to release her. "Wait. You don't want to do this."

The darker man rummaged in his pocket with his free hand. "Oh?"

Selena swallowed and glanced toward the townhouse. Perhaps fear would convince them. "This is the Duke of Childes's townhouse. He's wealthy and powerful, and I'm under his protection."

Her captor drawled, "Which is why the black witch paid us ten gold."

"*And* a powerful spell to use later." The darker man pulled his fist from his pocket.

Her stomach roiled. Ten gold was half a year's wages for men like these, and a powerful spell could be priceless. But perhaps greed would convince them. She forced a coy grin. "The duke would pay you more for releasing me."

The darker man bared his teeth. "But then the black witch would hunt us for betraying him. No deal." He tossed a fistful of mustard-yellow powder in her face.

When the bitter powder touched Selena, the gold gargoyle

nestled between her breasts warmed as it absorbed the powder's magic. She relaxed until her vision began dimming. The powder mustn't be entirely magic. Oh, Goddess! Ice flooded her veins. Why had she waited to tell Aragon she loved him? Now she never might. Her heart clenched. Then she collapsed as stygian blackness swallowed her.

CHAPTER 30

$\mathcal{W}$hen Aragon returned home, he grinned and slid from the saddle with Selena's melissa plant cradled against his chest. Then he tossed the reins to the nearest groom.

Rubbing his eyes, the groom almost dropped the reins. Odd for him to fumble.

Aragon frowned, but he burned to find Selena so he could give her the melissa plant, confess his love, then beg her to marry him, so he only said, "Give Nutmeg a good rubdown, plenty of water, and sweet oats. She'd a strenuous ride." He bounded up the townhouse steps, and as soon as the front door glided open, he asked, "Perkins, where's Selena?"

The butler arched his brows. "I believe Miss Midor is upstairs, but I haven't seen her since luncheon."

His heart quickening, Aragon nodded then trotted back to the conservatory, a room he seldom visited despite being the Minister of Agriculture. He preferred going outside instead. Although unfamiliar with the conservatory, he quickly found a pot and filched soil from an orenge tree for the melissa plant.

After potting and watering Selena's gift, he smiled and brushed off his hands. They were covered in dirt, along with his cuffs, shirt, and waistcoat. His stomach fluttered. He couldn't confess his love looking like that. Plus, he was ravenous since he'd missed luncheon. Bringing the potted plant with him, he dashed upstairs to wash, change, and eat.

Once he was finished, he tucked Selena's melissa plant under his arm and strode to her art room. He inhaled then knocked on the closed door and entered. "What are you sketching now?"

But the air in Selena's art room was still.

Aragon chuckled, warmth flooding his chest. She must be in her chambers. A bed would be convenient if she accepted his proposal. He loped back to the family hall. Again, he drew a steadying breath as he knocked on Selena's closed door and entered. "Taking a nap? How unusual."

Yet the air in her chambers was as still as her art room.

His pulse stuttered as he frowned and clenched the pot under his arm. Where was Selena? Perhaps she was reading in the drawing room, but 'twas unusual for Perkins to be mistaken.

Aragon barreled downstairs to the drawing room. This time he didn't bother calling. Like Selena's art room and chambers, the drawing room was empty. Where could she be? His throat constricting, he left her melissa plant in the conservatory then found Perkins in the wine cellar. "When did you see Selena last?"

Perkins blinked but followed him upstairs. "At luncheon with your parents. Miss Midor went upstairs when they left for the Campbells' garden party."

Aragon's heart lurched. So *where* was she? He forced a smile as they reached the entrance hall. "She wasn't upstairs or in the drawing room. Could you check if the other servants have seen her?"

Perkins nodded. "Of course, my lord."

As the butler strode away, Aragon forced himself to remain in the entrance hall. He'd make the other servants nervous if he hovered. Clenching his trembling hands behind his back, he paced while he waited. Please, Goddess, let this be a simple misunderstanding.

Perkins bustled back with a frown. "One of the kitchen maids saw Miss Midor slip out to the stables not long after luncheon."

A chill seized Aragon's chest. Why had Selena gone *outside* with the black witch at large? Although the house wards covered the stables, they were the wards' weakest point due to the stables' high traffic. A powerful black witch might know a spell to trick the house wards there, and the wards didn't prevent using spells inside them. 'Twas why he'd alerted the servants and hired guards in addition to bolstering the wards. But he'd never expected Selena to risk visiting the stables.

He yanked open the front door and pelted to the stables. His eyes leapt to the stalls for his mares. Ember stood beside Nutmeg like normal, but Selena wasn't with the sorrel mare. "Where's Selena?"

The head groom replied, "Miss Midor visited her mare an hour ago." He shifted with a cough. "I drifted off soon after. When I woke, she'd returned to the townhouse."

His stomach roiling, Aragon swallowed. The head groom never loafed. "You fell asleep in the middle of the day?" When the groom bobbed an embarrassed nod, Aragon asked, "What about the other grooms?"

The head groom winced. "They did too. We'd all been up late last night playing cards."

Aragon stiffened like a gorgon's stone victim. "I think 'twas more than that." The black witch was loose. "Did you or the other grooms notice anything odd?"

"Other than all of us falling asleep?" The head groom grimaced. "No."

Aragon leaned forward with clenched fists. All thirteen of the grooms falling asleep at once was odd enough. The black witch must have induced their slumber. "And Selena had vanished when you all awoke?"

The head groom nodded. "That's right, my lord."

"Damnation!" Fire flaring in his veins, Aragon punched a stable post and startled Mother's mare beside him. The black witch had kidnapped Selena despite all of Aragon's precautions. But the black witch's boldness wasn't surprising—a witch who could escape countless magic marshals would attempt anything.

Aragon whirled around. He must inform the magic marshals. They must find Selena immediately. The longer they took, the more peril she faced. He scowled at the head groom. "Saddle that stallion Hawke bought last season. Now." Hawke's stallion was ornery and not usually worth the effort, but his speed outweighed his flaws with Selena in danger.

The head groom blinked but bowed. "At once, my lord."

While they prepared the stallion, Aragon bolted upstairs and snatched Selena's hairbrush from her dressing table. The magic marshals could use her hair to perform a tracing spell. Then he raced back to the stables.

He vaulted into the saddle and thundered through Ormas. He wrenched the stallion to a stop before the main station for magic marshals in Ormas. He leapt down and tossed the reins to an apprentice marshal. "Here. Take him to your stables. Watch out—he likes to bolt."

He sprinted up the steps to the desk just past the entrance, like he had this morning. "I must see Master Marshal Thurston."

The marshal at the desk, different from the one earlier, cocked her head. "He's occupied at the moment, my lord."

Aragon set his jaw. He'd better be. "Yes, hunting that black witch I found. Tell him Lord Treyvan is here to see him again, and 'tis urgent."

The marshal's eyes widened, and she touched the communication crystal in her ear then muttered his message. After a moment, she gestured toward the stairs. "Go on up. Thurston is in the back office on the left."

Aragon managed a smile. "I remember." His pulse surged as he hurtled upstairs to Thurston's office.

Thurston sighed when he glanced up from his huddled conference with the three magic marshals from before. "Lord Treyvan, I know you're concerned, but we're hunting your black witch as fast as we can, and continually interrupting us doesn't help."

Aragon slitted his eyes as he halted before their desk. "I'm sorry to *interrupt* you again, but the black witch kidnapped Selena an hour ago." And Goddess knew what he'd done to her already. His stomach clenched.

The master marshal winced, and his brow furrowed. "Dear Goddess. Unfortunately, nothing we've tried has found the black witch or Adan Midor. The black witch is tricky as a djinn."

Aragon slammed a hand on the desk, blood rushing in his ears. They hadn't time for excuses. "Damnation! He has Selena. We must find him *now*." Before she was raped or worse.

As his companions leaned away, Thurston raised his palms. "I know, my lord. But panic accomplishes nothing."

Aragon glared as he yanked Selena's hairbrush from his pocket and flung it on the desk. He wasn't panicked. He was impatient. "I brought Selena's hairbrush for a tracing spell. Maybe *then* you can finally find the black witch."

Thurston removed some hair and dropped it into a glass bowl. Then he added several herbs and a silver potion. He stirred the concoction before waving his hand over the bowl with a muttered chant. After a moment, he frowned and repeated his gesture and chant. Then he sighed and shook his head. "My tracing spell isn't working. The black witch must be blocking me." When Aragon growled, Thurston added, "Let me contact Lady Juliet and see what she says. Although her earlier suggestions didn't help, perhaps she knows something else we can try."

Aragon grunted and crossed his arms as the master marshal turned to the communication mirror beside his desk then chanted a brief spell and waved his hand. Hopefully, Lady Juliet would be more helpful than Thurston.

The mirror's glass glowed white before the royal witch appeared. She arched a fashionable brow. "Yes, Thurston? Any luck with that black witch?"

Thurston shook his head. "Not as of yet, my lady."

Aragon clenched his hands. The master marshal was slower than a cold wyvern. He strode behind Thurston to interject, "And he kidnapped Selena over an hour ago and is blocking our attempts to trace her."

Lady Juliet blinked. "How bold." She glanced over Thurston's shoulder at Aragon. "Has Miss Midor continued wearing my protection charm? If so, we can't use an ordinary tracing spell to find her."

Aragon almost snorted. That explained Thurston's failed spell. "She never removes your protection charm." Even when she hadn't needed it. Because he'd given it to her? His heart twisted. "Not that it prevented her kidnapping. And now it's blocking our attempts to find her."

The royal witch's eyes narrowed. "My protection charm is for *magical* threats only, Lord Treyvan. That includes tracing spells. And my charm would do nothing against physical threats, as I mentioned when I gave it to you."

Aragon winced. "I remember." He must mollify the royal witch, so she'd help find Selena before 'twas too late. He leaned forward with an imploring smile. "I'm sorry for my outburst, but Goddess knows what the black witch is doing to Selena."

Lady Juliet's eyes softened. "I understand your concern, my lord, but perhaps Miss Midor's kidnapping is a boon."

As Thurston coughed, Aragon stiffened and echoed, "A boon?" Selena's kidnapping was no boon.

The royal witch chuckled. "Yes. The black witch could block an ordinary tracing spell, but regardless of his defenses, I'll be able to trace Miss Midor through my protection charm and find him." She cocked her head. "Unless he forced her to remove it and left it elsewhere."

Aragon's throat tightened. Selena knew that charm would be her only defense. "She'd ensure he didn't remove it." His brave lady would outwit the black witch like she had when she'd fled to the brothel. Please, Goddess.

Lady Juliet nodded. "Hold on while I perform a tracing spell." She slipped from her communication mirror, and the image shifted to show her workroom.

Aragon tensed and leaned over Thurston to peer at the royal witch in the mirror. How long would her tracing spell take? No matter how adroit, Selena had been kidnapped over an hour ago, and the longer the black witch had her, the more he could do. Aragon swallowed and fisted his hands behind his back.

Lady Juliet unfurled a map of Ormas on her desk then fetched a silver pendant. After a singsong chant, she dangled the pendant by its chain over the map. The pendant swung in a wide circle that gradually tightened to a point. The royal witch bent over the map. "My protection charm is inside Number Fourteen Sand Lane near the docks."

His heart leaping, Aragon began dashing from Thurston's office. At last! They could rescue Selena. Thank the Goddess. Please let the black witch not have harmed her.

"Wait, Lord Treyvan," Lady Juliet called. "I must scry the area first. No knowing what traps that sly black witch set."

He stalked back to the communication mirror. "Fine. But hurry, please." As the royal witch stared into her massive scrying bowl, he shifted his weight back and forth. Couldn't she hurry? Who knew what had already happened to Selena or what would happen before they reached her? They mustn't delay rescuing her.

CHAPTER 31

*W*hen Selena struggled free of the stygian blackness, her two kidnappers had propped her up with pillows and were tying her outstretched arms to a musty bed. Her pulse surged, but she shut her eyes and remained limp. Fighting now was senseless—her kidnappers could handily overpower her. She must wait until they left to slip free.

Soon the men clomped from the room, leaving her trussed to the headboard like a maiden sacrifice. Like? She was one.

Still feigning stupor, she choked back the hysterical giggle rising in her throat. She must gather her wits and concentrate on escaping. So she risked a glance about the room through her lashes. No one was there. She sighed and fully opened her eyes.

She pursed her lips as she scrutinized the room. Where was she? The shabby furnishings hinted at a poorer part of Ormas. But threadbare drapes covered the window, so she could be anywhere. And how long had she been unconscious? She wasn't hungry, so it must be before dinner. Had Aragon or his parents noticed she was missing yet?

Selena's chest tightened. She must escape before her uncle and the black witch auctioned off her virginity or whatever else they'd planned. She eyed the ropes tying her arms, and her breath hitched. Her kidnappers had used complex knots she'd no hope of unraveling, even if her hands had been free. They must have spent time as sailors.

She sagged and hissed a sigh. So much for slipping free. At least they hadn't tied her legs. She could kick anyone who got too close. But she'd best wait until in direst need to attempt that —'twould be easy for them to tie her legs too.

Selena set her jaw then wriggled her arms to loosen her bindings. Attempting escape was better than fretting and waiting for someone to appear. Her wrists had begun to chafe when the door creaked open. Her pulse stuttered as she stilled and closed her eyes to feign slumber. Goddess, would they notice her wrists?

A pair of gentleman's boots clapped across the floor. Uncle Adan, no doubt. Of course, the bounder was here. Air stirred when he leaned toward her. Could he tell she was awake?

Although her heart pounded in her ears, she forced herself to breathe evenly and remain relaxed.

Uncle Adan grunted. "Why hasn't she woken? Oh well." He slapped her cheek, the same one the darker kidnapper had earlier.

Her eyes flew open, and she gritted a smile as blood seeped in her mouth again. Her uncle was brave when it came to bound ladies.

Uncle Adan smirked down at her. "Afternoon, dear niece."

Forcing her jaw to relax, Selena blinked and glanced about the room to feign confusion. "Uncle Adan? What's going on?" The longer she could delay her auction, the better. Goddess knew when Aragon or the magic marshals would find her.

Her uncle snickered. "The black witch's men kidnapped you. So easily too. They were casing the Hawkes' townhouse when you entered the stables. So they decided to take you this afternoon rather than waiting until tonight."

She almost winced. Why had she been so reckless? She never should have risked visiting the stables. But no sense in crying for spilt unicorn water. She tensed and tilted her head. "But why did they kidnap me?"

Uncle Adan's teeth glinted in a cold smile. "Because the black witch has arranged an auction at midnight. He plans to sell your virginity to the highest bidder."

A chill skittered across her skin. An auction, just as she'd expected. But perhaps a lie would delay it. She laughed and lifted her chin. "My virginity? 'Tis too late for that."

Uncle Adan's eyes narrowed. "What do you mean?"

Selena forced another laugh. "I mean I'm no longer a virgin." Please let him believe her.

Her uncle snorted. "Impossible."

She slanted him an arch glance, struggling to appear nonchalant. She must play a brazen wanton to convince him. "You do recall I've been living with Aragon for over a month."

Uncle Adan arched a brow. "Along with his parents. The Duchess of Childes wouldn't present her son's lover to court."

Selena swallowed. Her uncle required more to convince him. Imitating Madam Lorelei, she purred a chuckle then shrugged despite her bound arms. "Probably not if she knew for certain, but Aragon and I have been discreet." So discreet they'd never made love.

Uncle Adan eyed her. "You're much too sanctimonious to have surrendered your virginity outside matrimony."

She shrugged again. She'd start her lie with the truth. "I abandoned my dreams of matrimony when I overheard your first meeting with the black witch. To escape being raped, I decided to sell my virginity in a brothel. The one on Mermaid Street. You're a patron, I believe."

Her uncle gaped at her.

Selena purred another chuckle, even though her pulse throbbed in her throat. Time to weave in falsehood. "Aragon is too. After taking my pesky virginity, he vowed to handle the black witch and have his mother find me a husband. Although that didn't stop him from seeking my bed in the meantime."

Uncle Adan's mouth snapped shut. "I can't believe it. But the black witch shall be able to tell for certain." He whirled and strode from the room.

She shuddered then sagged against the bed. Hopefully, her lie would delay them long enough for Aragon and the magic marshals to find her. Meanwhile, she resumed wriggling her arms, but halted when Uncle Adan returned with the black witch moments later. Her heart pounding, she lifted her chin to study them. She must be bold to outwit them.

His lanky frame now cadaverous, the black witch arched a brow. "No longer a virgin, Miss Midor?"

Selena flashed a sardonic smile to disguise her tension. "Not for the past month and a half."

Uncle Adan snorted. "She claims Lord Treyvan took her, but I can't believe it."

"Why not?" Her stomach fluttered as she tilted her head with a wanton smirk. "Would you care for me to describe his birth-marks to prove it? Or would describing his lovemaking do?"

The black witch's eyes gleamed. "Once Treyvan mentioned Midor and I realized you were under his protection, I always planned to kidnap you as vengeance. But to learn you're his lover as well makes it even sweeter."

Nausea swamped Selena. Oh, Goddess. Her lie had accomplished nothing. Her chest seized. How else could she delay them?

Uncle Adan glared at the black witch. "But she'll fetch less at the auction if she's no longer a virgin. Besides, she must be lying. Lord Treyvan is too *noble* to despoil a lady under his protection."

Which was why her desperate seduction attempt had failed. She suppressed a wince, but her heart softened. Aragon's chivalry was one of the reasons she loved him. She must escape, so she could see him again.

The black witch scratched his scraggly beard. "Your niece's questionable virginity is easy enough to prove." He raised his hand, muttered a spell, then gestured toward her.

The gold gargoyle nestled between her breasts warmed. Selena relaxed with a sigh. Lady Juliet's charm would absorb the black witch's spell, so he'd see nothing. Thank the Goddess.

The black witch glowered, and he repeated his spell with a sharp gesture.

The gold gargoyle warmed again. She almost smiled when the black witch growled. Although he'd managed to kidnap her, he couldn't match the most illustrious witch in Calatini.

Uncle Adan frowned at the black witch. "What is it?"

The black witch stormed toward Selena. "Something is protecting her from my spells. 'Tis fortunate that powder I gave the brothers was merely enhanced by magic."

Drawing herself fully upright, she arched a brow. "I've powerful and wealthy benefactors now. Purchasing a protection charm was nothing for them." Thank you, Aragon.

The black witch leaned over her with a scowl.

Selena tensed and resisted the urge to recoil. She'd not cower, no matter what the black witch did.

"The gargoyle, no doubt." The black witch seized the gold charm but shrieked and dropped it.

Uncle Adan winced. "What happened?"

"The cursed thing burned me." The black witch pointed at her uncle. "You try."

Selena almost snorted. Her uncle was a coward and would never touch something powerful enough to burn the black witch. Although the charm probably wouldn't harm someone without magic, so he could remove it if he tried.

When Uncle Adan shook his head, the black witch sneered and rubbed his injured hand. "Then I must devise something to neutralize that charm before the auction."

Her neck prickled, but she drawled as the black witch began to leave, "The Hawkes shall destroy you if you harm me." Would Aragon's influential family delay the black witch?

He paused in the doorway with a smirk. "But they must capture me first. And the power from your rape, regardless of your questionable virginity, shall secure my escape." He chuckled then swept from the room.

As her uncle began to follow, Selena glared at him. "You should be careful of the company you keep, Uncle Adan. Magic marshals are hunting your black witch and shall gladly apprehend you too. Then the Hawkes shall ensure you spend the rest of your days in prison. Forget ever gaining influence at court."

Uncle Adan shrugged. "I surrendered that after our skirmish at the sirenic play. Now I simply want your destruction as vengeance against Arias and the Hawkes. And the black witch assures me he has ways to block the magic marshals, so we'll depart long before they arrive. But we might leave your defiled body behind for them to find."

She shuddered as nausea burned her throat. "Mother would be ashamed of you."

His cheeks hollowing, Uncle Adan stiffened. "Isabel is *dead*, so her opinion no longer matters." He turned and strode from the room.

Selena sighed and leaned against the headboard, eyeing her outstretched arms. She'd not delayed the auction, and her wriggling hadn't loosened the knots binding her. Goddess, how could she escape? She'd probably only eight hours or so before the auction.

CHAPTER 32

a ragon clenched his hands behind his back as the royal witch continued staring into her massive scrying bowl. Would she ever finish?

At long last, Lady Juliet smiled and lifted her head. "Miss Midor is unharmed so far and tied to a bed on the second floor. The black witch and Midor are downstairs preparing for her auction. Nasty traps, both magical and physical, surround the rowhouse."

He relaxed and shut his eyes. Selena was unharmed, but for how long? He tensed again, his eyes springing open. He leaned toward the communication mirror. "When is the auction?"

The royal witch abandoned her scrying bowl to approach her mirror. "Midnight."

Aragon sighed. Now that they knew Selena's location, almost eight hours should allow them to rescue her well before the auction. And if they left at once, surely nothing would happen to her before they arrived. So she'd escape her kidnapping unscathed. Thank the Goddess.

Still seated, Thurston slowly nodded and rubbed his chin. "And no one else is in the rowhouse?"

Lady Juliet frowned. "Not at the moment. The black witch's

two lackeys are delivering invitations to the auction but shall return afterward."

The master marshal leaned forward. "Are they witches too?"

Lady Juliet snorted, her mouth twisting. "No, just ordinary ruffians."

Why were Thurston and the royal witch still talking? Aragon forced a smile and gestured toward the door. "Can we go rescue Selena now?"

Thurston waved for him to sit. "Not yet, my lord."

Aragon scowled and remained standing. Why delay rescuing Selena? His stomach hardened. Harm could befall her if they did. Yet he held his tongue as the master marshal began instructing his companions.

Thurston turned and pointed at the younger magic marshals. "You two, go scout that rowhouse and its traps. Make sure they don't spot you."

The young man and woman leapt up then strode from the room.

The master marshal eyed his other companion. "You, go prepare negation and sleep spells. We'll need lots when we raid the rowhouse."

As the other magic marshal left, Aragon's temples tightened. What was Thurston about? "Lots? Only the black witch and Midor are there now."

The master marshal nodded. "True, but there shall be more at the auction."

Aragon stiffened and narrowed his eyes. "At the auction? Why can't we rescue Selena now?" While she was still unscathed.

The royal witch interjected from the communication mirror, "Delay seems risky."

Thurston shrugged. "That can't be helped. We must capture the auction bidders."

Fire surging through him, Aragon bent and grabbed the master marshal's shirt. "I'm not waiting to rescue Selena so you can be *thorough*."

Thurston pried his hands loose. "Plus, we require time to prepare spells to defuse those traps. They'll be pernicious knowing the black witch."

Lady Juliet pursed her lips. "I can enhance the magic in the protection charm I created for Miss Midor. As its creator, I'm still linked to it, so the black witch shan't notice my magical signature if I take care. I can shield Miss Midor from physical attacks as well as spells."

Aragon relaxed with a sigh. Following the master marshal's deliberate plan would ensure Selena's rescue, and the royal witch could protect Selena in the meantime. Although he'd rather rescue her at once. "Please do. Thank you, my lady."

Lady Juliet inclined her head. "Goddess bless your rescue attempt, my lord." The communication mirror glowed white then cleared to reflect Thurston's office.

Aragon glanced at the master marshal, his chest tightening. "What should I do while you're preparing?" He'd go mad if he hadn't a chore.

Thurston eyed him. "Go procure dinner for everyone."

Aragon stiffened with a frown. 'Twas too early for dinner. Besides, who could eat with Selena in danger? "Why dinner?"

Thurston rose and clapped his shoulder. "Spell work requires a great deal of energy, and hunger causes muddled thinking. We all must be well-fed to capture the black witch and his cohorts."

Aragon grimaced but nodded. That made sense. And 'twas a chore to occupy him. "Very well."

After sliding Selena's hairbrush back into his pocket, he strode to a nearby tavern and purchased food for a dozen starving magic marshals. Staggering under its weight, he brought back the food to Thurston's office. He made himself eat with the magic marshals, although the food threatened to choke him.

As Aragon waited in Thurston's office, he forced himself to remain still—he must save his energy for rescuing Selena. Yet during the interminable wait, Selena being raped, killed, and everything in between kept flashing before his eyes.

An hour before midnight, Thurston gestured for Aragon to join him.

Finally! Aragon leapt to his feet and bound across the room. Then he and the magic marshals strode downstairs and rode to Sand Lane to meet the marshals scouting the rowhouse.

After he'd given his marshals orders, Thurston turned to Aragon. "Once we handle the magical traps, head upstairs to find your lady while we capture everyone. But stay hidden. We can't spare effort to protect you."

His stomach clenching, Aragon nodded. At least the master marshal was allowing him to help, and getting hurt or killed wouldn't help rescue Selena. He and the magic marshals turned their gazes to the rowhouse. He scowled as eight men concealed by dark cloaks skulked inside shortly before the auction. Degenerates.

When the clock tolled midnight, the magic marshals surged forward. They threw their spells at the black witch's traps. Booms and smoke filled the air.

Aragon swallowed then drew his paltry dagger. He slipped inside the rowhouse and sprinted up the first staircase. Which room held Selena? The royal witch hadn't said. He eased open the first door as the battle boomed downstairs, but Selena wasn't there.

He sighed and continued down the hall. With each empty room, he tensed further. Had the black witch moved Selena downstairs for the auction? Oh, Goddess. Then she'd be embroiled in the battle between the black witch and the magic marshals. He shuddered while he opened the fifth door.

Her eyes wide and outstretched arms bound along the head-board, Selena sat frozen on the bed. She relaxed when he entered the room. "Aragon?"

His throat too clogged to speak, he nodded and sawed through ropes binding her. He must get her out of here at once.

As soon as she was free, Selena threw her arms about his neck and buried her face against his chest. "Thank the Goddess!"

Warmth flooding him, Aragon dropped his dagger to crush Selena against him. He kissed her sandy-brown hair, her lymon scent filling his lungs. "Did they hurt you, my love?"

Selena shuddered in his embrace. "Not yet. But soon. The auction for my virginity had begun."

He shuddered too, his breath seizing for a moment. Then he kissed her hair again. "That's all finished." Thank the Goddess. "Come, allow me to escort you home." Where she belonged.

Selena nodded and slid free. "Yes, please."

Aragon sheathed his dagger then wrapped an arm about her. Now that he'd found her, he couldn't bear to release her. "We should avoid being seen downstairs. We don't want rumors to start." He'd marry Selena regardless, but rumors would irk Mother.

Selena flashed a wry smile as she grasped his hand dangling over her shoulder. "My uncle is being arrested for consorting with a black witch. I doubt we can avoid rumors."

He squeezed her hand and escorted her down the stairs he'd taken to avoid the battle still raging further inside. "True, but we can ensure 'tis only your uncle who's associated with the black witch."

Selena tilted her head as they left the rowhouse. "What if the magic marshals must speak with me?"

Aragon snorted. "They can interview you tomorrow." They seemed to appreciate waiting, and she needed time to recover. He lifted her into the saddle then leapt before her. Fortunately, Hawke's stallion had spent his orneriness earlier and remained still until Aragon urged him forward.

As they thundered through Ormas, Selena snuggled against him, heating his blood. He burned to kiss her again—this morning felt ages ago. But when they entered the townhouse, he restrained himself because his parents rushed to meet them.

Mother threw her arms about Selena. "Selena, thank the

Goddess! Perkins informed us you were missing when we returned from the Campbells. Are you well?"

Selena blushed in Mother's embrace. "Yes, Aragon rescued me in time." She drew back to dimple at him.

When his parents arched their brows, Aragon shrugged and shook his head. "I merely brought her home after the black witch kidnapped her."

As Father whistled, Mother captured Selena's arm and said, "Come, you should be in bed."

Aragon suppressed a sigh. He wanted time alone with Selena. But she'd endured a lot today and should rest before he proposed. His heart squeezing, he handed Selena her hairbrush then allowed Mother to lead her upstairs, but his gaze followed her until Father clapped his shoulder.

Father grinned at him. "Excellent handling of the black witch."

Aragon swallowed and shrugged again. He'd not done much. "The magic marshals and Lady Juliet handled him."

Father chuckled. "You're too modest. Who risked crossing a black witch to contact the magic marshals and the royal witch? Your dedication to pursuing justice allowed a dangerous black witch to be captured—twice."

Aragon blushed, his chest lightening at Father's approval. Perhaps dedication wasn't faint praise, after all. Although he'd not crossed the black witch for justice, but for Selena. "Thank you, Father."

He glanced upstairs again. With Selena abed, he should retire to prepare for his proposal. He said good night and strode upstairs, his mind awhirl. He'd approach Selena after breakfast and ask to speak to her alone. Then he'd give her the melissa plant, confess his love, and beg her to marry him.

Yet his plans were delayed when Selena didn't emerge the following morning. He visited the magic marshals to resolve matters instead. But when he returned, she still hadn't emerged. So after luncheon, he set his jaw and fetched her melissa plant from the conservatory. Inhaling the plant's lymon-like scent eased his chest as he strode upstairs to find her. His gift should prove to her he loved her.

Selena was staring outside the window with a frown when he entered her art room. At his knock, she swung to face him. "Are the magic marshals here yet?"

Aragon swallowed and tucked the melissa plant under one arm. "No, Thurston said they don't require us. They captured the black witch and immobilized him with a sleep spell until his trial to prevent another escape. The others at the auction await their trials in prison, and several, including your uncle, have already confessed." He eyed her. "Was the magic marshals' visit why you were hiding?" Or had she been avoiding him?

Selena blushed and bent her head. "No. I thought you'd prefer not to see me after all the hassle I caused yesterday. First, I tried to seduce you. Then I let myself get kidnapped."

Tingling warmth filled him. She was adorable. He captured her chin with his free hand and lifted her chin until her dark-gray eyes met his. "No hassle would make me not want to see you, my love."

CHAPTER 33

*H*er heart galloping, Selena stared into Aragon's dark-umber eyes. He'd called her *my love* like when he'd rescued her. Goddess, did he mean that? Even after her reckless and heartless seduction attempt? She breathed, "My love?"

Aragon smiled. "Yes. I love you. I should have realized sooner—you spellbound me from the start, I thought about you constantly, and I hated seeing you with other gentlemen. But I never dreamt love would be so tempestuous."

She winced and pulled her chin free. If he loved her, her seduction attempt had been even crueler than she'd realized. "And I inflamed that jealousy. I never should have done it. No matter my fear."

Aragon kissed her nose. "You were desperate to escape the black witch. I'm simply relieved you only wanted me. It made me hope you might love me as I love you."

Tingling swept through her. To forgive her so easily, Aragon was truly the most wonderful of gentlemen. And somehow he loved *her*. She threaded her arms about his neck. "I do love you. So much that I never want to stop when we kiss. You're the most enthralling gentleman I've ever met." She flashed a coy smile. "Dedicated too." With that, she kissed him.

Aragon wrapped one arm about her and deepened their kiss.

As they devoured each other, the scent of lymon blossomed from an object wedged between them. Her breath rapid, Selena grimaced and drew back. "We're crushing your lymon balm."

Aragon chuckled, offering her the herb. "'Tis for you—a melissa plant of your favorite scent. I meant to give it to you before I confessed my love, so you'd believe me."

Her heart fluttered as she accepted Aragon's extraordinary gift. Plants pollinated by melissae were more hardy, vibrant, and potent than ordinary plants—no wonder 'twas blooming over a month early. But if the nearby melissae took offense, melissa plants could be deadly to obtain. "You risked provoking the melissae for *me*?"

Aragon smiled at her. "I'd risk a great deal more to prove my love."

Selena brushed the lymon balm's white flowers. "You needn't risk death to prove your love. Simply telling me was enough." She inhaled the herb's refreshing scent. "Although I adore your gift. 'Twas perceptive of you to recognize my favorite scent."

Aragon blushed with a shrug. "Not particularly. I've kissed you enough that I'd have to be senseless not to recognize it. Besides, over the past few months, lymon balm has become my favorite scent too."

She sighed, a lump rising in her throat. "I've always adored lymon balm. So the summer before she died, Mother taught me how to create my scent. Wearing it reminds me of home and my parents' love." She caressed Aragon's face. "And now it shall remind me of yours too. If only I'd something for you in return."

Aragon kissed her left cheek. "Seeing your adorable dimple is all I need."

Selena tilted her head as tingling suffused her at his kiss. "Are you certain a dimple is enough? I could show you more."

Aragon chuckled, his eyes gleaming. "Are you offering to seduce me again?"

She smiled and set the pot of lymon balm on the window sill behind her. She'd not crush his extraordinary gift. "Yes, I believe I am. And not to escape the black witch either. Simply because I love you."

Aragon pulled her against his chest. "Do you love me enough to marry me as well?"

Warmth filled Selena as she twined her arms about his neck. "I love you enough to fetch mated griffin feathers if you asked." They were almost as deadly to obtain as melissa plants, and ardent lovers wore them to show their devotion equaled a griffin's to their lifelong mate.

Aragon squeezed her with a grin. "I don't need griffin feathers; I just need you. So will you marry me in a bloodbinding as soon as it can be arranged, Miss Selena Midor, formerly from Upper Ashville in Linwick?"

Her heart expanded until it ached. A bloodbinding like her parents'? That showed lifelong devotion more than griffin feathers. Only the most devoted entered bloodbindings since they could only bear each other's children and often died together. She beamed at him. "I will."

Aragon whooped then captured her lips in a deep kiss.

As Selena clung to him and returned his kiss, they stumbled against the window sill. The scent of lymon balm wafted about them again. Although her body throbbed, she wrenched her lips free with a chuckle. "We'd best stop, else my melissa plant shan't survive."

Aragon drew her away from the window. "We can't have that."

She almost sighed. Now that they'd ceased kissing, doubtless he'd withdraw like before. He was too chivalrous to go beyond kisses before they were married. She burned for more, but she'd stop if he wished, so she managed a tremulous smile. "Shall we find your parents and tell them our news?"

His arms still about her, Aragon shook his head. "My parents can wait."

Her pulse began to race. What did he mean by that? "Oh?"

Aragon brushed a kiss against her lips. "When I decided to beg you to marry me, I promised myself we'd make love like you wanted if you accepted."

Breathless, Selena blinked at him. Was her chivalrous gentleman offering to seduce her? "Truly?"

Aragon inclined his head.

She licked her lips as her breath quickened. "But you were so against it before."

Aragon shrugged. "Because I didn't believe we'd be making love for the right reasons. Now I know we are." When she blushed, he chuckled and asked, "So shall we take this to somewhere more suitable? Your chambers or mine?"

Selena dimpled at him. Goddess, he was perfect. "Whichever you pick is fine."

Aragon stepped back to take her arm. "Yours, I think. No one shall question your door being locked—they'll assume you're recovering from yesterday. Mine being locked would appear suspicious."

She blushed as he led her from the art room. He'd thought about this, proving how much he wanted her. Probably as much as she wanted him. "Makes sense."

When her door was locked behind them, Aragon hauled her back into his arms and kissed her.

Selena sighed into his mouth as passion consumed them again. After a timeless moment, she pulled back despite the hunger swamping her. "Swear you shan't withdraw like you have before."

Aragon rumbled a laugh. "I swear. I must make you mine and ruin you for anyone else."

She grinned and threaded her fingers through his seal-brown hair. "Likewise, my love, likewise."

Aragon began unlacing her dress. "Then tomorrow we'll

inform my parents of our decision to wed in the next month or two."

Selena purred as he kissed her neck and fire flashed through her. "Tomorrow?"

Aragon chuckled against her skin. "It'll take that long to thoroughly ruin you."

She grabbed his head to capture his mouth in a fervent kiss. When she paused to breathe, she said, "You ruined me for anyone else ages ago." Probably when he'd rescued her with no motivation other than kindness.

"Not as much as I'm about to." Aragon waggled his brows at her. "And I intend to *ruin* you for the rest of our lives."

Selena giggled. "I doubt your parents shall approve of that until we're wed." Especially the duchess.

Aragon finished unlacing her dress. "They shan't care as long as we're discreet."

Discreet? She clutched his hands as her dress rustled to the floor. "But what if I begin increasing before the wedding?" 'Twould be the opposite of discreet.

Aragon's brow furrowed. "What?"

Selena grimaced, fingering the gold gargoyle nestled between her breasts. "I don't have a contraceptive charm. The royal witch's protection charm destroyed the one Madam Lorelei gave me, remember?"

Aragon grinned at her. "Don't fret. Father gave me and my brothers contraceptive charms on our sixteenth nataldays."

She relaxed and released his hands. Thank the Goddess. 'Twould be painful to stop now.

Aragon feathered a kiss against her lips. "But we'll visit a healer tomorrow to purchase another for you. Never hurts to be cautious."

Selena sighed. And Aragon was always cautious, especially when protecting her. "I suppose you wish to wait until after that to continue making love."

Aragon kissed her until she was breathless then said, "No, I wish to make love now. I'm not letting you escape again. Unless you'd rather wait?"

"Goddess, no." Burning to touch his bare chest again, she yanked off his cravat and waistcoat then slid her hands beneath his shirt. "Now stop being chivalrous before I doubt you want me."

Aragon chuckled and discarded his upper garments. "Never doubt that."

He swept her across the room and tossed her onto her bed. Their hands and mouths ravenous, they came together at long last. Saving herself for the gentleman she'd love for a lifetime had definitely been worth the wait.

Afterward, basking in the glow permeating her, Selena snuggled against Aragon and drew patterns on his chest with her forefinger. "Is making love always like that?"

Aragon kissed her hair. "I suppose."

She rose to her elbow to study him. Didn't he know? "You suppose?"

Aragon blushed and shrugged. "I'm no rakehell like Hawke."

Light bubbled through her as she flashed a teasing grin. "Perhaps I should ask your brother instead."

Aragon flipped her beneath him. "You'll do no such thing."

Selena giggled and slid her arms about his neck. "But how am I to know?"

Aragon seized her lips in a fierce kiss. "We must practice to find out."

She hummed. More practice sounded perfect. She almost smiled as she tilted her head. "I suppose..."

Aragon kissed her again. "But later. I've heard virgins need time to recover."

Selena sighed then arched her brows. "If we aren't going to make love again, what shall we do for the rest of the afternoon?"

Aragon eyed the clock on the mantel. "'Tis almost time for dinner. I'll slip down to the kitchen and beg food from Cook. A lot of it."

Selena blushed when her stomach rumbled. She was ravenous as a gnome after a century-long, stone nap. She'd been too upset about Aragon to eat much before, and they'd had a vigorous afternoon. "Sounds good."

Aragon slid from bed and dressed. Except for the creases, he appeared almost normal. He kissed her again. "Lock the door behind me."

She nodded, her chest warm. She would, but she must fetch her sketch journal and melissa plant first. So after he left, she donned a dressing gown and darted to her art room. She returned to her chambers and locked her door then set the pot on her window sill. Humming, she began sketching the lymon balm while she awaited Aragon's return.

CHAPTER 34

*B*earing a tray laden with food and a bottle of sparkling wine, Aragon hummed as he strode back upstairs. No doubt the servants guessed what he was about, but they'd stay silent. The coins he'd slipped them would ensure that. He tapped on Selena's door with his foot. "'Tis me."

The lock clicked, and her door swung open. Selena dimpled at him. "Hello, me."

His heart swelling, he grinned back and entered her chambers.

Selena locked the door behind him as he set the tray on her tea table. While he poured them flutes of sparkling wine, she began uncovering the food. "I'm *ravenous*."

Aragon chuckled and handed her a flute. So was he. "Making love is strenuous." He toasted her with a playful leer. "To more such exertion."

Selena giggled as she sipped her sparkling wine. "Perhaps you're more like Hawke than you thought."

He almost snorted. Hardly. He'd not become a rakehell to avoid his love for his best friend. Once he'd realized he loved Selena, he'd burned to tell her. He winked at her as they sat at the table. "Only with you."

They fell on their repast like starving manticores, but midway through dinner, Selena asked, "If I spellbound you from the start, why did you keep denying our attraction and withdrawing?"

Aragon winced and coughed on his last spoonful of redkrab soup. "At first, I couldn't exploit your inexperience. I had to allow you to consider other gentlemen. Though I hated it when you did."

Selena tsked. "Silly man. As if I'd want other gentlemen when I'd met you. I only considered them because I believed you didn't want me."

His ribs squeezed while he devoured his fish pie. If only he'd realized that. "And when I did begin courting you, I couldn't rush you, but I burned to make love to you, so my restraint kept failing."

Selena dimpled and grasped his hand. "I should have realized your chivalry was why you kept denying our attraction."

Aragon threaded his fingers through hers then revealed dessert with a flourish. "Perhaps this karamel nut sweetice can atone for repeatedly withdrawing."

Selena giggled as she leaned forward and licked her lips. "Depends on how much of it you let me eat."

He slid beside her and offered her a spoonful, his pulse quickening. He'd barely resisted kissing her when they shared a bowl at the brothel, and now he didn't need to. "The entire sweetice. I recall how you adore it."

Selena hummed as she gulped that spoonful. "I do indeed."

Aragon leaned over and captured her mouth in a hungry kiss. She tasted as delicious as ambrosia fresh from a melissae hive. "I'll steal my portion from your lips."

Selena's dark-gray eyes gleamed. "Sounds perfect."

So he fed her dessert and stole kisses after each bite. With each kiss, his hunger deepened until his body throbbed.

After the final spoonful of sweetice, Selena moued. "No more?"

Aragon nodded, his eyes riveted on her lips. Goddess, she was spellbinding. "I doubt I could withstand more."

Selena flicked him a coy glance. "What are we to do with the rest of the evening?"

He shuddered when his body hardened further. Not make love—he must give her until tomorrow to recover. She'd been a virgin, after all. "We could play cards or read aloud."

Selena hummed, her gaze roaming her chambers until it paused on her window. "Perhaps I could sketch you again."

Aragon swallowed. When she'd sketched him at the picnic, he'd almost made love to her outdoors. Could he restrain himself this time? Yet he couldn't deny her. "If you like."

Selena dimpled and leapt to fetch her sketch journal from the window sill. "Go recline on the bed."

He stretched across the bed then stiffened when she adjusted his pose. He mustn't grab her like a lusty satyr. She required time to recover. He could restrain himself until tomorrow at least.

Selena dragged a chair beside him and began sketching. A smile curved her lips. "I always preferred landscapes to portraits, but I could sketch you for ages."

His body throbbing, Aragon clenched his hands to remain still. If he moved, he'd haul her into his arms. And he must wait until tomorrow for that.

"You've become my new inspiration." Selena whirled her sketch journal to show him her finished sketch. "What do you think?"

He suppressed a grimace. He wasn't worthy of her talents, but he'd continue posing since it pleased her. "Very nice."

Selena tilted her head and eyed her sketch. "I think you appear too tense. Perhaps if you were wearing less clothes."

Aragon jerked back as she reached for his cravat. "I can undress myself." He must if he was to restrain himself.

Selena giggled. "I was simply attempting to help."

Shuddering with desire, he stripped down to his shirt and trousers. Removing more would be dangerous.

Selena sketched him again. When she finished, she murmured, "You're still much too tense. Perhaps—"

Aragon snorted. "Removing more clothes would make me more tense, not less." And he'd burst if he was more tense.

Selena's lips twitched in a smile before flattening to a sober line. "Oh dear."

He eyed her. She was plotting something. "Selena, what are you doing?"

A coy look danced across her face. "Attempting to seduce you. Is it succeeding?"

Hunger roaring through him, Aragon groaned and covered his eyes. Goddess, give him strength. "Only too well. Now quit it. You require time to recover."

Selena slid onto the bed beside him. "I feel remarkably well. I'm certain I'll be fine."

He shook his head despite his painfully hard body. "I don't wish to hurt you."

Selena twined her arms about his neck. "Go slowly then. Please, Aragon."

His resistance crumbling, Aragon seized her mouth in a deep kiss. He caressed and kissed her everywhere as he slid open her dressing gown. When she attempted to yank off his shirt, he shackled her hands in her dressing gown. He made love to her with agonizing slowness, and they both sobbed with relief when they joined at last.

Curled against him, Selena nuzzled his chest. "Going slowly hurt worse than going fast would have."

He chuckled, his body finally languid. "Perhaps, but 'twas a good kind of hurt."

Selena's smile tickled his skin. "Cruel man." After several breaths, she added, "I should attempt some unclad sketches next. The masters were fond of those."

Aragon smiled at her new seduction attempt. She was adorable. "Not tonight. Now *I* require time to recover."

Selena sighed. "So do I. Tomorrow perhaps?"

He kissed her hair, inhaling her lymon balm scent. She could sketch him however she wished in private. "As long as they don't get shown anywhere."

Selena giggled. "Of course. I can't have other ladies knowing how perfect you are."

His heart full, Aragon kissed her hair again then drew the covers over them. Nestled in each other's arms, they drifted into slumber. Together at last.

THE FOLLOWING MORNING, Aragon and Selena were still entwined, and he woke her with a drowsy kiss. What a perfect way to greet the day. "Morning, my love."

Selena drew him back for another kiss. "Morning."

He glanced at the clock on the mantel, and his stomach tightened. "We're late for breakfast. Mother and Father shall hunt for us soon."

Selena chuckled. "And finding us in bed together is the opposite of discreet."

After a final kiss, Aragon sighed and slid from bed. "Right. We can tell my parents about our betrothal at breakfast." Then Mother would stop matching Selena with other gentlemen.

He changed then returned for Selena and escorted her down to the breakfast room. He paused before the door and arched a brow to ask if she was ready. At her nod, they swept inside and greeted his parents while serving themselves breakfast.

Her plate almost empty, Mother eyed them over her teacup. "What kept you two this morning? I was about to send servants to fetch you."

To divert attention from the blush tinting Selena's freckled cheeks, Aragon lifted his chin and replied, "Entirely my fault. We'd some private matters to discuss."

Father inclined his head. "About the black witch, I presume."

Only to start. Aragon grinned as he devoured his bacon. "No, I asked Selena to marry me."

Selena dimpled, laying her hand on his arm. "And I joyfully accepted."

Mother beamed like the reborn Winter Queen in a Longnight play. "Finally! I suppose Selena's peril prompted you. I'd hoped throwing other suitors at each of you would be enough."

His fork halfway to his mouth, Aragon stilled. "*That* was what you were doing?" He should have realized.

Mother nodded. "Your father and I always knew you'd ask for Selena's hand."

Father flashed a crooked grin. "Only a gentleman in love would rescue a lady from a brothel, a disreputable uncle, and a black witch."

Aragon and Selena exchanged a wry glance. His parents were dauntingly astute. However, he only said, "We wish to marry in a bloodbinding as soon as it can be arranged."

Father sighed and shook his head. "Unfortunately, as my heir, you must have children, so a bloodbinding is too risky. But if you still wish to, you can perform a bloodbinding after a child or two."

Aragon grimaced. Father's refusal was common for those needing heirs—bloodbound couples could only have children together and often died at the same time, so if one of them was infertile, heirs were impossible. "I'll still wish to," he glanced at Selena, "if Selena does."

Selena beamed back and threaded her fingers through his. "I will."

"You two are so romantic." Mother's eyes gleamed. "The ceremony shall be the beginning of next season, I think."

Aragon stilled. Next season? That was much too long. "We'd thought in the next month or two."

Still holding his hand, Selena nodded as she sipped her tea. "The wedding needn't be lavish."

Mother goggled at them. "Nonsense. Your wedding shall be a grand affair as befits our family. Elise's shall be nothing compared to it."

Aragon and Selena exchanged another glance. They should have realized Mother wouldn't allow a simple wedding. Too bad.

Father rose and clapped Aragon's shoulder. "At least your love shall live under the same roof while you wait."

His neck heating, Aragon jerked a nod as Selena blushed scarlet. True, but must his parents mention that? So embarrassing.

Mother pursed her lips. "We'll start by announcing your betrothal at another ball in a few weeks. So don't act possessive at court events before then." She accepted Father's arm, and they sailed from the room.

Aragon sighed then squeezed Selena's hand and slanted her an apologetic smile. "We could try eloping." Although Mother might never forgive them.

Selena shook her head. "We'd better let your mother handle the wedding." She eyed him beneath her lashes. "Although perhaps we should go riding today. If we take enough food, we can remain out past dinner. I doubt I can avoid acting possessive at whatever court events she's chosen."

Warmth filled his chest. Neither could he. He drew her upright and captured her mouth in a fervent kiss. When she yanked him closer, he lifted his head. Goddess, she was perfect. And his now. "I love you, Selena."

Selena caressed his cheek. "I love you too. Let's go before your mother notices." She winked at him. "If we race again, I might even let you win."

His heart fluttering, Aragon threaded his fingers through hers as they darted upstairs to change. "I already won when you agreed to marry me."

Want more?

*Order the next book **The Enchanted Bird** about Wren and Hawke* *today! Keep reading to learn more about the next book in the Calatini Tales.*

And sign up for my newsletter for exclusive stories and book extras, new book announcements, giveaways, and more.

LIKE THE SPELLBINDING COURTSHIP?

Please consider writing a review. Reviews truly help spread the word about the titles you love.

THE ENCHANTED BIRD

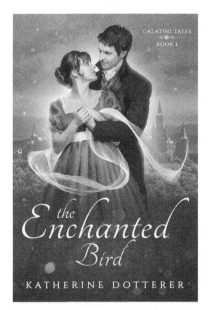

*C*alatini *is a kingdom suffused with magic. But strong spells come with high prices...*

Wren prefers a simple life of writing, reading, and volunteering at the orphanage to fashionable parties and balls at court.

If she attends at all, it's because Hawke, the best friend she's secretly loved forever, convinces her. So when she learns his mother has arranged his marriage, she knows she must act. All she desires is a single night in Hawke's arms, so though she distrusts magic, Wren turns to a witch to create the perfect masquerade disguise infused in an enchanted bird.

Lord Beza—Hawke, to his friends—is a notorious rake, but he can't stop thinking about the mysterious lady who seduced him at the summer masquerade then disappeared. Fortunately, she left behind a clue: a small enchanted bird. And his clever best friend Wren will surely help him in his search—after all, wouldn't she want him to find love?

Never having dreamt Hawke would hunt for her, Wren is desperate to convince him to forget his "mysterious" lady— otherwise the enchanted bird will extract a growing price from them both. But their night of passion is impossible for either of them to forget...

THE ENCHANTED BIRD IS HEARTWARMING, **Regency-inspired fantasy romance at its finest, perfect for readers of the Jane Austen's Dragons series, Mary Robinette Kowal's Glamourist Histories series, and Grace Burrowes' Rogues to Riches series of historical romance novels.**

WANT MORE? Order **The Enchanted Bird** *today!*

CALATINI TALES

The enchanting Calatini Tales includes...

The Spellbinding Courtship (Book 0.5)
The Enchanted Bird (Book 1)
The Nightmara Affair (Book 2)
The Secret Soulbond (Book 3)
The Goddess's Illusion (Book 4)

ABOUT KATHERINE

A lifelong creator of her own bedtime stories, **Katherine Dotterer** writes heartwarming tales of fantasy romance inspired by Regency England. Born and raised in Maryland, she still lives there in an almost cottage surrounded by trees. When not writing, she enjoys reading anything she can find, singing in local choruses, hiking in nearby parks, watching the wildlife outside her windows, and cuddling with her two cats. Visit her at KatherineDotterer.com to learn about her book releases, read her many book extras, and sign up for her newsletter.